Praise for the works (

The Convincing Hour

I'm a big fan of YA and this book in particular is very well written. This is the kind of YA that a teenager would like but this is absolutely a story for adults too. You hear authors always saying, 'write what you know', and that is exactly what Roberts did here which makes sense as to why this was such a well-done book. The prologue is a bit of a wow that hits you in the gut and after that, you can't put this book down.

This is not a light topic, but it's so well done and Story's character has so much heart, that as a reader you have to take this journey to see if she can somehow succeed. This is an easy one for me to recommend to YA fans. This book is very well written and I believe it is Robert's best-written standalone book and it might even be her best-written book period.

-LezReview Books

It's a great story and I'm rooting for a sequel. I would definitely recommend this book. Lessons are to be learned by everyone including the reader.

-Jane S., *NetGalley*

Dying on the Vine

The story is well-paced, with revelations coming bit by bit, whetting the appetite. The writing shows skill and a love of language. Ms. Roberts is extremely skilled at bringing her characters to life. It was a joy to read and is the kind of book to savour, like a large glass of your favourite wine.

I've read many Ann Roberts books, but this was my first Ari Adams Mystery. There is an excellent ensemble cast of characters, all of whom are nuanced, fully drawn, and intriguing. It's hard to say which is more interesting—the cast of characters and their relationships, the swift pace of the investigation, or the details of the art and science of winemaking. The relationships portrayed are genuinely adult and therefore complex and engaging. The culture around vineyards and winemaking is a passionate one and that passion is reflected in the characters and situations in the book. Highly recommended. I look forward to starting with the very first Ari Adams mystery and finding out everything I've missed.

Justice Calls

I must admit that I was sucked in from the first sentence because Ann Roberts has a way of crafting a story to keep her readers captivated. I definitely got a realistic portrayal of the gutwrenching pain, frustration, and anger that Ari and her father felt as they worked tirelessly to find out who killed Richie. I can't believe that I went through a gamut of emotions with every word I read and I just couldn't let Ari, Molly, or Jack go even when the story ended. If you're looking for heartfelt moments, character growth, timeless love coupled with an understanding that knows no boundaries and a compelling mystery, then this story is certainly for you!

A Secret to Tell

This is surely one story you should not miss out on reading. I can assure you, this story has the right amount of angst, mystery, comedy, and romance to keep you up way past your bedtime. From the first page I was completely sucked into the story due to the nonstop action and the steady flow of angst and excitement. The characters were realistic and the dialogue between them was fantastic!

-The Lesbian Review

Deadly Intersections

June, 2011, RLynne - Roberts has given her reader a wild roller coaster ride in a plot filled with dead bodies, intrigue, lies, and corruption. Her characters are very real with flaws and baggage, and very likeable. Set in Phoenix, Arizona, juxtaposes the bright sunlight with the very dark underbelly of the city. This is a book full of surprises with an exciting cliff-hanger of an ending.

-Just About Write

Vagabond Heart

The story starts off with a bang and kept my interest all the way through. It's been forever since I picked up a book that I had trouble putting down. This one could easily make it into my read-again pile. Both Quinn and Suda are interesting characters and their interactions didn't feel scripted or overplayed. The author managed to weave in several real-life xenophobic/bigotry issues which just made the characters feel like they were operating in real life without detracting from the story. In fact, I'd say it enhanced the story because we need to call more attention to these things. I've never been on Route 66, but based on the descriptions and the adventure it's on my bucket list moving forward.

-C-Spot Reviews

Beacon of Love

This is a well-written book about love, loss, redemption, and parenthood. Roberts intertwines her characters like a helix and slowly unveils the truth about each one… This is one of those books that sneaks up on the reader. There aren't a lot of bells and whistles, it doesn't shout at you, nor does it hit you over the head. It is, however, well written and in a quiet way, the characters and their story will stay with you long after you finish the book and put it aside.

-LambdaLiterary.org

A CAROL FOR KAROL

ANN ROBERTS

About the Author

Ann Roberts is the author of twenty-two novels, including the Golden Crown Literary Award-winning Ari Adams mystery series. A three-time Lambda finalist, Ann was awarded Best Mystery twice by GCLS and in 2014 she received the Alice B Medal for her body of work. She retired from public education in 2016 to focus on writing, coaching, and editing authors. Six years ago she and her wife traded the desert for the Pacific Northwest. When they're not running after their pets, AKA the "fur circus," they enjoy trips to the ocean, hikes in the mountains, and watching the University of Oregon Women's Basketball team and the WNBA. Ann loves to hear from readers and can be reached at her website, annroberts.net.

A CAROL FOR KAROL

ANN ROBERTS

BELLA
BOOKS

2023

Bella Books, Inc.
P.O. Box 10543
Tallahassee, FL 32302

Printed in the United States of America on acid-free paper.

First Edition - 2023

Editor: Katherine V. Forrest
Cover Designer: Kayla Mancuso

ISBN: 978-1-64247-500-5

PUBLISHER'S NOTE

Acknowledgments

By early 2022 I wasn't sure I would ever write another book. The muse had left on a Covid wing. In a last desperate attempt to find her, I visited the Tucson limb of my family tree and spent time with Aunt Judith, a painter, because sometimes creativity is contagious. One night my cousins, Josh, Tiffany, and Max, mentioned Winterhaven, an area of Tucson committed to celebrating holiday cheer each year. That got me thinking…

Then, Carolyn Goldschmidt, a dear friend and an HOA attorney in Tucson, proposed the idea of a community requiring homeowners to decorate the exteriors of their homes for the holidays. Thus, a story was born. She helped me navigate current housing laws and Covenants, Conditions and Restrictions (CCRs) that exist today. So grateful, Carolyn, that we chatted that night.

Julie Wycoff, Jennifer Pershing, and Trish Napier are leaders in the Winterhaven community, which does *not* require anyone to participate in their annual Festival of Lights each year. They let me step behind the scenes, sharing experiences, logistics, and stories about running one of the most successful, ongoing holiday celebrations in the country. I remind readers that the JOY neighborhood is fictional and is not modeled after Winterhaven, except for the shared vision of promoting kindness and cheer.

Leah Murray, the Executive Director of the Sheldon McMurphy Johnson House here in Eugene, Oregon, explained the processes for declaring a home historic and some of the unique features of Queen Anne Victorians. Her stories about the families and their daily life helped me craft a plausible, fictitious setting.

Bella Books is a fabulous community. I'm forever grateful to Linda and Jessica Hill and the entire Bella crew for their ongoing support. Also, my dear friend and fellow Bella author Cindy Rizzo served as sensitivity reader, providing insight about the religious aspect of the community seen in "The Court."

My editor, the incomparable Katherine V. Forrest, guides and teaches me, and the list of things I've learned is too long to enumerate, but the final product shines brighter under her care. Thank you, Katherine.

And of course, without my wife, Amy, I don't think there ever would've been a debut novel, let alone twenty-one after it. Thanks for sticking by me, honey, through these last few years.

Finally, to all of my readers, I am forever grateful to you. Regardless of when you read this book, may joy and kindness fill all your days.

For Judith

CHAPTER ONE

"Bette Davis was right," Karol Kleinz muttered. "Old age ain't for cowards, or whatever it was she said."

Unable to coax open the cellophane end of the new roll of packing tape with her fingernail, she dropped it on her bedroom floor. "Shit." It was yet another reminder that her fine motor skills were no longer up to par thanks to the arthritis in her hands, which seemed to worsen with each passing year.

She took a deep breath and gazed out her window at the New York skyline that greeted her. Thousands of lights punctuated the night sky. "I'll miss you, city that doesn't sleep."

She headed to the balcony of her Upper West Side apartment. Snow covered Central Park, the trees' bare limbs seeming to reach out for spring. She studied the buildings beyond the park. Each illuminated window indicated life—cleaning crews scurrying to prepare businesses for the next day; busy executives with corner offices, toiling to meet a deadline; families watching television; people relaxing with a favorite hobby—or having sex. In New York it could be anything at any time. The city was always alive. Most people couldn't tolerate life in the city, but she'd thrived on it. *What'll it be like in Boca Raton?* "Probably not as lively," she answered herself, "but hopefully not comatose."

A cold December wind whipped past and she retreated inside to face the stacks of half-filled boxes, rolls of Bubble Wrap, and the damn stubborn tape. She grabbed her tablet from an end table and pulled up her packing plan, not to be confused with her moving plan, her travel plan, or her Florida arrival plan. The movers weren't due for another week, and despite the apartment's disheveled appearance, she really was on track to finish ahead of schedule, according to the moving plan.

Three sharp barks interrupted the soothing jazz piano that wafted through the living room. "Manny," she called. "Where are you?" She scanned the room but didn't see Manhattan, her little Yorkiepoo. He was likely in a box as he favored small spaces. She stepped carefully around the detritus that covered every surface and the floor just in case he was hiding in plain sight.

Three more barks—and possibly movement—near the giant bag of giveaway clothes.

"Manny!" she called.

"*Ruff!*" came the response, closer to the boxes that lined the hallway.

"Manny!"

No bark. He was playing hard to get. She groaned and shook her head, careful not to tumble over the stacks of books waiting for a box. Why had she listened to the organization guru who'd advised that the best way to pack was to first collect similar items and then pack when they were all in the same place? Obviously that woman didn't have a Yorkiepoo whose favorite game was hide and seek.

"*Ruff!*" Over by the office door.

She looked in a box filled with recyclable packing peanuts, and there was Manny, his entire body submerged. Only his cute little brown head sat above the surface. He looked pleased that Karol had found him.

"*Ruff!*" The shifting peanuts indicated he was wagging his unseen tail.

"There you are!" She scooped him up and set him inside his little pen. "Sorry, bud. You gotta stay in the O.K. Corral for now. I don't have time for any reindeer games."

Manny barked his displeasure as Karol returned to the living room. She looked around and groaned. *Now, where the hell is my tablet?* She closed her eyes and focused, releasing her growing frustration. During every one of their sessions, Dr. Kennedy reiterated the importance of not sweating the small stuff, something that was truly a challenge, as she wasn't accustomed to losing things, forgetting things, or failing. She was a multitasker with a reputation for sharp wit. "Well, I used to be," she muttered.

Another minute and she found the tablet sitting precariously on the arm of a wingback chair. "Okay," she ordered herself, "tonight is photographs, art, and knickknacks."

She started with the most important photo: the black and white 8x10 of her with her family: her mother, Joyce; her father, Herschel; her maternal grandmother, Nana Hope; and her paternal grandfather, well-known New York attorney Eli Kleinz. She was only a toddler, sitting on her mother's lap. Her father stood behind his wife with Eli to his left and Nana Hope to his right. The picture said it all. The two men wore stern expressions and nearly identical three-piece suits while Nana Hope, her mother, and Karol smiled beatifically for the camera.

As usual her gaze bounced between her mother and Nana Hope, never really looking at the men. Her mother had died from breast cancer at thirty-four, when Karol was only eight, leaving her upbringing to her father—via the hired help—and sometimes Nana Hope. Many times Karol had begged to live with Nana Hope permanently, but her father recognized the leverage and sympathy he gained from being a widower, especially with the women he regularly bedded.

She quickly wrapped the photo and set it in a box and pulled an original watercolor from the wall, a beach scene. She loved staring at the detailed waves and the setting sun in the background. The Tucson artist who'd painted it, Judith Mariner, had told Karol it was a San Diego beach, but whenever Karol looked at it she thought of Boca Raton, the place that would become her new home in just a few weeks. After she made a stop in Tucson and finally settled Nana Hope's affairs and sold her house.

She'd avoided the home she inherited three years ago when Nana Hope had died of Covid. It had been much easier to hire a property management company to occasionally check on it, just to make sure the roof wasn't leaking or squatters hadn't taken up residence. She received a report twice a year, but what eased her mind was something Nana Hope had always said: "I have the best neighbors in the world."

Karol had met some of them. She knew that part was true.

Before she realized it, she was standing in front of the photo of her and Nana Hope outside the small Craftsman house with the wide, long porch. She and Nana had spent many afternoons sitting in the Adirondack chairs playing Go Fish, while the neighbors strolled by and waved or came up the walk to chat.

There were also other kids in what had come to be known as the JOY neighborhood for its Christmas affiliations, mostly boys, but she couldn't remember them specifically, and there was one other girl with dark, curly hair and a mischievous smile. They'd always had fun and her name was Carol too, but she spelled it differently and went by CJ. There had been several afternoons underneath the giant Aleppo pine behind the field… eventual kisses and a long-distance, preteen "romance," destined to fizzle. It was a first love that navigated her toward women. She still thought of CJ occasionally.

Where was that picture of the three of them with Hope?

She hadn't been back to Tucson and the Craftsman house since her preteen years. Her father had moved them to San Francisco for his computer job, so Nana Hope, since she was retired from her job as a civil engineer, always came to them. Then, after Karol's mother passed, they rarely saw her. Nana always invited Karol to come visit again, but as she grew older there was always a reason to say no—a chance to see friends, a big law school final, or the demands and expectations of an up-and-coming junior associate. Whole decades flew by and the only tether between Karol and Nana Hope was this photo and the memories that surfaced each Christmas when she'd make Nana's famous gingerbread people for her colleagues, neighbors, and friends.

She wiped a few tears off the picture, remembering one of Nana's favorite expressions. "If you don't bother with me when I'm alive, don't worry about me after I've passed."

Karol hadn't even gone to her celebration of life.

Her cell pinged with a text from Stella, her paralegal. *I just splurged and bought a crap load of sunscreen.*

Karol laughed. Stella Plotz was queen of the bargain. She replied with a thumbs-up, and suddenly remembered what she wasn't supposed to forget: Stella's retirement gift. Despite four different reminders in four different places, she still hadn't wrapped the present.

"Shit. Let's just pray I don't have dementia."

She rustled through the items on the couch and found the Macy's box that contained a lovely light-blue cashmere sweater. All it needed now was a fancy bow. Karol had vowed to learn new things in retirement so instead of heading down to the gift-wrap counter, she'd stopped at a craft store and picked up some red wire ribbon. How hard could this be?

She cleared a spot on the dining room table and pulled up a picture of a handsome five-loop bow. She studied it for a moment, cut off a hefty piece of ribbon and tried to re-create the picture. After three attempts, she'd severely mangled the ribbon. She held it up and groaned. It looked like a starving red balloon animal.

She laughed and opened her YouTube app. There were endless choices for How to Tie a Bow with Wire Ribbon, but the first video had over nine thousand "likes" and the smiling woman holding the bow was definitely Karol's type—curly salt-and-pepper gray hair, lovely green eyes and a wide smile. Karol was a sucker for a great smile. She tapped on the play button.

Some upbeat violin music started and the words, *It's All JOY* filled the screen followed by the same woman sitting at a dining room table. She introduced herself as Carol and spoke in a soft, lilting voice. There was something very familiar about her, but

Karol didn't have time to dwell on that. She needed to get this bow done and return to her packing.

Carol methodically outlined the steps, gave clear directions, anticipated the mistakes beginners would make, and three minutes later, Karol did indeed have a lovely bow for her present. At the end of the video, Carol asked the viewers to stay tuned for a special announcement, and Karol felt obliged to listen, since Carol had done such a stellar job.

Holiday music played while Carol narrated a video of a neighborhood exploding in Christmas lights with ice skating, sleigh riding, even a reindeer petting area. Hundreds of people milled about, drinking hot cocoa and eating gingerbread people. "...so if you're anywhere near the Tucson area," Carol said in the voiceover, "come visit the JOY neighborhood this holiday season. JOY will fill your heart with joy."

Karol gasped. "Carol is CJ! That's *my* CJ!"

A laughing little girl filled the screen. Then the camera pulled back to include her entire family standing in front of a house made up to look like Santa's Workshop, complete with elves, sacks of presents, and a real sleigh with Santa waving at the camera. Fake snow covered the lawn and the roof. Karol stared past them—to the long front porch with the Adirondack chairs, the swing, and the front door painted bright red.

Again she gasped. "That's Nana Hope's house! My house!"

CHAPTER TWO

CJ Joy sipped her coffee as the sun inched past the Rincon Mountains. She concentrated on her breathing and focused on the yellows and oranges that quickly upstaged the surrounding tans and green splotches of the desert landscape. Her second-story balcony, a one of a kind in the JOY neighborhood, provided an unobstructed view of each sunrise thanks to the pair of elevated barbershop chairs CJ had installed. They were like a humble version of a throne. She wasn't trying to look like a queen. She just wanted to sit high enough so the balcony railing didn't obscure the view.

Houston, CJ's brawny and brindle rottweiler/pit bull mix, rubbed his face on her sweatpants and she automatically scratched his head. "You're such a good boy, Huey." Happy with the attention, he dropped onto his nearby bed.

CJ gazed across the Douglas and Spruce intersection. A four-way stop, there had never been a need to install a traffic light, even during the JOY Extravaganza, which everyone called "Ganza." Tucson folk were patient and only one accident had occurred during the seventy-eight-year existence of the JOY neighborhood—and it wasn't the fault of a drunk or inattentive driver.

It had been Teddy Ruxpin's fault. Not the real Teddy, but the enormous teddy bear on a float built in homage to the toy craze of 1987. It split in half as the float wrangler attempted to turn left and return the float to the staging area after the annual parade. The front half made the turn, so a few of Teddy's smaller furry replicas were unscathed, but Teddy himself forked to the right and his enormous, stuffed chicken-wire buttocks landed on the hood of a cherry-red Porsche convertible.

CJ smiled and shook her head at the memory. Fortunately, the Porsche couple were unharmed and bubbling with Christmas spirit. They even laughed when Teddy's bottom was extricated from their car, the hood of which looked like a thousand little chicken feet had discoed the night away.

Yes, there was only a four-way stop now, but for how long? The JOY neighborhood sat on the northwest corner and the Joy family business, Tucson Ice and Big Wave Shaved Ice, sat across from the neighborhood on the southwest corner. The delivery trucks were already loading up, and since Salma and Shea's Prius was in the parking lot, she guessed the co-managers of Big Wave were in early to do inventory. Shaved ice proved profitable every day of the year in the desert.

The southeast corner and the acreage behind it comprised the Desert Springs Cemetery where many of Tucson's local heroes resided, as well as CJ's parents and grandparents, Christopher and Elizabeth Joy, the architects who designed the entire neighborhood.

And Nana Hope.

Several families had migrated to the Southwest from the East Coast, following CJ's grandparents, but Hope came later. She and Elsa, CJ's mother, had been college roommates. They became inseparable, sharing similar goals about careers, family, and motherhood. When they graduated they separated but wrote letters constantly and Hope eventually found her way to Tucson.

And after Mom died…

CJ had thought a lot about Hope in the last few hours—after she read the terse email from Hope's granddaughter, Karol. It had been quite surprising, vandalizing the few memories CJ had of their special summers.

At least they were special to me.

She sighed and stared directly across the street at the northeast corner, once home to Orozco Farms and the Orozco Market. This was the trouble spot. The parcel was seventy-five acres and extended almost to the base of the Rincons. Most of those acres had been some of the best farmland in all of Arizona, cultivated, nurtured and nourished by five generations of the Orozco family. They had turned the hard, unworkable southwestern clay into rich soil and were rewarded each year with fine harvests of alfalfa and sorghum.

When Reynaldo Orozco became the head of the family, he looked to expand the business to include vegetables—after his recently arrived neighbor, former Navy commander Christopher Joy, CJ's grandfather, suggested such an addition would be supported by the new subdivision he was building across the street.

And thus, the Orozco Market was born. A giant red barn and parking lot were constructed and within a year the lot was always full as word spread about the new "organic" vegetables. One good turn deserved another, and just like Commander Joy had suggested the market, Reynaldo Orozco introduced Christopher Joy to a new product: shaved ice. And Big Wave Shaved Ice was born.

The Joy and Orozco families had been friends for decades. CJ had wonderful memories of helping the Orozcos at harvest time, going for hayrides through the pumpkin patch, running through the cornrows…and sliding down the banister of the Orozco's magnificent old house, *Tierra Celestial*, Heavenly Ground. More than once the top piece of the Newell post had popped off when one of the Orozco children crashed into it to end their slide.

Built in 1875 by the original owner of the land, Dr. Claude Blankley, the grand Victorian structure had withstood foundational cracks from the earthquake of 1887, a kitchen fire in the 1920s, a monsoon that took out nearly every window, and general neglect by the current owner, Rubio Orozco, the great-great-grandson of Reynaldo. All the generations between Reynaldo and Rubio attempted to preserve Dr. Blankley's vision and the original structure, which was a one of a kind in Tucson.

Until recently, CJ and Rubio had been cordial, and it helped that Rubio's mother, Valentina, had been one of CJ's best friends growing up. Still, Rubio, an immature thirty-year-old, wouldn't listen to CJ when it came to the future of the property, and both Valentina and her husband were gone, as well as Valentina's two childless siblings. Everything belonged to Rubio and he was determined to sell it all. CJ understood his reasoning. He didn't live in Tucson and there wasn't anyone left in the family who wanted to farm or live in "that old, drafty pile of sticks," as Rubio referred to Tierra.

The selling part didn't bother CJ. It was the buyer. A national big-box retail chain was the current frontrunner, and CJ would do everything she could to keep her majestic balcony view from turning into a giant rectangular blob with air-conditioning units scattered all over the top. The JOY Homeowners Association (HOA) had immediately started researching their options. It helped that Rubio had asked CJ to keep an eye on the place—and given her copies of all the keys. JOY's head of security, Blair Nicol, walked the grounds twice a month, and as CJ enjoyed her morning coffee, she'd perch on her chair with her binoculars and periodically do a cursory inspection.

Rubio had abandoned the property in 2010 after Valentina passed. By 2013 word was out that no one lived there, and Blair regularly escorted squatters from the premises until Rubio agreed to install a chain-link fence around the market and the house. That had solved the problem until 2020, when a contingency of homeless people, mostly folks displaced by Arizona's raging summer wildfires, had cut a hole in the fence and taken up residence inside the market. They had been stealthy and CJ hadn't noticed them during her morning coffee check surveillance, but Blair had found the squatters during a bimonthly walkabout.

CJ and the rest of the HOA board then walked across the street and into a different world. The twenty-thousand-square-foot barn had been turned into four zones by the small group of self-appointed leaders: a quiet area, an eating area, a school, and a Covid area. CJ learned that outside, directly behind the barn, was the playground, an area impossible to see from her balcony. Since the farm sat on the eastern Tucson border where there was little traffic, and across from a cemetery, only the dead knew the secret.

The HOA board flew into action and with Rubio's help, because he did have a heart, the utilities were turned on and the barn became a way station for hundreds of people throughout the pandemic, all with the help and support of the JOY neighbors who volunteered every single day, raised money, provided food, and farmed a few acres. It truly was neighborliness at its finest, and by 2021, all of those they'd sheltered had moved on, physically and figuratively.

It also prompted Rubio to start the process to sell the property, and the JOY HOA played the one card they had: get Tierra Celestial declared a historic structure. There were many reasons it hadn't been done before, all of which were flimsy excuses in CJ's mind, but they were pressing forward now. She'd had an audience with the head of the Historic Preservation Society and they were slowly gaining media attention. Rubio wasn't speaking to her anymore, but fortunately he hadn't asked for his keys back—yet. He was a good businessman even if he had no interest in the past.

CJ swapped her coffee mug for her binoculars and adjusted the focus on the chunky four-foot-by-five-foot FOR SALE sign that sat near the intersection. "Let's take a look," she muttered. She slowly swept across the decrepit barn, much of its paint faded and curled. The market sign had slipped, one of its screws gone. "Hmm. That's new."

She looked left and right through the fields until she settled on Tierra Celestial. Despite its dilapidated appearance, she always marveled at the craftsmanship and magnificent detail that defined all Victorians—the turrets, the towers, the ornate gables. *Well, they used to be ornate.* From the upper-pitched roof down to the red brick that formed the broad front porch, it all needed renovation. And the cupola. The glass dome on the top of the roof had been Dr. Blankley's nineteenth-century man cave.

"And it will happen if we win, Houston," she whispered.

She knew Tierra was a place of secrets. She'd overheard several stories when Valentina's mother, Maria, would visit. They'd found a hidden door, a dumbwaiter, even a secret wine cellar with a few very old bottles of wine. Dr. Blankley had been a rich eccentric, fancying himself an inventor who enjoyed surprises and intrigue. Maria was convinced the family hadn't uncovered all of Tierra's secrets. She told the story of an unfortunate butler who flipped a metal handle and nearly fell through a trapdoor that opened beneath him.

CJ followed the line of the structure, wallowing between sadness at the horrible degeneration of the house and ennui with the exercise—until she saw a figure in one of the upstairs windows. She jumped and nearly dropped the binoculars. Houston barked and immediately circled the balcony, unsure of the problem. "It's okay, boy, settle down," she cooed. When she positioned the binoculars again and found the window, there was no one there. She took a deep breath. It probably was nothing. Maybe a shadow or the sun playing tricks on her eyes.

As she approached sixty, she reflected, it seemed much of life was a trick. After Mary died, an army of JOY residents with good intentions had descended upon her, but she politely and graciously declined most of their assistance, proving to herself that she was still self-sufficient. But after her double-nickel birthday things started to change slowly. She forgot things, lost things, and what used to be minor injuries that she recovered from in a few days became much larger problems that required convalescence, a word she'd never used to describe her own situation. Her best friends, most of whom sat on the HOA board with her, were the first to notice. People were now always at the ready to help her move furniture, paint a room, haul tree branches or chop wood.

She adjusted the binoculars again and homed in on the window. She sat there for a good two minutes but saw nothing else. She lowered the binoculars and sighed. It was probably just a shadow.

The warehouse next to CJ's house was abuzz with activity when she arrived for the HOA board meeting. The JOY Extravaganza was only three days away, and there were a hundred things still to do. Much of the warehouse currently hosted the parade floats, all in various stages of completion: the float celebrating the upcoming Chinese New Year was still missing its key component—the actual dragon. The fairytale float only had two of the Three Little Pigs so far, the tribute to the Hohokam was just moving into production, and in CJ's opinion, the most disturbing sight was the seven headless dwarves on the Snow White float. Doug, the chief float builder, assured CJ that all dwarves would have a good head on their shoulders by the time the parade started.

Before she joined the board meeting in the conference room, she stopped by the food and beverage cart for another coffee and a bagel. She grabbed a few dog treats from the jar and tossed them to Houston, who waited patiently next to her. She knew Merry would have at least three plates of goodies for the board to enjoy, but CJ was trying her best to resist sweets and lower her A1C level, the measurement used to determine type 2 diabetes, since it seemed another reality of growing older was being prediabetic.

She was the last one to slide into her chair just as Merry Burris-Cisneros, CJ's best friend and the president of the JOY HOA, rapped her candy cane gavel on the table and announced, "I call this meeting of the JOY HOA to order. Let's keep it moving, people. We need a lot more time workin' and a lot less time flappin' our gums." She pursed her red lips and flipped the tail of her Santa hat back with her green fingernails. Her makeup was always perfect and while the hat covered some of her blond hair, most of it cascaded over her shoulders. In addition to her Santa hat, Merry's gold-framed prescription glasses sparkled and matched her glittery gold pants. Her Christmas sweater had four 3D presents across her front, and CJ imagined Merry's husband, Juan, who sat to her right, had made many jokes about her "gifts." She made eye contact with each of the five other HOA members. Everyone nodded their agreement.

"Instead of talking, please enjoy the banana muffins, apricot tarts, and some of this year's gingerbread people that I made this morning in the communal kitchen." She gestured to the middle of the table and the mouthwatering baked goods that smelled heavenly. CJ's willpower melted. Like everyone else, she grabbed a gingerbread person.

She realized that anyone who walked into the meeting and saw their group would burst out laughing. Everyone sported holiday headgear: Santa hats, reindeer antlers, elf beanies, and Taylor's new acquisition, a menorah headpiece: she would make sure Hanukkah was done well and done right during Ganza.

Juan Cisneros was also decked out in a red-and-white Christmas sweater that announced *There's no such thing as an ugly holiday sweater*. While Merry had just celebrated her fifty-first birthday, Juan was fifteen years her junior. Underneath the big sweater, which CJ guessed Merry had made for him, were rippling biceps and a six-pack that had earned him a spot on the Tucson firefighter calendar. He stroked his goatee and smiled lovingly at his wife.

Next to Juan's hulking bulk was his opposite, Blair Nicol, skinny as a stick, rockin' an Elvis pompadour and dressed in a black T-shirt and green plaid kilt. It didn't matter what season it was. Blair celebrated their Scottish heritage by wearing the same thing every day and glitzing it up with jewelry that accentuated their fiery red hair. Today they donned a necklace that read HOHOHO in gold.

CJ loved looking into Blair's cornflower blue eyes. Their calming voice and logical mind kept the board from going off the deep end as they navigated contentious issues, like whether to repaint the Santa sleigh with semi- or high-gloss paint.

CJ sat at the end of the table opposite Merry, and next to CJ was Taylor Zilberman, the board's secretary, the marketing whiz and computer expert. CJ imagined that Taylor, who was the youngest board member, would eventually run the JOY Ganza. She was a petite firecracker with dark hair that usually was pulled back into a ponytail, but today it flowed down her back so the menorah hat could stay atop her head. At twenty-two she'd started her own website-design business and judging from the extravagant vacations she took during the summers, she was doing just fine. In May she would receive degrees in journalism and computer science from the University of Arizona.

Ming Zhou, the treasurer and neighborhood seamstress, sat between Taylor and Merry. She was always sewing or mending something, regardless of where she was or what else required her attention. Her daughter's teacher had been understanding when Ming brought a torn elf costume to parent-teacher conferences, but the Tucson judge she encountered during her jury duty threatened to put her in jail if she didn't set aside the ripped wise man robe she was fixing during voir dire. He wasn't from the JOY neighborhood and didn't understand Ming's complete commitment to dressing the entire Ganza, which meant she worked for eleven months straight. Ming wasn't a woman to mince words and told the judge she was sure she could do her mending and find the person guilty at the same time. That earned her an immediate dismissal, and fortunately the judge liked Christmas enough not to throw her in jail for contempt.

Whereas everyone else on the HOA board took notes, Ming did not. She was always the first to report to the group since her sharing lasted less than ten seconds. CJ was certain today would be no exception.

Merry said, "First order of business, as usual, Ming's treasury report. Ming?"

Ming looked up over her glasses at the group. "I sent you the latest financial report. We're on target with our projected expenses. Receiving the grant from Tucson For All has ensured we stay in the black, even with the expense of the extra porta potties. Cookie sales are going well, and we've already received an extra five thousand in donations from people around the world. Finally, our anonymous benefactor has reached out again."

Merry clapped her hands. "Ooh, I'm excited."

"He or she or they will double this year's donation."

Juan smacked the table. "Two million dollars. That's what I'm talkin' about!"

"Three cheers for the benefactor!" Merry cried.

Once they'd "hip, hip, hoorayed" the benefactor, Ming said, "So we're all good." She returned to a split in Santa's pants.

"Are you sure we're on track with the costumes, Ming?" Merry pressed. "We have—"

"Three days, I know," Ming sighed. "No worries. Move on."

Merry saluted and turned to Juan, her face melting into a smile. "Whatcha got, baby?"

Juan winked and a titter went through the group—except for ever-focused Ming. The energy between Merry and Juan dripped sugary sweet all the time. CJ couldn't recollect a single fight or harsh word between them. They both seemed crazy for the other as the rest of the world watched from the fringes.

Juan cleared his throat and spoke like the fire department commander he was. "Most everything in the operations department is ready for tonight's run through of the lights. We have some more extension cords to fix, and I think I've finally convinced Mr. Palmutter that he cannot have seven cords plugged into one outlet."

Taylor asked, "How'd you do that?"

"Showed him the scene from *Christmas Story*, like six times."

Everyone laughed, recollecting the part of the movie where the "Old Man" creates a spark in the outlet from overloading it.

Juan looked down at his notes. "And…We've also secured the baby Jesus into the Stromans' nativity scene. There's no way Goldie, or any other dog, can grab him out of the crèche this year."

It had been hysterically funny to see Goldie, the Birch's golden retriever, and the biggest thief in all of JOY, running up and down the street with the baby Jesus in his mouth—until he stopped in a yard and shook it severely, causing Jesus's head to pop off. Several children screamed and cried at the decapitated holy savior until a quick-thinking elf scooped up the head, withdrew a gingerbread person from her pocket, and coaxed Goldie to give up Jesus's body.

"Everything else on my checklist is done or almost done."

"When are the reindeer arriving?" CJ asked.

Juan grinned. "Tomorrow. But we're not saying anything until tonight. We want it to be a surprise for the littler kids."

Blair crossed their legs and asked, "You're really keeping that a secret from Juanito?"

"*Especially* from Juanito," Merry commented about her son. "That boy couldn't keep a secret if his Christmas presents depended on it."

The return of the reindeer was a huge celebration and expense for Ganza. Decades before, CJ's grandfather had struck a deal with the owner of a Christmas tree farm in northern Arizona, who happened to own three reindeer. Commander Joy agreed to pay for the reindeers' food for the entire year if the farmer would breed or acquire five more, and then bring them to Tucson for Ganza, weather permitting. There had been a few winters that were too warm and the reindeer were canceled, much to the dismay of everyone. When they did arrive they were treated like royalty to maintain their comfort and health.

"What time?" Blair asked.

"Early, as usual," Juan replied. "Gotta get 'em out of the morning sun, even if it's only going to be forty-two. Probably between six and seven."

Blair nodded and made a note. No doubt the security force would need to be present, ensuring no one scared or spooked them accidentally.

In CJ's opinion, Blair's responsibilities were the most difficult, as they dealt with the City of Tucson and various private entities, like the local cable company and Tucson Electric, in addition to all of the JOY homeowners. CJ had personally witnessed the overt prejudice Blair faced when CJ and Blair had met with a city official about the difficult parking situation that happened every year. He took one look at Blair, dressed in their kilt and sporting pink nail polish, shook his head and smirked. Eventually he came around because Blair was exceptional at public relations and had managed to finagle a grant from Tucson Electric, but in CJ's mind, that city official represented all those who still couldn't understand the idea of nonbinary persons.

"Blair, how are things shaping up with the city?" Merry asked.

Blair quickly finished the last of their gingerbread. "The city's done what it can about the parking issue. We'll have a shuttle to and from the main gate, but state law says we can't prohibit other people from riding the shuttle even if they're not coming to Ganza."

"That's ridiculous," Juan said. "We're trying to help the environment and discourage so many cars."

"Now, Juan," Blair mocked, "when has the Arizona legislature ever cared about the environment?"

"Touché," Juan replied, picking up an apricot tart.

"The real issues," Blair continued, "are the preachers and the porta potty placements—"

"Say *that* ten times fast," Taylor joked.

The neighbors hated the porta potties, but after decades of finding visitors squatting around the sides of houses, the HOA authorized the expense in the '80s, recognizing bathrooms as a necessary evil. A rotation schedule was created and each street hosted the potties once every six years.

"This year it's Santa Street's turn," Blair explained, "but Mrs. Jones is insisting the crappers are put in the middle of the street rather than next to the sidewalk."

"But that's against fire regulations," Juan said. "The trucks couldn't get through if there was an emergency."

"I explained that to her so she's lobbying for placement on the other side. I've almost got the Prudhommes to agree, even though their side had the potties last time it was Santa Street's turn." Blair waved a hand. "I'll figure it out. We don't need to discuss it. I am, though, looking for ideas about the preachers."

"They're coming again?" Merry whined.

"Yeah. Preacher Joe says they won a lot of new recruits—er, followers—from last year."

"I still don't get why we can't kick them out," Taylor said. "I know the whole First Amendment thing, but when they're actually pointing at visitors and calling them 'whores,' that's gotta cross a line."

The rest of the board voiced their loud agreement until Merry was forced to bang the candy cane gavel. "Order! Order!" When they all quieted, she said, "We can't solve this issue right now. But everyone needs to be thinking of strategies to persuade the preachers to stay away."

CJ shook her head. "I never thought I'd be trying to dissuade people who are supposedly Christians from coming to an event that, for many—if not most—of our visitors, has clear *Christian* roots. With that said, we cannot have another confrontation like we did last year."

"But that was justified," Taylor argued. "I've taken an entire class on the First Amendment, and when those preachers pointed at the high school cheerleaders, called them whores and harlots—in front of their parents, boyfriends, and girlfriends—they shouldn't have been surprised when the entire football team jumped them. The preachers crossed that line, the one that doesn't allow you to shout fire in a crowded theater."

"That may be true," Ming said, "but the police didn't have time to sort that out. So they did the one thing they could do to restore order: shut down Ganza for the evening." Ming's son, a Tucson police officer, had been the supervisor on duty that night and had made the difficult call.

"I think shutting us down was the point," Blair said.

Merry nodded. "And that's why we need to use tactics that keep the peace."

"My grandfather is probably turning over in his grave," CJ muttered.

"I know," Merry said quietly. "Make yourself feel better and try the banana muffins. They're delish."

CJ nodded and reached for one.

"Taylor?" Merry asked. "Your turn."

Taylor held up a blue handout and said, "I emailed you each a copy of this, and it's been sent to all one hundred and fifty-one homeowners. It's got all the social media links, buzzwords to use, a link to our website. Now it's time for everyone to do their part like they always do," she added quickly and glanced at CJ, who winked in support.

CJ had offered to coach Taylor when it came to speaking in front of the board and interacting with people who were twice her age and had been planning and executing Ganza for decades—without any help from technology or social media. While Taylor, Blair, and Juan represented the youth and future of the HOA, the three other members, CJ, Merry, and Ming, were starting to think about Medicare. Taylor was quick to accept CJ's offer and she'd come a long way, learning patience and adopting a tone the elders didn't find condescending. In the process, Taylor and CJ had become such good friends that CJ felt like her mom.

"The only other thing I need to report," she continued, "is a potential hack into our server. Somebody tried to steal the recipe for the gingerbread men—I mean, gingerbread people…" she corrected with a quick smile at Blair.

"Oh, my!" Merry gasped. "Please tell me they weren't successful. I'm always so nervous about all this technology."

Everyone stared at Taylor—and even Ming looked up. "It's okay, Merry. Nothing happened. That's why we have three layers of security. I know everyone complains when I change the passwords every other month and I made us add facial recognition, but it all helps."

Merry took a deep breath. "Thank goodness. That recipe…"

She didn't need to finish her sentence. The gingerbread recipe, created by Nana Hope, the honorary JOY Grandma to All, was a huge draw to Ganza, and some people waited all year for the cookies and cocoa. Nana Hope had been approached by a cookie company to sell her recipe, which she'd politely declined, and the cookie maker went off and tried to replicate Hope's creation, only to fail miserably.

CJ and Merry, the only JOY residents entrusted with the recipe by Nana Hope, had recruited a small army of bakers who had already disappeared into the commercial-grade kitchen and would spend the holiday season making batches of Nana's cookies. Last year the JOY baking brigade had churned out nearly fifty thousand gingerbread people, a new record.

Merry took another deep breath. "All right, I think my heart rate is back to normal." Juan squeezed her hand and she blushed. "Thanks, baby."

"Sorry, Merry." Taylor winced.

Merry waved a hand. "No worries, honey. I continue to work on my internalization of bad or potentially bad news. It's still my growth area, according to Dr. Doan." Her gaze swept the table, over the people who truly cared for her. CJ knew, even though she had no blood relatives left, that these people were her family.

Merry said, "I just want us to get picked this year. I don't want to be another runner-up..." She fanned her face so the tears wouldn't come, and Juan leaned over and comforted her. Everyone knew Merry's competitive spirit was unmatched.

Blair shifted in their seat. "I think we're gonna get it this year. I really do."

"Me too," Taylor said.

It was the CUDL Award. CUDL stood for Christmas United Display of Lights, the highest honor that could be bestowed on a neighborhood Christmas festival. Five neighborhoods were chosen each year as finalists and then one received the grand prize. In addition to international attention, the grand-prize winner won $25,000. JOY had been a runner-up twice in the last ten years. Three years prior, when a CUDL official was spotted at Ganza, the board was certain they had the award in the bag until the gentleman visited the reindeer petting area, and just as the judge reached out to pet Barry the reindeer, Barry shook his head and shed his antlers, one dropping on the judge's foot.

"I know we have a great chance," Merry said, crossing her fingers and closing her eyes. She mumbled, "Think positive, think positive, think positive." When she opened her eyes, she looked at CJ. "Anything from you?"

"Unfortunately, yes. I got a message through my YouTube channel...from Karol Kleinz, Hope's granddaughter."

Suddenly everyone spoke at once, and Robert's Rules of Order, possibly Robert himself, were thrown out the window. Merry finally smacked her candy cane gavel on the table, silencing the board.

"Now," she said, "before we overreact about a communication from a person who hasn't been to JOY in several decades and couldn't even be bothered to attend her own grandmother's celebration of life…" Merry inhaled and closed her eyes. "Happy place, happy place."

As the board was familiar with the multitude of coping strategies Merry employed to deal with anger, frustration or just general pissed-offness, they waited patiently. Taylor had learned this the hard way during her first meeting, when she dared to interrupt Merry's sixty-second de-stressing chant.

"What are you doing?" Taylor had asked innocently.

Merry's eyes had popped open and she let out a primal scream that scared Taylor so much she fell over in her chair. It was also later reported that the scream had been so piercing, all the dogs in JOY howled in solidarity.

"Apparently," CJ continued, "she saw the promo we did for last year's Ganza, and she saw Hope's house as the workshop. She's asking why she wasn't informed since it's legally her property, and she wants to make sure it's *not* included in this year's Ganza."

"Well, of course, it's included!" Merry cried. "It's the gosh darn center of the whole show!"

Ming looked up again. Twice in a single meeting, CJ thought. Had to be some kind of record. "I thought the property management company was in charge of that," Ming said evenly. "They gave us permission."

"Yeah," CJ said slowly, "they did. And since they were…*are*… the agents for Ms. Kleinz, they had every right to authorize it. So they're in the clear for past actions."

"But now that she's aware…" Taylor said.

"She can revoke it," Blair finished.

"Boris, the property manager, told me that Karol's rarely communicated with them since inheriting the property. He didn't think she'd care. He said he put the information in an email the first year she owned the house and she never responded."

"Fu—…function Covid!" Merry spat, replacing the first word of her expletive with the family-friendly word she used regularly. "Hope should still be here!"

Everyone paused and a moment of silence fell upon the meeting. CJ had thought the loss of her would get easier with the passage of time, but Hope had been a second mother to her, just as CJ's mother, Elsa, had been Hope's best friend. Hope's house had become a refuge for CJ when Elsa developed ALS.

"Why don't we just tell her okay, we won't use it?" Juan offered. "She doesn't really care about this place, so she'll never know."

Taylor leaned forward. "And in case she gets on YouTube to check, we could make sure all the promo films use angles that don't show Hope's actual house. Juan's right. She'll never know."

"Except for the fact that she's coming here," CJ said.

The meeting devolved into more pinkish swear words—not the hardcore ones—exclamatory phrases and whining about another lost CUDL competition because there wouldn't be a Santa's Workshop. Merry became so distressed that she went to a corner of the room and put herself in time-out.

CJ just watched. She was agitated as well, but her anxiety had a secondary cause: memories of the past…kisses, some fondling, certain emphatic statements…that she'd exchanged with a preteen Karol Kleinz under the Aleppo pine. Her memories of those six weeks strewn across three summers were hazy at best. She remembered only moments, especially their physical connections, enjoyed at such a confusing and hormone-filled time of life. One feeling stood out and had followed her through adulthood: homeliness. She didn't think she was ugly but standing next to Karol had always made her feel inadequate, and she'd figured the only reason Karol had made the effort was to have a gal pal for the summer, one who was funny even if she wasn't very attractive. When Karol hadn't visited JOY after that third summer, CJ knew she'd been correct.

"CJ?" Merry asked, tapping her arm. "Anything else?"

"Uh, no."

The meeting broke up and CJ leaned over to Blair and asked, "Can I see you for a moment?"

Blair nodded and followed CJ outside. "What's up, besides everything?"

"I know you're crazy busy, but when was the last time you stopped by Tierra Celestial?"

"Uh, last Thursday. About a week ago. Why?"

CJ suddenly realized she shouldn't have bothered Blair. It was probably nothing. She glanced at Blair's "I'm-all-in" security face. She had to tell them something, so it might as well be the truth. "When I was out on my balcony this morning with my binoculars, I thought I might've seen someone in the second-story window."

Blair's usual blank expression remained just that. "Which room, west end or east end?"

"East end. But like I said—"

"The master. Huh."

"Did you notice anything unusual when you were out there on Thursday?"

Their beautiful blue eyes looked away but CJ could tell their gears were turning. Their cheeks turned red and they checked behind them before whispering, "I don't think it's related to what you're talking about, and I wasn't going to mention it, but I saw Noel out on the swings behind the barn. And I'm rather certain the person with her was Heather Coughlin."

CJ couldn't hide her surprise. Noel was Merry and Juan's fifteen-year-old daughter and Heather Coughlin was the shyest teenager CJ had ever met. "What were they doing?"

"Swinging…and not swinging."

"Oh."

"It was really harmless and I wasn't going to say anything to Merry and Juan. I was just going to talk with Noel about trespassing. I don't want to make a big deal of it. I don't think it's my place."

"I get that."

"But I'm mentioning it because if it wasn't their first time on the property…"

CJ nodded. "They might've seen someone. I'll talk to them and leave you out of it, okay?"

Blair exhaled and their shoulders dropped. "Thank you. I hate human drama."

"I know. Don't worry about it. I'll keep you posted."

Blair split their time between the JOY neighborhood and northern Arizona, working on the reindeer farm and other ranches. When they weren't wearing their reindeer antlers for the holidays, they were sporting a cowboy hat with their kilt. CJ had seen Blair ride a horse in their kilt and they did it with incredible grace and style.

"Thanks again," Blair said, squeezing CJ's shoulder. "Give me a pack of angry reindeer over a histrionic teenager anytime."

CHAPTER THREE

In her window seat on the plane, Stella snored softly next to Karol, a tousle of blond hair shrouding her face. Karol couldn't help but be a little envious. Stella was sixty-three and five years older than Karol, but she looked forty-five. Whenever they traveled for business and Stella flashed her AARP card for discounts, she was met with scoffs and bewilderment. Sometimes she did it just for the compliments, but hey, if ya got it, flaunt it. That's what Stella always said. Her lean, tall frame and smooth skin were the result of hard work, attention to skin maintenance, and mainly good genes. She was the definition of self-care.

Karol herself was fit from years of aerobics because Stella served as her teacher and personal trainer, but all the moisturizer in the world couldn't erase the deep creases in her face and the crow's feet. And unlike Stella, whose blond hair was mostly natural, Karol had a standing appointment with her stylist each month to keep her roots dark. The last time, though, the stylist, who sometimes served as Karol's therapist, broke the news to her: it was time to wave the white—or gray—flag. Her hair was too damaged to hold the color anymore. But if she gave up, in six months she'd be as white as hotel sheets.

She leaned back in her seat and reclined it. Thank God for business class. She wouldn't mind sitting in coach except for the lack of leg room and seat size. She was five foot eight and riding in coach felt like being trapped in a flying closet. She couldn't imagine how a tall person, like a WNBA player, could ever fit in one of those seats. Of course, Stella complained about the price of business class, until she stretched out in the leather seat and ordered a martini, which immediately helped her sleep—that and the Xanax she took in the gate area.

Karol was wide awake. In fact she hadn't slept at all in the last twenty-four hours. After seeing the video of Nana Hope's house, she'd fired off a message to CJ, ordering them to leave Nana's house. Then Karol had phoned her partners at Gentry, Kleinz and Rose, telling them she was officially retiring a week early. They didn't have to worry, though. She'd still show up for her not-really-a-surprise retirement party at the Ritz.

Her partners should have known not to trust Stella with a personal secret. When it came to business and confidential legal information, like literally where the bodies were buried, Stella wouldn't crack—ever—but tell her anything about a promotion, an engagement, or a plastic surgery appointment by the coffee maker in the staff lounge, and the news would be all over the office before the receptionist had made the second pot.

They were still two hours away from Tucson. Karol would've preferred a nonstop flight, but Manny, who was tucked away under her seat, needed to tinkle around Kansas City which had been their last stop. He was such a good little traveler and he made fur friends wherever he went. At the dog rest area in KC, a toy poodle made her amorous intentions clear, and the much-embarrassed owner could only apologize.

Manny took it all in stride. A good snuggler. A good *friend*? Maybe that wasn't the right word, but he was more loyal than her last few lovers. After Leslie dumped her, she kept her vow to stop dating, but she was definitely lonely.

She'd start anew in Boca. She was already taking stock of who she was in retirement, focusing on her next act. She needed to be busy but it had to be purposeful. While she enjoyed the community aspect of being an HOA and estate attorney, the pro bono work she'd done on behalf of unhoused people looking for permanent homes had been her personal North Star. The next stage in her life had to have similar purpose.

She drained the rest of her red wine and wiped her tired eyes. She'd spent hours combing through any article, video, image, or review she could find about the JOY neighborhood. One of the first things she learned was that the community had legally changed its title to all capital letters in the '60s.

"Free love and all caps," she muttered. "Makes sense."

She'd been there a few times during the summers, and it just seemed like a nice place, like any other neighborhood in the summer, nothing special. And summers in Tucson were slow and sweltering. It was nearly as hot as Phoenix and everyone stayed inside or found a pool. She suddenly felt cheated. Why hadn't her father sent her to JOY for at least one Christmas? Why had they always stayed in San Francisco? She liked Christmas, probably not as much as these people, but still…

She refocused on the website and what she could learn. It dawned on her that her request to eliminate Nana's house from the extravaganza would make her look like a grinch or a scrooge. They had a great website, put together by a cutie named Taylor, who, from the look of her, Karol guessed was a spitfire. Other than CJ, the only other person Karol had met during her summer visits was Merry, the HOA president. A memory of a little girl with beautiful golden hair, wearing a Peanuts Christmas shirt and skipping down Nana's walk during August, stuck in Karol's mind. As an olive branch she'd brought the photo of the three of them making cookies with Hope. Her "cease and desist" email from the night before seemed very harsh when she reread it in the morning.

She'd viewed all twenty-five of CJ's "how to" videos, and should anyone need to make a wreath, wrap an unwieldy present, buy a host gift, recycle glitter—and a multitude of other needs—

Karol knew just the video series they could watch. She hit the pause button any time she recognized something familiar—CJ's smile, her laugh, the way her curls bounced as she moved her head to the left or right. There were just enough similarities to confirm CJ's identity and then plenty of "additions" like the sound of her sweet voice! Karol loved listening to CJ's soft and melodic voice, tones meant for an audiobook.

The other person featured in a JOY video series was Merry. It was apparent she lived for Christmas. Whereas CJ's place had a clear southwest vibe with Saltillo tile and adobe walls, Merry did the holidays every day of the year. She even had summer Christmas attire, such as Santa shorts, modeled by her shirtless and very buff husband, Juan. He apparently loved Christmas as much as Merry, so much so that they kept the tree up in the living room year-round.

Karol looked through the queue of Merry's vlogs. She'd just finished learning about obscure and overlooked holiday music. Music that, as Merry described it, could replace that far-too-often-played Mariah song and any rendition of "Little Drummer Boy." Karol agreed with Merry on that point, and she'd added a few more songs to her holiday playlist based on Merry's recommendations.

The last vlog was apparently Merry's first one, filmed about seven years before. Karol had noticed the further back she went through the catalog, the more amateurish the vlogs seemed. Over time graphics had been created, music added, as well as a second camera, and editing. That cutie Taylor probably produces them now, she mused.

She wished she'd started from the beginning and worked her way to the present, but the older ones had a comical side that made her laugh. Merry was forever asking her husband the cameraman if they were "rolling," and her lapel microphone dropped into her abundant cleavage at least once during every filming, and he could be heard making suggestive comments whenever she had to fish the mic out from between her boobs.

Karol hit play and Merry's pleasant face appeared. She wore her reindeer antlers, her glasses with candy cane-striped frames, and a bright green sweater. She was looking at someone, probably her husband.

"We're on? Right?" She cracked a big grin. "Hello, this is Merry. I'm here today to assure you that fruitcake is not the enemy."

She let the heavy statement hang in the air while she mustered an earnest expression. "Now, I know most of you have never tried fruitcake." She raised a hand as if listeners would try to contradict her. "Nu-uh, I know it's true. Over the last few decades fruitcake has been maligned by many late-night TV hosts, ridiculed in countless Lifetime movies, and once was even used as a weapon during an assault." She shook her head as if in disbelief.

"According to our friends at Tucson Waste and Disposal, fruitcake is one of the most trashed holiday goodies, second only to blinking Christmas light necklaces. Oh, don't get me started on those. Mine went to Goodwill the same day I got one. If you watch my show," she said as a feline strolled into view, "you've met my cat, Mr. Chestnut."

Karol shook her head. Mr. Chestnut had appeared in a few of the later vlogs. He had to be one of the oldest cats in America. Karol guessed he'd been born a calico, but now he was practically bald. Merry had vaguely explained that there was an incident with candied apples and "Chesty" got the business end of the sweet treat. For whatever reason, when much of his fur was cut off, it never grew back. He also had an underbite that gave him a surly expression. Karol figured if she looked as homely as Mr. Chestnut, she'd be surly too.

Merry continued about the Christmas necklaces. "So Chesty saw those lights and entered a hypnotic state, falling off the top balcony of his kitty tree. In the moment, I couldn't be sure if his fall was related to the necklace, but when I bent over to see if he was hurt, he looked at those lights, his eyes got big as saucers, and he pounced on my front, tryin' to rip those little bulbs off me, which he did, along with several layers of skin.

"For a while I looked like I had a giant tattoo across my chest. Any time I wore my favorite V-neck Christmas sweater, my husband, Juan, always one to find the positive, commented that it looked like the Parthenon and perhaps Chesty had hidden artistic talent. We both had a laugh at that."

Merry sighed and said, "Well, back to the fruitcake. We're here today to make a fruitcake you will eat. A fruitcake you can be proud to serve guests or take to a holiday party." She motioned to her left and said, "And this is the premier fruitcake maker in all of Tucson, probably the entire Southwest, a fabulous baker and one of my best friends, Hope."

Nana Hope stepped into the screen and Karol gasped.

From next to Karol, Stella's blond head twisted toward her. "You okay?"

"Yeah," she replied absently.

It was like staring at a ghost. Nana Hope looked exactly as Karol remembered her—white hair in a bun, a bright red apron circling a waist wide enough to suggest she sampled the baked goods she made, a sweet round face with permanent laugh lines, and warm brown eyes, just like her daughter's...Karol's mother.

Nana looked into the camera with a kind smile and Karol closed her eyes to stop the tears. Nobody smiled like Nana. She did so with her entire face, as if there were a switch that honed all her features to sincerity.

"The steps to making fruitcake aren't difficult, but you must follow them precisely, and you can't skimp on the fruit." She stepped toward the counter. "Let's try it together, shall we?"

Shall we? How many times had Karol heard that phrase? Whenever she fell down—literally or figuratively—Nana offered a strong hand, not to make it all go away, not to do it for her, but to guide her. Those two words made most everything possible—*shall we?*

Karol watched as Nana pointed to the ingredients on the table, the garnet ring she always wore glimmering for the camera, the one Nana's mother had given to her and should've gone to Karol's mother, Joyce. *Except she died.* The ring turned out to the be the last communication Karol had had with Nana Hope. Although Karol skipped the celebration of life, too ashamed of her absence and apathy toward Nana's life, a package arrived a week after she was buried. It contained the deed to the house, the ring and a note that simply said, *All my love, Nana.*

Karol leaned toward the screen and smiled. She watched the video over and over. Nana's voice, her laugh, and her movements surfaced forgotten memories, like the time Nana taught her to use the standing mixer. Karol had turned it on too soon and the liquid ingredients splashed all over the cabinets, Karol's face, and Nana's good Christmas sweater, which had been left unprotected when Nana allowed Karol to wear her special holiday apron. After Nana hit the off button, they stared at each other, the rich smell of vanilla covering them both.

Karol immediately gushed apologies, expecting Nana to explode in anger. That's what usually happened at home when Karol or her mother made a mistake and Karol's dad was there to witness it.

Instead Nana had swept a finger across her chin and tasted it. "Mmm. I taste good. What about you, Miss Karol?"

Karol wiped her own chin, tasted, and nodded before they both burst out laughing.

"Passengers," the captain announced, "it's time to stow away those large electronics as we begin our descent into Tucson."

Karol sighed, relieved and regretful that she had to stop watching her screen. Any longer down that rabbit hole and she would've been bawling, something she didn't want to explain to Stella. Yet as she tucked the laptop back into the case, it was comforting to know Nana's voice and smile were just a few keystrokes away.

CHAPTER FOUR

CJ pulled into Christmas Card Court, Houston beside her. Tonight was the Electricity Dress Rehearsal. Opening night was now forty-eight hours away, and tomorrow would be the full dress rehearsal. As lights were the most crucial factor, they were tested first, just in case the JOY electricians, Karin and Becky Watts—that really was their last name—needed to be contacted.

Out of all the streets in the JOY, "The Court" was the most solemn, representing five different belief systems—Catholicism, Protestantism, Judaism, Buddhism, and Greek Orthodox. The lawns were devoid of all secular holiday representations as agreed upon by the neighbors and the cul-de-sac had a truly spiritual vibe. Some visitors spent a large part of their JOY Extravaganza experience in The Court, while others skipped it completely.

She stopped at the Stromans' place and double-checked the nativity scene, specifically the baby Jesus. She didn't doubt Juan's efforts to secure him in his cradle, but some of the neighborhood teenagers enjoyed pranking the event, although the "Jesus incident" had been ruled a complete accident. Most of the time the teenage antics made the HOA board laugh, except for Blair, who felt anything unexpected was a potential security issue.

A few stunts had crossed the line. In 2019, the teens made an extra batch of gingerbread people, ones that included very specific anatomical parts that separated the males from the females. When Merry found some amidst the gender-neutral cookies, she blew her cool and bit off the offensive bits, but not before one of the teens caught it on video. Merry earned the TikTok monicker "The Gingerbread Lorena Bobbitt" until Taylor removed the video.

CJ hopped out and waved at Steve Stroman, who was up on his roof with his son, Stevie, one of the teenagers CJ and the board kept tabs on during Ganza. The Stromans were devout Catholics, and CJ imagined that Steve had long confessions with the parish priest, and probably confessed to occasionally wanting to throttle his eldest son. She knew Stevie had been the ringleader of the gingerbread caper but he'd never admitted it. The code of silence that CJ remembered from her high school days seemed to pass from generation to generation. Protecting your friends was a part of teenage genetics.

Father and son were testing the bulbs of the giant cross that spanned the pitch of their roof. CJ guessed one bulb was dead or not screwed in correctly. "Anything I can do to help?" she called from the driveway.

"Actually, yes," Steve replied. "There's a sack of spare bulbs on the front porch, can you hand those up to me?"

CJ retrieved the bulbs and climbed the ladder to join them on the roof. "Hey, Stevie, how's it going?"

Stevie flashed his humble All-American boy smile, the one that got him off with a warning instead of a traffic ticket, detention from the assistant principal instead of suspension, and the cushy assignment of video game reviewer at the local paper. "It's all going great, CJ. How's everything looking?"

Stevie had his father's strong jaw and the male version of his mother's stunning features. For a brief time he'd been a child model, but he couldn't sit still long enough for a photo shoot. Nobody wanted to believe such a pretty face could be involved in anything slightly despicable, but CJ knew better.

"Is it true the reindeer get here tomorrow morning?" Stevie asked innocently.

CJ shrugged and shook her head. "Where did you hear that?"

"Around."

Stevie knew better than to tell her, because if Blair found out one of their elite "Reindeer Wranglers" was a leak...

"Stevie, you know I don't mind most of the pranks your crew has pulled. Putting the Olsons' sleigh over a Go Kart and driving it around the neighborhood was my favorite."

"And the year all the presents jumped out of Santa's bag was classic," Steve added.

Stevie beamed. "Thanks, Dad."

CJ frowned. "But the reindeer are completely and totally off-limits. You cannot pull any stunt or prank involving the reindeer. You got that, right?"

"Of course," Stevie said, his face so covered in sincerity that CJ almost believed him—almost.

"The HOA is uber-careful with them. You know why, right?"

"Yes. Because of the special relationship your grandfather established with the deer farm three generations ago," Stevie said, reciting the standard line the JOY children learned when they were young.

"And Blair would flog you if something happened," CJ concluded.

"And I'd help," his dad said, quickly looking toward the sky and adding, "Sorry, God."

Stevie held up his hands as if he were surrendering. "I got it. Really, CJ, I mean it. I know how important the reindeer are to the neighborhood. It might be cute to decorate their antlers or paint their hooves pink, but my life would be hell for the rest of the year."

"Hell is right," CJ agreed. "Okay, I'm glad we're on the same page."

Steve replaced the last bad bulb and suddenly brilliant white light flooded the roof. CJ quickly put on her sunglasses. "Nice," she said.

She waved goodbye and climbed off the roof, hoping she'd made her point with Stevie. She wanted to believe him, but the fact that he'd already outlined two pranks to pull on the reindeer suggested the window for mischief was wide open.

She and Houston slowly circled the cul-de-sac. None of the other residents were outside since their displays were completed. That happened every year. The Court finished first. While most of the other JOY neighbors would toil through all-nighters for the next two days, The Court was its own enclave, with a mini version of an HOA board. They all worked together to ensure their displays included the important symbols and representations of their individual beliefs, while conveying a central theme, a thread that connected them all. This year that thread was charity and philanthropy.

The Stromans always erected the nativity, but they'd also posted collection boxes in front of life-size versions of gold, myrrh, and frankincense, encouraging the visitors to donate money to the local mission. CJ noted the sturdy padlock on each box.

Enormous Bible quotations about giving and receiving covered the Wallaces' yard, done up like a series of movie marquees. Glowing white bulbs outlined each marquee, and stage footlights bathed a vertical gold cross in the center of the yard.

The Epsteins had a menorah in their window, but on their roof white lights spelled out Black Lives Matter. Near the sidewalk, a spotlight shone on a sign defining the word, *TZEDAKAH*, as righteousness, justice, and charitableness. A handcrafted tzedakah box, featuring the tree of life on its front, was ready to take donations. Three booths, currently empty, sat in the driveway. CJ imagined three different community organizations would be invited to hand out information and answer questions during Ganza.

The Kouris family was coordinating the yearly blanket and food drive. Anyone who'd ever been to the JOY Extravaganza knew not to show up empty-handed. It was a tradition CJ's grandparents, Christopher and Elizabeth, had begun at the very first Ganza. All those who donated got cookies and cocoa, and if those cookies tasted as good as the test batch at the morning's HOA meeting, there would be record-high donations. As the bulk of the Kourises' work was done at the two entrances, the display in their yard was simplistic. A sign that read Love One Another as I Have Loved You sat in front of three life-size thermometers, one for food, one for blankets, and one for "other stuff." The thermometers would fill with sand throughout the extravaganza based on the donations received. CJ couldn't remember a year when the thermometers hadn't filled to the brim by Christmas Eve.

Finally, the Gilbert family, devout Buddhists, had placed their statue of Buddha, which normally sat in their backyard near their yoga studio, in the center of the front yard, electric candles forming concentric circles to the yard's edge. Within each circle were pictures of pets in the JOY neighborhood, photos of relatives who had passed, and favorite quotations about love and kindness. A sign posted at the sidewalk explained the concept of Loving Kindness, or Metta, the compassion toward all sentient beings. CJ scanned the circles for the two photos she'd donated: one of Houston and the other of her grandparents with her mother. She smiled when she found the one of her family, the people who had made the JOY neighborhood a reality for her and thousands of others.

"C'mon, Houston, we've got a lot more to see."

At the mention of his name, Houston stopped sniffing a picture of Albie, one of Merry and Juan's Chihuahuas, and caught up to CJ. While she loved all of the displays in JOY, The Court was her favorite. It really brought the most joy to JOY.

While The Court was quiet and solemn, ready for opening night, the other streets were humming with energy. CJ liked these nights as much as the actual event. Neighbors held potlucks, everyone chowing down on dinner together before returning to their individual yards and getting to work. A few streets went house by house, all the neighbors helping each other to complete each vision one at a time, while on most streets, families tended to their own houses and called out if they needed more hands or extra help.

Indeed, it took many strong people to erect the enormous Snoopy and his decorated doghouse that had delighted young and old for the past twenty-five years. The Kentons challenged themselves each year to re-create scenes from favorite Christmas shows with life-size cutouts and props. Visitors meandered amid the display arranged in chronological order to "see" the movie or holiday classic like *Frosty the Snowman*.

By far the most elaborate display, one that had a national following, was the "Steampunk Holiday Show," created by the musical Clayton family. They sang original songs and often incorporated the always-present audience into their show. Steampunk, the style that combined nineteenth-century fashion and industry with futuristic esthetics, held a twist of Christmas that had earned the Claytons several neighborhood awards. Each year they erected a metal-framed stage with a large movable watch gear as the backdrop. During their performance the gear turned around and flashed green and red lights. Their costumes were elaborate Victorian-era designs. Mother and daughter wore tight bodices, flowing red skirts and corsets with metal headpieces displaying dials that looked as though they came right out of an old car. Father and son sported Christmas-green morning coats and top hats fitted with aviator glasses around the brim.

The new displays were always balanced by the traditional ones erected by the original owners, all of whom had a sign announcing their longtime commitment to the neighborhood. In CJ's mind they were the standard-bearers, the backbone of the community.

As she zipped up and down the streets, answering questions, problem-solving various placement issues, helping out homeowners who needed one more set of hands, her own holiday spirit soared. While most of the displays were still in disarray, and every construction and craft material imaginable was strewn across lawns and driveways, just seeing the twinkling lights was enough. And while she was busy making a list of those homeowners who would indeed need the help of the "Completion Crew" because they weren't terribly organized or they had bitten off more than they could chew, she was certain it would all come together by opening night, December 12th.

It wasn't just about Christmas. Indeed, all of the celebrations that occurred at the end of the year had been celebrated throughout the existence of the JOY neighborhood—Kwanzaa, Boxing Day, and Hanukkah to name a few. She remembered the first time the Yule festival, a celebration of the winter solstice by Wiccans, had been acknowledged back in the '80s. There were raised eyebrows and a few protests from nearby neighbors until Aura and Mage, the two Wiccan residents, held a party in their front yard and explained the celebration.

She'd just waved goodbye to the Zendejas family after helping them untangle twenty-five sets of lights when her cell phone rang. *Blair.* "Could be good or bad, Houston," she said as she answered. "What's up?"

"Hey, can you please come over to Santa Street?"

This had to be about the porta potties, but Blair's voice indicated nothing. "Um, sure. I'll be right there."

She pocketed her phone and quickly pulled Houston's collapsible dish from her backpack along with a bottle of water. After they'd both rehydrated, they headed toward the most southern street in the neighborhood, CJ mentally noting all the homes they were bypassing that she still needed to visit because they were owned by new residents. There was a lot of pressure about Ganza, especially for new homeowners who often felt overwhelmed the first time they participated. Anyone could "decorate" the exterior of their house, but to be a part of a collective effort, one determined to send a message about peace, kindness, and...well, joy, in a display that potentially would be seen by over 100,000 people over twelve nights... That often raised the stakes—and the anxiety.

When she turned down Santa Street, she immediately saw the problem. Twenty of the twenty-five potties followed the curve of the right side of the cul-de-sac and CJ was grateful to see they weren't in the middle of the street. However, the last five and the handwashing station were clumped together at the mouth. In recent years the board had ordered twenty potties, but visitor feedback from the previous year overwhelmingly indicated that was not enough, so five more were ordered— but no one had measured Santa Street to confirm the additions would fit.

Blair stood in front of the extra potties, surrounded by the neighbors. Nearby was Fergus, the delivery guy, perched atop his small forklift, a gingerbread person in one hand and a cup of coffee in the other. He looked amused at the scene unfolding in front of him. When he saw CJ, he grinned and held up the gingerbread person, nodding in approval.

She waved and pulled up beside Blair, who was speaking with Dr. St. John, an original owner and the informal mayor of the street. He informed CJ, "I'm all about following the rules and taking our turn as the 'pee hosts,' for lack of a better term, but this is too many for one street, and not just because of their size. The smell for two weeks is unacceptable."

Other neighbors grumbled their agreement.

Dr. St. John shifted his weight, his hands resting atop a cane. *When did he start using that?* She adored Dr. St. John, a retired professor of African American studies at U of A. His yard alternated between a display for Kwanzaa or a Santa's House— with him as Santa.

"Okay," Blair said. "Let's brainstorm a solution."

Angela Sands, a fourth-grade teacher, raised her hand. "I know we've talked about finding a central location for the potties, but it just hasn't happened." She quickly turned to CJ and said, "No offense, really. I know how hard the HOA works." CJ nodded. Angela had been the HOA secretary for five years. "I just know we're at that point maybe where necessity could at least be the second cousin of invention?"

"I'm all for that," Blair agreed. They looked around and asked, "Where can it go?"

Everyone fell silent, thinking. CJ already had the solution, but as it involved the city, the HOA had been hesitant to broach it. Every year it seemed they asked the city for something—and usually got it—but CJ hesitated to ask for too much all at once. They'd already spoken to the city about the parking. But as Angela had said, this had turned into a necessity. *If only my grandfather could've imagined a hundred thousand people visiting JOY…he'd have made a place for bathrooms.*

"How about this," CJ began. "There's an easement over by the north entrance. There's not a lot of room right now because of those six palm trees scattered about, but there is room for five units. Let's use the standard twenty units here on Santa Street with the handwashing station, have Fergus take the last five to the easement for use this year, order another handwashing station, and in January we'll open the discussion with the city about relocating those six palms so that next December that whole area could be for the porta potties."

"That is an excellent plan," Dr. St. John said, beaming. "And I'll be happy to volunteer if we need to do any research or legwork to get the city to agree."

"I can help with that too," Fergus called from his perch on the forklift. "I got friends in Tucson Environmental Services. We'll get it done."

"Great," CJ said, typing a note on her phone. "I'll put it on the board's agenda. Anything else?"

They all offered effusive thanks and dispersed to their respective yards, but Blair stayed and touched CJ's arm. "Thanks. I figured that's where you'd go with a solution, but I didn't want to put it out there without your or Merry's blessing, and she's stuck in cookie baking land."

"I get it."

"One other thing…" Blair opened their phone and pulled up a picture. "Do you recognize this car or driver?"

The car was a red Ford Focus. "Nothing like standing out," CJ murmured. There were two people in the front. She stretched the image to get closer to the driver, which pixilated the face and made it nearly indiscernible. *Something about it…* CJ looked at the back window and laughed. "Did you notice the dog?"

"What dog?"

"The Yorkiepoo, or at least I think it's a Yorkie."

"Huh. So much for my superior skills of observation."

"You see plenty," CJ said.

For the nine months of the year that Blair lived in the JOY neighborhood, spending the summers with the reindeer in northern Arizona, they made it their business to know which cars belonged to whom, and when Blair saw one they suspected didn't belong, they followed it through the neighborhood until it either reached a destination, which happened most of the time, or the driver hit the gas and peeled out of the neighborhood, no doubt there to case houses or see what online goodies had been delivered to the JOY porches. Blair was always extra cautious during the extravaganza prep. A few years prior, their attentiveness had foiled a destructive prank perpetrated by an ex-husband of a new resident. Thanks to JOY's security force of one and those who covered in the summer, JOY's crime statistics were the lowest in Tucson.

"Any idea where they went?"

"Not really. I snapped this right before I got pulled into the potty discussion. I got a pic of the rear plate, too, but my friend from the DMV isn't picking up. I've got a hunch it's a rental."

CJ stared at the photo. She knew that face. "Which direction were they going?"

Blair tossed their chin east. "Toward Candy Cane Lane and Christmas Avenue."

Nana Hope's house was on Christmas Avenue.

CHAPTER FIVE

"According to GPS," Stella announced, "you just need to turn left at the dancing sugar plum fairies and you'll be there."

Karol smirked and made the left turn. Stella's long nap on the plane had refueled her sarcasm tank and Karol realized it was a mistake to bring her on this reconnaissance mission. If they interacted with anyone, especially CJ, Stella's complete inability to make a good first impression would leave a lasting imprint that wouldn't help their position.

They passed a little red brick wall with the sign: Welcome to the JOY Neighborhood. A bed of colorful flowers burst from the ground, confirming the welcome—and the joy of cool weather in the desert.

Stella pointed at the sign. "Emphasis on *joy*, with capital letters," she announced as they turned onto Angel Avenue and entered the community.

A group of neighbors standing in the middle of the street stepped to the side, but not before they all stared into Karol's rental. When they saw Manny peering out the open back seat window, they smiled and waved. Karol waved back, hoping the gesture made her look less like an outsider. She glanced at the rearview mirror and saw someone in a skirt—no, a kilt—taking pictures of the rear license plate. "Great," she muttered.

Stella pointed to the residences on her right. "This street looks post-apocalyptic, if the apocalypse happened at the North Pole."

She had a point. Strewn across each yard were large wooden cutouts of animals, candy canes, Rudolphs, Santas, Snoopy and his decorated doghouse, Charlie Brown and his sad little tree… and some Karol didn't recognize. Cartoonish signs and deflated Christmas blow-up figures lay atop bushes and cars. Most lights glowed on each house, but some sat in the various driveways, people kneeling in front of them testing and replacing bulbs. Karol had seen enough video of the JOY Extravaganza to know the community would pull it all together. They still had two days before the opening, and usually disarray and chaos preceded awe and amazement.

Stella continued her commentary but Karol tuned her out as memories surfaced—making cookies with Nana Hope, playing gin rummy on her porch at night, and taking long walks with her in the early mornings. Karol visited in August and daytime temperatures catapulted to triple digits by noon, sending Nana Hope inside her air-conditioned house. Nana Hope was the center of almost every memory of visiting JOY—almost.

Karol made another left turn onto Peppermint Parkway, knowing Stella would comment if she happened to see the street sign. She missed it, but she leaned forward, studying the streetlamps. Karol had been fascinated by them too when she first saw them as a child. They looked like the old oil lamps used before electricity, but these were modern and had been adorned with red and green garlands. At the top of each was a Santa hat.

"Okay, those are adorbs," Stella said.

"Agreed."

Karol pulled into a large empty parking lot. She guessed no one was around because all the homeowners were in their yards. She scanned the open field, which looked completely different than she remembered. A large building with red and green doors stood directly in front of them, its sign reading *Elizabeth Joy Community Center*. Well-lit basketball courts sat south of the center, and to the north, where the basketball courts used to be, were pickleball courts. In the rear was a smaller, completely full parking lot near a nondescript building. *That's new too.*

Only the giant Aleppo pine remained from her childhood.

"I take it you came here when you were a kid?"

"I did. Spent a lot of time on the basketball court that used to be over there."

"You played with CJ, right?" Stella asked, her voice dripping with innuendo.

"Yeah."

"And you did more than shoot hoops."

Karol stared at her but said nothing.

"That answers my question. Will it be weird for you to see her?"

"After forty-five years, I doubt it."

"Good. We don't need any distractions."

Manny barked and jumped on the front seat console. "Okay," she said. "Let's go stretch our legs."

"You go and I'll wait here." Stella leaned against the headrest and closed her eyes.

Karol was grateful for a few minutes alone. She automatically headed toward the Aleppo wrapped in colored lights that ascended to the highest branch. At the top was a shiny gold star. Manny sniffed around the base, leaving his mark in several places, while Karol gazed toward the pickleball courts, remembering how she and CJ had found each other by accident one day when Karol took her basketball to the playground during Nana's nap time. Although Nana complained about the Tucson heat, it didn't bother Karol to shoot hoops in the midafternoon. The heat in Arizona was dry, nothing like the sweltering humidity of the East Coast that she experienced when she visited her paternal grandparents.

She'd come upon a shorter girl about her age practicing free throws. Karol stayed next to the giant Aleppo and watched her. They dressed alike—gym shorts and tank tops—but while Karol's skin was tanned thanks to her Mediterranean ancestors, the other girl was milk white, almost ghostlike. She had dark curly hair and a stocky build. Karol imagined that she easily held her position on the floor during a game. She made more free throws than she missed, and those she missed were close, just clanking off the iron.

When the ball hit the front rim and bounced toward Karol, she stepped away from the tree and scooped up the ball, acting as though she'd just walked up. The girl grinned and held out her hands. Karol smiled and passed her the ball.

"Thanks." She glanced at Karol's ball. "You want to play? I'm CJ."

"I'm Karol. What do you want to play?"

CJ shrugged. "How about HORSE or Around the World?"

"HORSE is cool."

"Have you played on this court before?"

Karol shook her head. "First time. I'm just here visiting my grandma, Nana Hope."

CJ's blue eyes widened, and Karol swore they were twinkling. "Yeah, Nana Hope is cool. She said you were coming for a visit." CJ turned to the hoop. "Let's just practice awhile so you can get used to the basket. It's kinda bent at the front."

They shot around, showing off their trick moves, making small talk about families and school.

"I'm actually Carol, too, but I go by CJ. I've never met another Carol."

"I was named after my dad's favorite aunt, but I'm Karol with a 'K.'"

Manny now barked to move on, the Aleppo pine fully inspected. Karol ignored him and closed her eyes, remembering the sweet kiss she and CJ exchanged at the end of the summer, the night before Karol left. Up to that point they'd held hands, hugged, and leaned against each other in the movie theater. She hadn't wanted the summer to end. That kiss... It was the first time she'd ever kissed a girl—anyone—and it confirmed her sexuality.

They had kept in touch for a while through phone calls and letters, but neither of them was great at long-distance communication. Karol had sent CJ a present for Christmas, a copy of *Ruby*, a story about a teenage lesbian girl. She'd found the book in a store on Castro Street in San Francisco. Inside the cover she'd written, *See? We're normal!* Then the next summer they picked up right where they left off, kissing under the Aleppo pine that first night.

They were teenagers now, and they'd seen R-rated movies and felt so mature. While they never went "all the way," there had been a lot of touching and kissing, and even an "I love you." Karol came back to Tucson for one more summer, but CJ had been away on a family vacation. By the end of that summer, her father had decided they'd move back east, closer to his family, and she hadn't been back to Tucson since. But you should have, she again scolded herself, you should've been back for Hope's celebration of life!

The car horn honked. Karol rolled her eyes. She gave Manny's leash a little tug. "C'mon, boy. Auntie Stella's ready to go."

They loaded back up and Karol pulled onto Christmas Card Boulevard.

"Are we almost done?" Stella whined. "I feel like I'm stuck in a Hallmark made-for-TV movie."

"I just want to see Nana Hope's house."

"That's a good idea. We need to make sure that all of the holiday decorations have been removed, in accordance with Judge Hurwitz's orders."

Karol glanced at Stella. "You do know, technically, he has no jurisdiction in Arizona."

"True, but many people don't know about judicial overreach, and of course the law is on your side as the owner of the property. Maybe they…"

The thought died on Stella's lips as Karol pulled up to Nana Hope's house. If anything, more decorations had been added and a sign with flashing neon lights sat next to the driveway announcing SANTA'S WORKSHOP. Sitting on the porch in

Nana Hope's Adirondack chairs were CJ and someone that Karol thought was wearing a kilt.

It had taken a half hour longer than CJ expected, but finally the rental car Blair had photographed rolled up in front of Nana Hope's house. She'd barely recognized Karol from the distant photo Blair had taken, but the shape of her face looked familiar. Now CJ stood up from her Adirondack chair and took a deep breath as Karol got out and opened the sedan's back door, flashing her familiar smile at the dog. She came around the front and the Yorkie bounded up the sidewalk. Karol avoided CJ's gaze, focusing on the tall woman exiting the passenger's side. *Equally as attractive as Karol, so probably her girlfriend or wife. And she's dressed for business.*

"Here we go," Blair murmured. "Which one is Karol?"

"The driver," CJ whispered. "I think." Karol really didn't look anything like CJ remembered, but nearly fifty years of absence will do that. Her dark hair was much grayer, and she'd filled out, especially her chest. *Why am I noticing that?* She wore designer jeans and a short-sleeve denim shirt with a gold necklace and gold earrings. Her makeup was understated, but in CJ's opinion it was completely unnecessary. She'd been a beautiful girl and now was an equally beautiful woman. CJ almost sighed. She'd never understood what Karol had seen in her—the frumpy tomboy.

"Well," Blair observed, "she's very attractive, as is her friend. Girlfriend?"

"Maybe," CJ said, suddenly hoping the other woman was a colleague, a bodyguard—anything but Karol's girlfriend or wife.

Karol and the passenger started up the walk together, and CJ had roughly thirty feet to process so many emotions and memories that she didn't really have time for right now, seeing as Ganza's list of things to do was still four pages long. She did her best to push it all away and just smiled pleasantly.

She had no idea how to greet Karol. They were in weird relationship purgatory. She vividly remembered sliding her hand under Karol's tank top during one of their kissing sessions, the exciting shock of touching female breasts not her own. Karol decided the greeting when she pulled CJ into a brief hug.

"It's good to see you, CJ," Karol said.

CJ wanted to believe she was sincere. "Good to see you, too."

"I'm Stella," the tall woman said, thrusting out a hand to Blair. "I'm the person who will live in the other half of the duplex we bought in Boca Raton, assuming we can get this old house sold."

"I'm Blair," was the easy reply.

"Love your kilt," Stella said.

"Thanks."

"Do you take pictures and profile all the cars traveling your thoroughfares or just ones you don't recognize?"

"Exactly," Blair replied, and Stella was momentarily speechless.

Stella looked younger than Karol, CJ thought, but that could easily be attributed to a good surgeon and fancy beauty products. She wore a business suit and her blond hair messily draped over her shoulders, which just made her more attractive. Whereas her hair was mussed, her makeup was perfect.

Blair turned to Karol. "Hi, it's nice to meet you. Your grandmother was one of the best human beings I've ever known."

The smile Karol had plastered on her face cracked and her eyes puddled at the mention of Hope. She swallowed hard and managed, "Thank you."

Blair squatted to Karol's dog and said, "Who's this cutie?"

"That's Manny," Karol said. "His real name is Manhattan."

As if on cue, Manny sat up and offered his paw. Blair shook it and laughed. "Pleasure is all mine, Mr. Manny. That's quite the long name for such a little guy."

Stella looked at her watch and then at Karol, whose gaze had focused on the kitchen window.

CJ thought Karol was remembering the hummingbird feeder that sat just outside that window and the many times Hope had called them over to watch the birds with her.

"Hey," Stella said, "Earth to Karol. Remember why we're here?"

Karol seemed to drag herself back to the conversation. "Um, yes." She looked at CJ uncomfortably.

"I take it you got my court order," Stella said.

CJ grinned. "Oh, yes."

Stella gestured to the yard, covered in fake snow, Santa's sleigh filled with presents. "Then why hasn't it been heeded? It was very clear and written in English. We would've expected at least part of the yard here to be gone—"

"Stella, stop," Karol said curtly.

"No, please keep going," Blair said, folding their arms. "Please inform us how a New York judge has any jurisdiction here in Tucson."

Stella's gaze slid up and down Blair's physique. "Are you an attorney?"

"Former paralegal," Blair said, looking coolly back at her.

"You are?" CJ asked. "How did I not know this?"

"Because I never talk about it. It was one of the worst times in my life. A time when I sold my soul and prostituted every fiber of my being for the almighty dollar." They cocked their head to the side and asked Stella, "And what do you do?"

Stella cracked a smile. "Just a soulless paralegal."

Nana Hope's front door creaked open and suddenly Michael Bublé belted the chorus of "Holly Jolly Christmas."

"Shit!" Stella said, jumping back.

"Oh, my! Language, please," Merry shouted over the chorus. "Children are present."

Juan and Juanito followed Merry onto the porch. Juan shut the door, silencing Mr. Bublé. At the sight of Karol's dog, nine-year-old Juanito immediately fell to his knees and Manny rushed into his arms, licking his face.

"Manny," Karol scolded, but she didn't pull him away.

"Does that always happen?" Stella asked, pointing to the door.

Juan crossed his arms. "Do you have something against a true Canadian national treasure?"

"No, I'm just thinking prospective buyers might find that particularly annoying."

"Then, frankly, they don't belong here," Blair said. "Everyone in this community is dedicated to holiday cheer, and *this* house in particular..." Blair looked away and Merry patted their shoulder.

"You can't keep this house from Karol!" Stella cried. "It's hers. She gets to decide if lights go up or not, if it's going to be Santa's Workshop or...a Hell's Angels clubhouse, whether she wants Michael Bublé or Herman's Hermits for a doorbell ring."

"What's a Herman Hermit?" Juan asked.

"Papa," Juanito said, looking up, "Herman's Hermits was a British pop band from the sixties. They're the ones who recorded 'I'm Henry the Eighth, I Am.'"

Juan frowned. "I hate that song."

Juanito faced Karol. "Excuse me, ma'am. First, I'm Juanito and this is my father, Juan, and my mother, Merry."

"We know each other," Merry said primly.

"Oh, well, would you really kick Santa out of his workshop just a few weeks before Christmas? Would you deply—"

"Deprive, honey," Merry corrected.

"Oh. Would you *deprive* children of meeting him and telling him what they want for Christmas?"

Karol crouched and looked him in the eye. "I understand this is an important part of the Extravaganza, but—"

"Seriously," Stella interrupted, glaring at Merry, "you coached your kid to say this stuff? How low can you go?"

"I did no such thing," Merry insisted. "Juanito is incredibly bright."

Stella harrumphed, "That's what they all say."

Juanito stepped forward and said, "I've got this, Mama." He turned to Stella. "Ma'am, I'm encouraged to use my advanced vocabulary even if I make a mistake. *Yo tambien hablo dos idiomas.* That means I also speak two languages. Can you say the same?"

Looking disconcerted, Stella shook her head while Juan and Merry giggled. From the look on Karol's face, CJ guessed he'd effectively dressed down Stella.

Stella put her hands on her hips. "Look, kid, sometimes things don't work out. We need to get our business done here and get gone." She looked over at the adults and added, "I'm sure some other house could be Santa's Workshop. Right?"

"Not in time," CJ said, stepping to the doorway. "Opening night is in forty-eight hours."

"Forty-six," Blair corrected.

CJ nodded. "Not that you have any legal authority to shut us down—"

"For now," Karol said curtly.

CJ paused and stared at her stony face. *How much have you changed?*

"True," CJ conceded, "but you being an attorney, I'd think you'd want all the facts before you make that decision. Can I give you a tour so you can see all the hard work that's been done, primarily to keep your grandmother's memory alive?"

Karol's expressionless veneer cracked and she cleared her throat and muttered, "Um, not tonight."

"Figures," Merry said. "You couldn't be bothered to come to her celebration."

"Merry," CJ hissed.

Karol held up a hand. "No, I deserve that."

"You should at least read the plaque," Merry added, pointing to the bronze engraved testimonial next to the front door. The small crowd parted and Karol shuffled to the plaque.

Home of "Nana" Hope Yates
May 1, 1921 – March 15, 2020
Grandmother to All
Nana Hope put the joy in JOY!

Karol stood perfectly still for much longer than it would take anyone, especially someone who produced legal documents for a living, to read and comprehend the short message. She slowly raised a hand and settled her fingertips on her grandmother's name and bowed her head. CJ wasn't sure if she was praying, crying, or both, but she felt a strong desire to wrap comforting arms around her.

Suddenly Karol turned, her expression again like stone. *Definitely her lawyer face.* She ostentatiously looked at her watch, and said to Stella, "I think we should go to the hotel now. It's late and we can deal with this tomorrow."

"Let's deal with it right now. We need—"

"I said tomorrow."

All the bluster evaporated from Stella's face. She looked genuinely hurt. "Fine," was her curt response.

Karol looked around. "Where's Manny?"

"He was just here," Blair said, crossing to the far side of the porch and glancing around the house. "Manny!"

"I'll look around on the other side," Juanito said.

"I'll go with you, son," Juan offered.

"Maybe he went inside while we were talking?" Merry suggested. "Does he like gingerbread cookies?"

Karol rubbed her temples. "He likes to hide."

"Gotcha. I'll check inside. There's lots of good places."

Stella went in the same direction as Blair, and Merry disappeared, Michael Bublé emoting a few more measures before the door closed behind her, leaving only Karol and CJ on the porch. Cries of "Manny!" came from every direction.

Karol crossed her arms and stared at her loafers. A breeze swept across the porch, signaling that winter chill had arrived. Good news for the reindeer, CJ thought. "Would you like my sweater?"

Karol glanced at her. "No, thank you. I'm okay."

"I'm guessing there's a lot of memories on the other side of that door."

Karol nodded. "I haven't been here since…I'm not sure."

CJ cleared her throat. "Since August of nineteen seventy-seven, specifically, August fourteenth."

Karol shuffled her feet and CJ willed her to look up, remaining silent. Eventually she did. CJ had forgotten Karol's green eyes.

"You remember the exact date?" Karol murmured.

"Yeah. I remember a lot. Do you at least remember…some things?"

Karol smiled. "Of course."

Suddenly CJ shivered. That was Karol's secret smile, the one meant only for CJ and offered when Nana Hope or other adults inquired about the time CJ and Karol spent together.

CJ smiled back and held her gaze. "You know, if you're going to sell the house, you need to go inside and see it. For all you know, Nana Hope might've installed a greased pole in her bedroom."

Karol laughed and CJ enjoyed how rich and deep it was, just as she remembered. CJ had said or done whatever she could to hear it every day they were together.

"I'll go into the house tomorrow. I didn't realize...until we walked up the steps...And there's that plaque." She sighed. "Wow, it's a good thing my law firm's founding partner isn't here to see me stumble over my words. He never would've hired me."

"I understand. You left and never came back, not even for her celebration of life. A lot of people never forgave you for that. Some people—"

"Did you?"

"Did I what?"

"Forgive me?"

"I did. I figured you had your reasons, and even though we waited nearly a year for the service, a lot of people were still afraid to fly. I thought that might've been your reason—at least that's what I told Merry."

"Did she buy it?"

"Considering most of us, especially Merry, would've done whatever it took to be there for Hope...no." CJ pointed to one of the Adirondack chairs. "Do you remember that?"

They'd spent many evenings sitting on the porch talking. Over the years, any time CJ walked up the steps to visit Nana Hope, a single image came to mind: Karol in the chair, throwing her head back and laughing, usually at something stupid CJ had said.

Karol shrugged.

CJ gasped. "I'm disappointed." She rotated the chair, revealing their initials burned into the back crossbeam.

It was Karol's turn to gasp. "My birthday present! That wood-burning pen."

They squatted and studied their decades-old handiwork. Karol traced their initials with her index finger, and for a moment CJ felt the years of absence dissolve. When Karol turned and smiled, CJ knew she felt it too.

CHAPTER SIX

Karol's phone alarm chirped at five a.m. the next morning. She debated whether to get up or just sleep in. After all, she was retired. She didn't have anyone left to impress, no judge's schedule to follow and no junior associates to supervise. She could stay in bed. Then she remembered what CJ had told her last night.

If I get up, I can go see reindeer!

She had less than an hour to get ready and make the ten-minute drive over to the JOY neighborhood. She'd be free from Stella for a while. She'd forgotten how exhausting Stella could be outside the workplace.

Since they all but lived at the office, most of the time it had been easy to keep Stella focused. Such was not the case now. In the last twenty-four hours Stella had fried Karol's nerves more than once, and a shadow of doubt crossed her mind about the move to Boca. While they would each have their own side of the duplex, they knew no one else, so for at least a while they would rely solely on the other. *Is that really what I want?*

The drive back to the hotel from the JOY neighborhood last night had been ten minutes of a Stella rant about the kooky people stuck in holiday mode and their complete disregard of the law.

"The nerve of them—and I mean all of them—not just Blair," Stella qualified, "to think they can do whatever they want with *your* house."

Karol knew the touchstone of Stella's anger was the judge's order. Stella had called in a favor with Judge Hurwitz to sign it, a favor that was now spent for no profit, although Karol couldn't imagine either of them would need favors anyway from a New York judge after they retired to Florida.

They had been bested by a paralegal with disdain for the legal system, and Blair had clearly gotten under Stella's skin. Karol wasn't sure if that meant interest—at least on Stella's part—or dislike.

"I can't believe Blair!" Stella had bellowed. "And what is it with that 'they' thing? I really don't understand it."

"Why don't you ask them?" Karol offered.

"I don't want to seem ignorant—"

"You mean old."

"Don't say that!" Stella growled and then shut up. It was blessedly silent in the car until they arrived at the hotel. Stella's last words before she slammed their connecting door shut were that she would find a Tucson judge who would do the right thing.

Just rehashing their conversation last night was enough to propel Karol into the shower. By the time she was dressed, Manny was ready for his kibble and his walk outside. When she pulled out of the parking lot, she still had fifteen minutes to spare. A part of her was excited to see a reindeer. *Or are you really excited to see CJ again?*

As she crossed into the JOY neighborhood, most everyone was outside in their yards. Some were preparing for Ganza, as CJ called it, but many sat in lawn chairs holding cups of coffee and eating pastries as if they were waiting for a parade to start. In the daylight, the neighborhood looked stately—old one-story ranch homes, mostly constructed from red brick on large plots of land. Palms and paloverde trees were prominent, and most "lawns" consisted of desert landscape to preserve Arizona's most precious resource: water.

A few more turns and she pulled up in front of Nana Hope's house. Just like last night, her mouth went dry and she felt a lump in her throat. She clutched the steering wheel for a little longer, willing her hands to stop shaking. She took a cleansing breath, and willing away further thought, she got out of the car and smiled when she saw CJ sitting in one of the Adirondack chairs. Manny ran ahead to greet CJ, and Karol was almost embarrassed when he jumped right into her lap.

"I'm so sorry about his manners."

"No need. I understand pushy dogs." CJ pointed to the large rottweiler mix who'd risen to his feet at Manny's brazen invasion of his space. "This is Houston, Huey for short."

Karol squatted to give Huey a scratch behind the ears, and Manny ducked between Karol's legs and sniffed Huey's enormous mouth. He seemed relaxed and friendly but clearly Manny could be an hors d'oeuvre for him.

CJ handed her a cup of hot coffee and pointed to the pastries on the small table. "Help yourself. If you need to doctor your coffee, there's some stuff just inside."

"Thanks, but I just like it black."

"Me too."

Karol momentarily prickled at CJ's familiarity with Nana's property, but she quickly reminded herself that CJ had visited Nana thousands of times and probably helped her with a multitude of do-it-yourself tasks. If anyone was the outsider, it was Karol.

"How did you know I'd come over this morning?"

CJ offered a lopsided grin. "Well, I didn't *know*, but I thought you might. I hoped you might."

A crackling voice cut through the air. "CJ, what's your ten-twenty?"

CJ pulled a walkie-talkie from her belt. "I'm over at Hope's house with Karol."

"Ten-four. We've got about fifteen more minutes. They hit a bottleneck on I-17, so they're a little behind."

"Gotcha."

CJ started to refasten the walkie-talkie when Blair said, "Is Stella there too?"

CJ looked at Karol, who pressed her lips together, suppressing a grin. "Hmm. Interesting." She pressed the talk button and said, "That's a negative."

A female voice chimed in, "Stella and Blair just sittin' in a tree—"

"Hey, knock it off, Merry," Blair barked. "This channel is for security business only."

"Yeah," Merry drawled. "Right. Hey, honey, did you have a chance to stop by Mrs. Singer's place this morning?"

"I did," a male voice replied, and Karol assumed it was Juan. "She's doing…okay today."

"I'll check on her later while I'm giving a tour," CJ replied. She smiled at Karol. "At least, I hope I'll be giving a tour."

"Karol," Merry said, "you definitely want to take a tour with CJ. With the neighborhood all gussied up right now, it's like going behind the scenes at Disneyland, only without It's a Small World, thank God."

"Or Pirates of the Caribbean," Juan said. "That's Juanito's favorite."

"And the monorail," Merry added. "I wish we had a monorail. But not the Bear Jamboree. That thing gave me a headache."

"Did I mention this is a security channel!" Blair snapped.

Everyone stopped talking and CJ holstered her walkie-talkie. She shook her head. "Sometimes our professionalism goes sideways."

"It seems like you all care for each other. What's the situation with Mrs. Singer?"

"She's nearly eighty and lost her husband last year and is living all alone. We try to keep tabs on her and help with things she can't do. She's not ready to give up her independence and take a place in our assisted-living group home."

"You have a group home for the elderly? In this neighborhood?"

CJ nodded. "It happened organically. One of the neighbors just kept building rooms onto his house. He eventually moved to the Pacific Northwest, and we had an elderly couple who just couldn't live on their own anymore. So I bought the place and we had it rezoned as a group home. There's a spot there now for Mrs. Singer when she's ready."

"That's incredibly generous and kind of you."

"It's what my parents would've wanted." She took a deep breath. "Thank you for sending the flowers after my mom died. That was equally kind. Hope brought them over, but she said you paid for them."

Karol knew she was blushing. "It was the least I could do. Your mother was so nice to me."

CJ glanced at Hope's front door. "What about going inside today?"

Karol looked away and took a deep, meditative inhale and closed her eyes. Only when she exhaled did she open them again. "That's a maybe. I thought coming here and taking care of the house would be easy, just business. I didn't think about the emotional aspect. I mean, I did, but I'm surprised."

"Can I ask why you didn't come to the celebration of life?"

Karol set her coffee down and grabbed one of the napkins near the pastries. She dabbed at her eyes and stared at the street. She couldn't look at CJ. "I was so ashamed. I didn't feel like I had the right. Nana used to always say that if you didn't care about me during my life—"

"Don't bother with my funeral," CJ finished.

"Exactly."

CJ reached for and gently took Karol's hand. "I know she didn't believe her favorite quotation applied to you. She was so proud of everything you'd accomplished and the woman you became."

Karol cocked her head to the side, absorbing the warmth and firmness of CJ's hand. "How would you know? Did she talk about me a lot?"

CJ cleared her throat and blushed. "So, do you remember that night we hung out over here while Hope went to bingo over at the church?"

Karol suddenly shivered. *Am I having hot flashes? What is going on?* "I remember that night. It was very special."

They had told Hope they were making cookies and watching TV, which they did, but as the night grew longer, they moved closer and held hands. Soon they were kissing...and touching. When CJ slipped her hand underneath Karol's tank top, Karol surprised her by guiding her hand up to her breast. Soon they were topless.

"I'll always remember that night," CJ whispered. "That's when I knew I was a lesbian."

Karol squeezed her hand. "Me too."

"And apparently that's when Nana Hope learned we were lesbians."

Karol gaped at her. "She did? How?"

"Well, she told me several years later that when she came in through the back door, we must not have heard her, probably because of the TV. She saw us and decided to slip back out and come in again, much louder than the first time."

Karol laughed. "I remember that part. I put on my bra so fast."

CJ was grinning. "Me too." She paused and studied their entwined fingers, noticing how much their hands had aged. Finally she said, "I think Hope wanted us to get back together, so she gave me periodic updates about you. When you graduated from high school, when you decided to go to law school. Did you know that we were less than a hundred miles from each other during those years?"

"Really?"

"Yeah. While you were at Columbia going to law school, I was in Philly at the Wharton School of Business getting my MBA."

"Why didn't you call me or try to get in touch?"

CJ pursed her lips and Karol shook her head. "Stupid question." She sighed and leaned closer. "I just want you to know that just because I stopped visiting and didn't stay in touch—"

The walkie-talkie crackled and Karol pulled her hand away quickly and reached for her coffee.

"Okay, they're in the city limits," Blair squawked. "Security, at your places, please."

"That's our cue," CJ said. "We're not security but we're the official hostesses."

"*We?*"

"Unless you're afraid of reindeer or think they're ugly."

"Are you kidding? I'd love to meet them!"

CJ put a finger to her lips. "And that's the first rule. Quiet." She pointed to a golf cart in Nana's driveway. "Let's go. And I hope we can continue that other conversation."

They hopped onboard, Manny between them and Houston lying across the back seat with a seatbelt fastened around him. They retraced the route Karol had followed. More neighbors had gathered on the sidewalks, and Karol noticed how still and subdued everyone was, even the kids. A few offered a thumbs-up to CJ, and she nodded as if to tell them it was almost time.

"You'll see everyone talks in whispers and all the folks out on the sidewalks don't talk at all," CJ said. "It's a silent parade. No cheering, clapping or making noises. It helps the reindeer. They're not thrilled about the travel, so we don't want to stress them out."

"Makes sense," Karol said.

As they approached the turn to exit the neighborhood, CJ veered east, down the last street. Karol realized they were headed toward the Joys' house that CJ's grandparents had designed. She'd been inside many times but she couldn't remember much about the place. It seemed she'd excised many JOY neighborhood experiences from her brain as if they were tumors in need of extraction. *Unbelievable how many of those memories are returning at light speed!*

The road forked, the path on the right leading to CJ's, the only two-story house in the neighborhood. Like its neighbors, it was red brick with dormer windows and lovely white trim. Perfectly shaped hedges bordered the front windows and a bright red door was festooned with an enormous wreath.

The left fork, the one CJ took, led them to a large red barn and a red warehouse. In between the house and the other buildings was a sprawling grassy area with old-growth Aleppo pines that reached to the sky and shaded the structures behind them.

Karol pointed at the warehouse. "That wasn't here when we were kids, was it?"

"No, my parents had it built once Ganza got so large and involved. Nobody could store all the decorations, sculptures, costumes, and oversize stuff. We had the most land, so my mom decided to build it. It's not only for storage. It houses the food pantry, the nonprofit offices—"

"You're a nonprofit?"

"Yeah, we got our 501c(3) status about thirty years ago. Our tax guy was throwing fits every year because of all the breaks we were missing out on, and when I moved home, it was my first order of business."

"And you run a food pantry?"

"I call it that, but really we're the middle man between a lot of places that have excess food, like grocery stores and restaurants, and places that need food like domestic violence shelters and food banks. Did you know that America's food *waste* is actually the third largest producer of CO_2 in the world?"

"I had no idea. That's really cool that you're trying to be part of the solution."

"Emphasis on the word *trying*," CJ said. She pointed to a red-and-green van pulling onto the road. The depiction of a long table with the words *Full of JOY* stretched across its side. "That's one of our vehicles. We have a small fleet."

"Sounds like quite the operation."

"It is and it's mostly funded by donations. Know anyone who's an expert at organization? Our scheduling director, the person who organizes the moving parts of this operation on a daily basis, is retiring at the new year."

"Oh, no. Who's going to do it until you find someone?"

CJ sighed. "Who do you think?" She cocked her head and flashed her smile. "Seriously. Do you know anybody?"

Before Karol could reply, the walkie-talkie crackled. "We have arrival. Passing through the north entrance now. CJ, are you in place?"

"Roger."

She parked the golf cart in front of the barn and they walked the perimeter to the back where seven workers were busy preparing for the reindeer's arrival. Each wore reindeer antlers, red flannel shirts, jeans, work gloves, and a brown vest with a fanciful nickname stitched on the front, like "Griswold," no doubt a reference to *Christmas Vacation*. On the back of the vests were the words Reindeer Wranglers and a smiling reindeer. They each greeted CJ and Karol with only a wave as they were completely focused on the job at hand.

As they opened the enormous rolling doors, a gust of cold air hit Karol's face. "Brrr," she said, zipping up her jacket. Not only was the temperature low, but the entire barn floor was also covered in snow. "If I'd known we were actually going to the North Pole…"

"Pretty amazing, huh?" CJ whispered. "One second you're in the desert and right behind this door you're in a completely different atmospheric zone."

"It's incredible."

"This barn is unlike any other, I guarantee that. The temperature doesn't go above forty while the reindeer are visiting. Those large silver tubes snaking around the perimeter blow in our version of snow. We can replenish it if needed. We just have to move the reindeer outside for a little while because the process freaks them out."

CJ took Karol to a small room filled with coats, hats and gloves. She grabbed a parka off a hangar. "Here, put this on over your jacket."

Karol suited up, adding gloves and a scarf to her outfit. CJ opened a storage locker and withdrew two baseball caps—with reindeer antlers. "If you want to work the reindeer, you've got to don the right gear."

Karol was grinning. "Are you suggesting the reindeer will think we're reindeer if we're dressed like this?"

CJ laughed. "No, it's about team spirit among the humans. No one is above looking a little silly." CJ looked down at Manny, who'd been uncharacteristically quiet the whole time. "I might even have something for you."

First CJ strapped some antlers on Houston, who didn't seem to mind at all. Karol sensed he'd worn lots of headgear. Then CJ found a tiny set of antlers and Manny was more than willing to dress up after receiving some treats.

"Oh, my gosh," Karol cried, "I have to take a picture of this."

Karol snapped a photo of Manny alongside Houston and sent it to Stella in a text. When Stella replied with a smiley face seconds later, Karol was surprised. She assumed Stella would sleep until noon.

CJ led their little group around the corral to the far side of the barn. "This is where the guests come in." She pointed to a series of ropes that formed a line.

"I'll bet this is very popular," Karol said, noting the stanchions that zigzagged throughout the space.

"Oh, yeah. The reindeer petting area's been voted Best Holiday Attraction three times by our Tucson paper." They heard the rumble of a truck and CJ smiled. "Here they come."

Northern Arizona Refrigerated was plastered on the side of a truck that slowly backed up to the doorway. Without any verbal communication, four of the wranglers moved pieces of metal fencing in place to create a path from the truck into the corral. The other three finished the final prep on the corral. When everyone gave a thumbs-up, the truck driver and one of the wranglers slowly raised the door while four others hopped into the truck armed with pouches labeled "Reindeer Food." Each wrangler clipped a leash to a reindeer's harness and coaxed it down the ramp with the food as incentive. Seven wranglers, seven reindeer.

"Oh, my…" Karol whispered. She couldn't find words for what she saw. Each reindeer had a unique set of antlers that were two- to three-feet tall, matching its massive size. Three of them, though, were nearly double the size of the other three.

"Reindeer are also known as caribou. The larger reindeer are males," CJ told her. "Normally by this time of year they've shed their antlers, but these bulls have been castrated so they'll probably keep theirs through Christmas. The females will keep their own antlers until spring, as they're most likely pregnant."

"Have you ever seen one shed its antlers?"

CJ sighed. "As luck would have it, the year a judge for the CUDL award was visiting, one of the males shed his antlers right on the guy's foot. That killed our chance that year. A bunch of people caught it on video and it went viral."

Karol couldn't help but chuckle. "Sorry," she said quickly.

"It's okay. It's an amazing feat of nature. You can easily find the video online if you want to see it."

"Is there a meaning to having one wrangler per reindeer?" Karol whispered.

"There is. That reindeer becomes that wrangler's responsibility."

"How did you choose?"

"We didn't," CJ laughed. "The reindeer chose."

"What? How?"

"Well, each year, at the end of Ganza, we invite anyone who's applied to be a wrangler to come down and meet a specific reindeer whose handler is moving on."

"A reindeer meet and greet."

"Exactly. Usually the reindeer takes a shine to a certain person."

"How interesting."

CJ pointed to the far side of the corral. "Look, your little dog has a new friend."

Karol gasped. Across the barn Manny was nose to nose with one of the reindeer. "Oh, my God. I didn't even realize he'd left my side."

CJ took her arm and said soothingly, "He's fine. That's Maureen, everyone calls her Mo. She's very gentle and incredibly curious. Manny's not in any danger. I can tell from his posture he's not any threat to Mo. See? He's wagging his tail, and by lying on the ground, he's showing submissiveness."

Indeed, Manny was backside on the snow and Mo was sniffing him.

"You're sure Mo's not going to step on him?"

"I'm sure. Karis, Mo's wrangler, is right there. She knows Mo the best and can pick up on any anxiety or negativity. If she's not concerned, I'm not concerned." CJ grasped Karol's hand. "C'mon, you can meet Mo too. See if she's good enough for your little boy."

They walked hand in hand across the barn. Karol expected Manny to rush to her, but he was too busy circling Mo, sniffing each of her hooves. When he'd completed his inspection he sat down in front of her, tail wagging, making a little snow angel behind him. Karol pulled out her phone and started snapping photos. She almost burst out laughing when Mo leaned down and once again came nose to nose with Manny.

"Will you look at that," Karis said quietly. "I think Mo's in love." She handed Karol some treats. "Go ahead and say hello."

Mo quickly turned to Karol, who held out her palm. Her heart pounded as she stood next to the majestic creature. "Their antlers are so intriguing."

"Each one is unique," Karis said, "as unique as their individual personalities."

It took some extra treats, but Karis managed to move Mo away from Manny, but not before the entire HOA board gathered to get a look at the odd couple.

Merry clapped her hands and looked like she might cry. "This is the most adorable thing I've ever seen. Mo and Manny sittin' in a tree…"

"I'm so glad Mo finally found someone," Taylor said.

"Are the rest of the reindeer in relationships?" Karol asked hesitantly. As a lawyer who *always* knew the answer to any question before she asked it, she felt completely ignorant.

"They have been," Blair said, "but Mo never took an interest. I guess now we know why. Mo's into canines."

Feeling bolder, Karol asked, "How come they don't have the traditional reindeer names?"

Blair nodded as if they got this question a lot. "The guy who owns the deer farm, which you and Stella should definitely come visit some summer, is a total character and he's a late Baby Boomer. Grew up in the seventies. He has nine reindeer and he named them after the cast of *The Brady Bunch*. Not their character names, the actors' names. "So, this is Maureen McCormick." Blair pointed to a deer who was much larger than Mo. "That's Barry Williams. And next to Barry is Mike Lookinland."

Karol laughed. "Well, that's unique. So if only seven made the trip, who's missing?"

Karis answered, "Robert and Florence, or Mike and Carol Brady."

Taylor scoured the corral. "Where's Ann B.?"

"Over in medical," Blair said. They turned to Karol and explained, "The first thing we do after they arrive is check them out individually. Make sure they've not been impacted by the trip."

"Okay, this should do it."

The woman named Ming held up Manny's reindeer antlers. When she'd noticed how lopsided the antlers fit Manny's little head, she'd pulled out her sewing bag, which apparently she always had with her, and made a few adjustments. "Here, Manny," she called, and Manny went to her, and for a few reindeer treats allowed Ming to situate the antlers squarely on his little head.

"Those are truly adorable," Blair said.

"He's one of the herd now," Juan said.

CJ looked around. "Where's Juanito?"

"Helping Dr. Charlotte," Blair said. They looked at Karol and added, "Juanito showed an interest in veterinary medicine at a very young age. So each year Dr. Charlotte allows him to assist."

"It's actually part of Juanito's homeschooling science unit," Merry added quickly. "We started homeschooling because Juanito wasn't challenged."

"Well, it's very cool that he gets to help." Karol imagined Juanito would have the vet's job by the time he was fourteen.

"CJ, have you asked Dr. Charlotte if she's hanging around for a few days?" Merry asked in a transparently innocent tone.

CJ's ears burned red and she shrugged.

"She is," Blair said with a grin.

CJ nodded and looked at the ground. The huge pause in the conversation told Karol everything she needed to know. With a feeling of desolation she realized that CJ and this vet were involved. *Why am I disappointed? I'm going to Boca.*

Merry's phone rang and she stepped away to take the call.

Karis reached for Mo's harness. "Okay, they're motioning me in. Guess they're done with Ann B." Mo grudgingly turned to go with a glance back at Manny, who tried to follow, but Karol scooped him up.

"Oh, no, Casanova. You're staying out here."

"How about a real breakfast?" CJ asked Karol.

"Just the two of us?"

"Um, yeah. And Manny and Huey, of course. Then I'd gladly give you a tour if you want one."

"Sounds great."

They went to Locale, a no-fuss breakfast place on Alvernon Way. It reminded CJ of a corporation's cafeteria with its simple square tabletops, Naugahyde chairs, a cash register where you paid, and wall art or kitsch everywhere. The kitchen was hidden in the back, but that was the place where magic happened. Whatever Locale didn't spend on decor, they spent on cuisine.

CJ wondered what Karol would think of the place, but her blank expression didn't change when they strolled up to the counter. She'd said hardly anything on the drive over, and her change in demeanor seemed to coincide with Merry's insinuating comment about Dr. Charlotte. A thought surprised her: *Could she actually be jealous?*

"Anything you'd recommend?" Karol asked as she pored over the menu.

"I always get either the cinnamon roll pancakes or the breakfast sandwich but everything is good."

"How would you know that if you always get the same thing?"

"Uh, well, I guess I can't?" CJ stuffed her hands in her pockets and stared at her shoes, regretting the breakfast invitation. *What was I thinking? It's not like anything is going to happen between us. She's moving to Florida!*

They placed their order and CJ insisted on paying. She handed their table number to Karol and went to the restroom. If she stayed in there a few minutes, it might be long enough for the food to arrive. Then their mouths would be amply busy, excusing them from conversation. She texted Merry. *Call me in twenty minutes.*

Why? Merry replied. *Is something wrong?*

Not really. I just want an excuse to drop Karol at her car.

Got it. Okay, I'll call you back with a crisis. By then we may have one.

CJ headed back to the table. The food had arrived and Karol was waiting for her, sipping her coffee.

"Oh, you should've started," CJ said.

Karol shrugged. "Mother always made us wait till everyone was at the table. Old habit. Got you a coffee too. Black, right?"

"Yeah, thanks."

CJ focused on her breakfast sandwich, cutting it into small pieces. The restaurant wasn't busy so there wasn't much chatter, amplifying the few sounds around them—knives scraping on plates, ice tinkling in the water glasses. Karol was nearly finished with her pancake, but everyone ate faster than CJ. She'd also been dropping a few bites to Huey, who sat patiently by her chair.

"I've never seen anyone cut up a breakfast sandwich like that," Karol observed. "Do you do that with all of your food?"

CJ nodded. "When I was fifteen I came home before a basketball game with only a few minutes to drop off my stuff, change into my uniform, and snarf down some carbs. I took a big bite of a sandwich and couldn't get it down. Fortunately, my mom was home or I would've choked to death. She had to perform the Heimlich maneuver. That feeling of not being able to breathe..." She shook her head and picked up one of the bite-size pieces. "Thus my lifelong habit of cutting up my food. I've trained myself to chew each piece thoroughly. Most of us, at least Americans, don't chew enough." She raised her fork. "Sorry. TMI on your simple question."

"No, not TMI for me. I get what you're saying," Karol said, cutting a piece of pancake. "My picture is probably in the dictionary next to the word, *snarf.* I think I coined the term."

She blushed and dropped her gaze to her plate while CJ stared at her long eyelashes and full mouth. There were wrinkles and laugh lines too, but they only added to her beauty. She suddenly blurted, "Well, you look fantastic."

Karol met her gaze, and CJ remembered how much she enjoyed staring at those lovely green eyes.

"Thanks for the compliment."

CJ vowed she wasn't going to look away. She'd make Karol do that first. But Karol didn't look away either.

They stared at each other until CJ was sure Emily Post was twirling in her grave over the breach in etiquette. Weirdly, the longer they gazed across the table, the more comfortable CJ felt, as if the years they'd been separated were being whittled away to nothing.

Then CJ's phone rang. And rang.

"Aren't you going to get that?" Karol murmured. "It's less than a week before the Extravaganza—Ganza, sorry."

CJ nodded. "Hello?"

"Okay," Merry said, "So remember when I said a little while ago that by the time I called there might be a real crisis?"

"I do."

"Well, it's happened. Two of our bakers caught Covid. I've got a couple of temps coming this afternoon from the bakery over on Speedway, but until then we're short folks and that'll mean fewer cookies. I need a baker!"

"Okay, I'll be back shortly and we'll figure something out."

"The clock is ticking!" Merry announced and signed off.

"What's wrong?" Karol asked. She was snarfing down the last of her pancake.

"We're short bakers. Two of them got Covid."

"What are you baking? The gingerbread people?"

"Uh-huh. We sold fifty thousand of them last year."

Karol's eyes grew big. "That's unbelievable. How?"

"Lots of online orders besides those folks who ordered them in early December for Santa's arrival."

"I'll bet. I could help. I make them every year."

"That's right. You're actually Cookie Maker Zero."

"I'm what?"

CJ discarded her fork. There wouldn't be any more time for food. "The board had this debate one day about who Hope trained first. Merry and Ming claimed it was them, I knew it was me out of the board group. But before us there was you. When we met, you already knew the recipe. Merry and Ming never thought Hope had taught you because you never visited for Christmas."

"That's true, but we made them in July."

CJ chuckled. "Right. And Merry and Ming forgot that."

"In fact," Karol said, grabbing her purse and rustling through it, "I found something while I was packing up my apartment..."

She pulled out an old photo. It was a black and white, printed on the paper that had scalloped edges. Nana Hope stood in her kitchen with CJ, Karol, and Merry, whose head barely reached over the tabletop, smiling for the camera. In front of them were trays with dozens of gingerbread people, all ready to be decorated—CJ's favorite part of the process.

"Well, here's the proof." She looked at it again. So long ago... "You need to show this to Merry," she said, returning the photo.

"I'm not sure Merry's that pleased with me right now."

"Understandably so, don't you think?"

Karol looked around the restaurant. "Probably. I know it sent a terrible message when I didn't show up for the celebration of life." She shook her head. "I just want you to know this wasn't some big plot I devised. Like, how can I ruin the JOY Extravaganza? It wasn't like that at all."

"I believe you. The question is..." She paused until Karol looked at her. "What are you going to do with what you know now?"

When Karol didn't reply, CJ thought it best to take advantage of what Karol *would do* for them. She needed to get her back to the bakery and she'd just have to convince Merry that Karol wasn't a spy or a pariah. The photo would help. They went back out to the car.

An awkward silence remaining between them. CJ decided to return the back way to check for trespassers at Tierra Celestial. As she slowly passed, she saw two figures go through the gate—Noel Cisneros and Heather Coughlin.

"Okay if we stop? I see some trespassers going into the old Orozco Market. I need to talk to them."

"I'm the passenger. I go where you go."

They pulled up to the gate and Karol peered through the windshield. "Wow, I'd forgotten about the market. Hope and I went there once a day when I visited. Isn't it funny how you forget certain things, even stuff that was relatively impactful to your life, and remember ridiculous trivia?"

CJ laughed. "No kidding. Why can I sing the theme song to *Gilligan's Island* but I can't remember anything that happened during eleventh grade?"

"Really? Nothing during your junior year?"

"No." She paused and glanced at Karol. "That was the year my mother was diagnosed with ALS."

She reached for CJ's hand, resting on the center console, and gave it a squeeze. "Then it's completely understandable." She tried to pull it away but CJ held on.

"Just for the record, all that talk about me and Dr. Charlotte is just that. We went out a few times, but we're much better as friends. Merry just hasn't given up on it because she doesn't want me to be alone. My partner passed away five years ago."

Karol glanced at their entwined fingers. "I'm so sorry. And as for the good doctor, I wish you'd told me that on the drive over to breakfast. We could've squashed my jealous streak and spent all those minutes of silence reminiscing—"

"Or singing the theme to *Gilligan's Island*." CJ squeezed her hand once more and pulled away.

As Karol got out she sang, "Just sit right back and you'll hear a tale…" She motioned for CJ to join.

"A tale of a fateful trip…"

On their way to the market they sang the rest of the song without stopping and then burst into giggles. *It's like I'm twelve years old again.*

CHAPTER SEVEN

By the time they stepped into the market Karol was emotionally unraveled. She visualized being at court and summoned her steely lawyer persona, the invisible shield she donned around her heart anytime she had a case with a highly emotional component like an abused animal or child, a duped elderly person who'd lost their home due to an illegal HOA rule—anything that was out of the norm unjust. If it weren't for her lawyer persona she'd completely break down during a cross-examination or her summation. Rarely did she ever need it outside of her job, but she'd summoned it several times since arriving in Tucson. *Is my personal life so sanitized I feel no emotion? C'mon, Karol. What personal life do you have?*

She took in the large empty space that used to have aisle after aisle of produce. They checked the old walk-in refrigerator and the delivery area. CJ explained the status of the Orozco property, the person she'd glimpsed in the window of the old house, and the teenage lesbian trespassers.

When they peered through the back window, they saw Noel and Heather sitting on the rusty old swing set behind the market.

CJ said, "I should probably go talk to them alone. They don't know you and they're already in trouble."

"That makes sense. Why don't I go back out through the front and check out the area near the house?"

She gently touched her arm. "Just be alert. I don't know who was in that window, or if there really was someone there. It seems the older I get, the more I question myself."

"I hear you," Karol groaned. "But I'll look sharp."

CJ headed out the back door and Karol watched her approach the girls, wondering if the teens would run. They immediately jumped off the swings, but CJ must've put them at ease, because they just stood there wearing penitent poses.

Karol headed back out the market's front door and turned toward the large looming Victorian up the road. It was sad to see chain-link all around it. She'd never been inside, but she'd seen it during its glory. She and CJ had hung out there a few times with the Orozco's daughter, who Karol had thought might have liked her, which made CJ a little jealous.

And on the topic of jealousy... *Why did you tell CJ you were jealous? What were you thinking?* The old Karol never would've admitted those types of feelings so soon into a relationship. *But I'm not in a relationship with CJ. At least not now.* She knew Stella would be furious if Karol shared—or if Stella even noticed—the obvious energy between them.

She walked to the front of the house, continuously gazing up into the windows, but the glare from the bright December sun made it impossible to distinguish anything. CJ wasn't a hundred percent sure she'd seen someone, and Karol understood the doubt that came with middle age and deteriorating eyesight. As she made the turn behind the house, she noticed two square wooden vegetable boxes stacked up against the inside of the fence. *Odd...*

Her curiosity was gaining steam. That had happened with some of the cases she'd litigated over the years. She'd become part sleuth, helping her investigators piece together a chain of events. She'd toyed with the idea of working for a PI firm in Boca as her "Second Act." Stella had scoffed at the notion, announcing that her Second Act involved a martini, a beach, and possibly a fling. Nothing else. *Am I sure I want to go to Florida with this woman?*

Stella. She had to be up and about by now. She pulled out her phone and saw that she had four missed texts from her: *Where are you? Why did you leave without me? I guess I'll Uber. Call me when you can.*

Karol shrugged, pocketed the phone, and stared at the two vegetable crates again and had an idea. There were two enormous Aleppo pines ten feet away, the area completely shaded. She walked between them and found what she was looking for—two more vegetable boxes.

She scoured the area, finding another piece of her childhood she'd lost until that very moment. On the north side of the Victorian was an enormous rock, tall enough for a child to feel a sense of accomplishment after climbing it, with a top flat enough to sit upon and enjoy the sun. As kids, she and CJ, and anybody else whose parents happened to be shopping at the market, scaled the rock or played tag around it.

Karol rubbed her arms, feeling the chill and wishing she hadn't left her jacket in CJ's truck. She climbed up the sun-splashed rock and took advantage of its warmth. She missed the Arizona sun and the mildness and light of the winters. She imagined CJ was still with the teenagers, so she went ahead and called Stella. The phone rang only once.

"So, after you abandoned me at the hotel—"

"I didn't abandon you. I let you sleep in. I thought you'd like that. I had no idea you wanted to see reindeer, or maybe you wanted to see Blair."

Stella scoffed, "Are you kidding? Why would I care if I saw them?"

"Well, they asked if you were with me when they called on the walkie-talkie."

Stella made no reply. Karol stretched her legs, relishing the warmth on her face.

Eventually Stella said, "So, they specifically asked about me?"

"They did."

"Well, I doubt they will again, especially after they see what I've done."

Karol took a deep breath and slid down off the rock. She leaned against it, propping her feet on the tree stump next to it. "What have you done?"

"I found a lawyer who lives in a well-to-do neighborhood not far from JOY. He hates the Extravaganza because of the parking nightmare, and he would be happy to file an injunction on our behalf."

"*Our* behalf?"

"Hey, this affects me. I want a Christmas in sunny Boca Raton. Every day we're stuck here in the Old Pueblo makes it that less likely that I'll be wearing my two-piece bikini on Christmas Eve."

"When will he file?"

"Probably before close of business tomorrow. His name is Burt Ozer and he's a sole practitioner with a dinky office and a part-time paralegal who answers his phone. He can get the injunction done later today."

Karol scratched her head and sighed. Ozer. *Why does that name sound familiar?* She looked down and realized she literally was standing between a rock and a hard place.

"What's with the sighing? Why aren't you thrilled?"

"I'm conflicted. This is harder than I thought."

"Don't be conflicted. There's nothing to be *conflicted* about. Since you're not selling your apartment in New York, we need that money for Boca. I'm good at making deals but not that good." She paused and then added, "Has something changed? Are you even going to Boca?"

Stella simply knew Karol too well, and she knew what was coming. This was the key difference between them. Stella was a shark, unwilling to make any concessions. Sometimes it worked and the client was pleased, but other times Karol had to bail the firm out, be the one making a compromise that made her look like the bad guy to the client.

"I repeat," Stella said, "don't be conflicted. Why are you having second thoughts?"

"Because I owe it to Nana Hope."

"Hope is dead. She gave you the house to use as you see fit. She didn't leave an addendum to her will requiring you to hang Christmas lights each year. Pardon me, I meant holiday lights." She audibly inhaled and said, "So what's the real reason you're conflicted?"

"This place is from my past—"

"What's the real reason!" Stella bellowed.

"I'm not sure I should sell!" Karol blurted.

"Of course! Oh, my God, Karol! What's happened to you in the last twenty-four hours?"

"Coming here has brought up a lot of feelings, a lot of reflection and definitely some regrets. And you yelling at me isn't helping."

Stella sighed loudly. "I...apologize...mostly. I'm just trying to keep us on track with our plan. I knew this wasn't going to be a picnic for you. I remember when Hope died you didn't come to work for five days. In lawyer life, that's like six months. Remember where I found you?"

"In the kitchen."

"And?"

"And I was making gingerbread people in honor of Hope."

"How many ginger people did you make? Do you remember?"

"A lot," Karol mumbled.

"No, not just a lot. *A lot* is how many Grand Slam tournaments Billie Jean King won. *A lot* is how many women I've slept with. You passed *a lot* and went straight for *mind blowing gobs and gobs*. If all your ginger people held hands, we could've completed Hands Across America, the cookie version."

Karol almost laughed at the thought of Hope's gingerbread people stretching across the width of America, the way the Hands Across America effort had tried to decades before. She spied CJ coming up the road. "Stella, I've got to go. Look, all you see is the end game—the money and life in Boca. For me it's a lot more complex."

"Really? It sounds like you've totally forgotten there *is* an end game." She clicked off.

After escorting Noel and Heather out the front gate, CJ hung back by the market, gazing up the road at Karol, who was on the phone. Some of her body language—waving a hand and rubbing her forehead—suggested the conversation wasn't friendly. *Probably talking to Stella.*

CJ just stared. She was surprised by the connection she felt to Karol, but she wasn't sure how much was chemistry and how much was nostalgia. She needed to get Karol into Nana's house. Once she saw what they'd created, maybe compassion for the kids would kick in. There wasn't any way they could reconstruct a different property to be what was the heart of Ganza. The whole community collaborated on Santa's Workshop, which, after the reindeer petting area, was the second most visited place. It made spiritual sense, too, for it to be at Hope's house, as she really was the heart of the neighborhood.

"I could have Juanito turn on the charm," she muttered. That boy could pull heartstrings all day.

As CJ strolled up the path, Karol ended the call and motioned for CJ to join her by the fence. "You're smiling, so I assume it went well with the girls?"

"Well, they've been out here four or five times. They think they may have seen someone about a week ago. A middle-aged guy in a blue T-shirt. Maybe Hispanic. They didn't get a good look because they got out fast. They were really worried about being caught."

"How have they been getting in?"

CJ frowned. "I'm not the only one with a key. I doubt Merry even knows hers is gone, what with everything going on right now."

"Ah, so Noel's been taking it. How's Merry going to feel when she finds out?"

CJ shook her head. "I'm not going to tell her, but I told Noel if it ever happens again, I will." She gazed at Karol, whose expression seemed to question CJ's choice. "Heather's parents don't know she's gay so the girls have been hiding in more than one way."

Karol winced. "That's tough. I understand what Heather's going through. Telling my dad cost me a lot."

"Oh, I'm sorry. But...Weren't you living in San Francisco? I'd have thought—"

"The gay Mecca would rub off on everyone?"

"Well, yeah. Not true, huh?"

"Not when it came to me. And by the time I came out we'd moved back east." She pointed to the boxes and changed the subject. "I think I found something. So those two boxes are against the fence, but over there, behind those two Aleppos, are two other boxes." Karol paused but CJ only shrugged.

"Sorry, I'm not that quick today. My brain is on overload. While I was with Noel, Merry texted three times wanting to know when you're showing up."

Karol held up a hand. "I'll help. We'll get there. But here's what I think about your intruder—or intruders. They're using the boxes to get over the fence. The fact that those boxes are pushed up to the inside fence—"

"Means they're not here right now."

"Exactly. And I'll bet when they're here, it's reversed. The outside boxes that they use to get a leg up and gain entry will be against the fence, and once inside, they'll put those boxes that help their landing somewhere else." She pointed to the cellar doors. "Like maybe in there. Then it doesn't look so obvious."

CJ stroked her chin. "Rather ingenious. You should've been a detective."

Karol chuckled, "That was definitely not in my father's plan, but I occasionally thought about it."

"Oh, really? I could see you as a sexy female PI."

Karol suddenly stopped and pulled CJ against her. The abrupt action caught CJ completely by surprise and she gasped. Karol caressed her cheek and said, "Sexy, huh?"

Like the first time we kissed. Her pushing me against the Aleppo pine and touching my face. Impossible, someone as beautiful as her would never want someone as plain as me. But then...she'd leaned in and her soft lips...

"Hey, CJ? Are you with me?"

CJ blinked. Karol had cupped CJ's face between her hands, but the sexy look had been replaced by worry. "I…I was just lost in the past. Sorry."

Karol pulled her hands away and took a very deliberate step back. "We both keep doing that. Have you noticed?"

"Yeah."

Karol wrung her hands and winced. "Why?"

"Why what?"

"Why did I just grab you?" She groaned. "That was really inappropriate and if we were in a workplace—"

"But we're not."

"And we've only known each other a total of five weeks. Do you realize that? We only were together for five weeks. *Five weeks* of our entire lives. And not even five good weeks."

CJ frowned. "You didn't enjoy being together?"

Karol shook her head. "Not what I meant. I'm talking about that time of life. We were preteens, still figuring ourselves out. Stuck with our little adolescent brains. What the hell did we really know? And how much could we really learn in just five weeks? And not even consecutive weeks."

CJ shoved her hands into her front pockets and suddenly a laugh burst forth.

"What the hell?" Karol shouted. "I'm pouring out all of my anxieties to you, and that's your reaction?"

CJ covered her face with her hands, trying to control herself. "I'm not laughing at you," she insisted, although she guessed it was hard to understand what she was saying behind her fingers.

"Sure looks like it," Karol said.

CJ needed to do something else with her hands, so she closed the distance between them and caressed Karol's shoulders. "I've got my own anxieties too."

"About what? Ganza seems expertly planned."

"No, I meant I have anxiety about us, well, actually about me." Karol looked puzzled so CJ added, "At least when we were younger, I was a cute young butch. Now…"

Karol melted in her arms and whispered, "And you're as adorable as you were then. I won't be disingenuous and suggest

Vogue will be calling, wanting you as their cover model, but you have the kindest eyes and the cutest face. And frankly, I like a woman with a fine chest."

CJ's phone dinged again. "That would be Merry."

Karol kissed her cheek, took her hand and they headed to the padlocked gate. CJ suddenly wanted to learn as much as she could about Karol. So many decades had separated them. "So, it sounds like your dad had a lot of control over your life."

"Oh, he had the whole thing figured out for me. Some of it I agreed with and some I did not. Being an attorney was a good career choice. Being a housewife married to a man...never gonna happen. I dug in when it came to my personal life."

"So did you really want to be a lawyer?"

As they started up the cobblestone path that led to the wide front porch, Karol's gaze floated to the tallest turret and CJ followed the lovely curve of her neck. She had a great profile.

"Sort of," Karol replied to her question, and CJ had to think hard to remember what she'd asked. "I also wanted to be a baker. Guess where that came from?"

"So he tipped the scale toward lawyer?"

"He did. He offered to pay for college and law school but not culinary school. Since I really was torn between the two, I hypothesized that baking could be a hobby, but practicing law could not."

"Hmm. I've met a couple of awful attorneys who I'm rather certain were just playing lawyer." She scowled. "In fact, one of them is actually the attorney in charge of this property."

"I think I've met them too," Karol said, looping her arm through CJ's as they headed to the front door. "This place is a little creepy now."

"Yeah, it is," CJ agreed, flipping through her thick ring of keys for the two Rubio Orozco had entrusted to her. "But if we can get it declared historic by the state, the great-great-grandson, Rubio, won't be able to sell it."

"Is that a hard process?"

"It's a lot of paperwork, but basically we have to prove it's unique."

Karol looked around and said, "Don't see too many Victorians in this area."

CJ laughed. "Exactly. And this house is the only kit house erected in all of Tucson."

"Wait. A kit? Like a model airplane kit?"

"Yeah. From Montgomery Ward," CJ said as she pushed open the chain-link gate.

"Amazing."

They trudged up the twenty-five stairs to the front door. Karol's gaze roamed all around. "I don't remember much about it as a kid."

"I doubt you ever went inside. I counted Valentina as a friend and during those years from about second grade to sixth grade we went back and forth between our houses. But like most kids, once we became teenagers, our circle of friends changed."

"Was there a particular reason you separated from her?"

CJ shook her head. "I'm not sure. It was so long ago." She froze as she put the key in the lock. *There's a memory that's important…*

"You okay, CJ?"

CJ turned the key and pushed open the door. "Fine, I'm fine. I just remember there was something that happened between our families. There was a while when we wanted to see each other and couldn't."

Karol patted her shoulder. "If it's important, it'll surface. It might be at two a.m., but you'll remember it eventually."

"Yeah, two a.m. is about right."

They stepped inside the small foyer, and CJ imagined the Orozcos' maid welcoming people and taking their coats to the closet located next to the modest staircase. Karol admired the sleek wood railings that ended at wide, chunky Newell posts capped by enormous wood orbs.

CJ patted the wood ball, which was as big as a bowling ball, and said, "We'd all slide down this banister and more than once Valentina's brother broke this cap off when he smashed against it." She led them through a grand arch and into the living room. "This room still needs a lot of work."

Sunlight streamed through the bank of windows that wrapped around two sides of the living room, revealing all of Tierra's flaws they hadn't yet addressed—the drooping wallpaper, the scuffed and water-damaged hardwood floors and the rusty heating grates—victims of a main floor flood in the '60s. Although a few pieces of furniture were tucked away in the corners and covered with thick tarps, the room was otherwise empty.

They crossed the entryway again and stepped into the parlor. Karol said, "Oh, this is what it should look like." Unlike the living room, the parlor was ready for display with polished wood floors and clean red velvet drapes cinched with a sash. "I was expecting something more like *The Addams Family*."

"Yeah," CJ agreed, "everyone who comes inside says that. I figured that if we want the place declared historic, then it must be presentable."

"So, does that mean you're paying for the upkeep?"

CJ nodded. "Yes, but I'm also doing some of it myself and the HOA board pitches in. I can still polish the floors and clean the heating grates...stuff like that."

"This looks like a lot of work."

"It is," CJ conceded. "We've dealt with things we weren't expecting, termites and dry rot. But once it becomes historic, we can give tours, make some money. Potentially, it could bring in a *lot* of money. You see, it's got several features most houses don't have."

"Such as..."

CJ looked around. "I wasn't old enough to be told all of the secrets, but I remember a few." She crossed to the wall between the parlor and the living room. The patterned wallpaper hid what she was looking for—a camouflaged light switch. "Ah, here it is." She flipped the switch and part of the wall swiveled, creating a pass-through.

"Oh, my gosh!" Karol exclaimed. "A real secret passage."

"It was more for practicality, really, allowing the servants a quick way to the living room during a party." CJ pointed to the kitchen just beyond the parlor. "Instead of walking all the way around the parlor, they just stepped through. Guests did as well, I assume. It's a cool novelty."

"It is." Karol stepped onto the platform that turned the wall and studied the setup. "Wow. Really cool."

"We could even make it part of Ganza. Maybe it could be Santa's Workshop...in the future."

Karol bit her lip and nodded. She gravitated to the window seat and sat down on the oak bench. The sunlight hit her face and she looked upward, as if giving it permission to wash over her. She looked beautiful, and CJ stuffed her hands into the pockets of her jeans as she resisted the urge to sit beside her and pull her into an embrace.

"I've always wanted a window seat," Karol mused.

"I like mine," CJ said.

Karol gasped. "That's right. I'd forgotten about the window seat in your family room. Your mom loved sitting there reading a book."

"Yeah."

CJ shuffled her feet and looked away. She became misty-eyed whenever she thought of her mother in certain places, a certain expression on her face, or doing certain things—moments of still life CJ cherished. The window seat was one of those pictures.

Her phone dinged. A text from Merry. *Where are you? Where's Karol? Quit making googly eyes and get her over here!*

CJ's neck warmed and she guessed she was blushing. She glanced at Karol, who was still staring out the front window. "We need to hustle through here and get back to the neighborhood. Your cookie-making talent is requested. Demanded."

"Gotcha," Karol replied, hopping up and beelining through the formal dining room and into the kitchen, CJ following behind.

They rummaged through the cabinets, finding nothing but dust. Her crew hadn't yet started the kitchen renovation, but CJ vowed to get it done once the holidays were over. The refrigerator was empty and turned off, and a cobweb in the oven suggested it had also been untouched for a very long time.

"If anyone's living here," Karol said, "they're not prepping meals."

"Seems that way," CJ agreed.

She opened the back door and they stepped onto the screened porch, the place where people had slept during summers before air-conditioning or swamp cooling. All that remained were a couple of built-in benches, the cushions discarded long ago.

CJ pointed to the back staircase originally intended for servants. "Let's go up this way, and then we'll come down the main stairs. That way you'll get the full tour experience."

The stairs were steep and compact, and CJ couldn't picture balancing a tray with dishes while she plodded upward, but indeed that's exactly what the first owners, the couple who'd built the house, had expected.

As if reading her mind, Karol asked, "Who owned the house before the Orozcos?"

"The Blankley family."

"I assume they were white?" Karol asked as she reached the second floor.

"They were. He was a doctor."

"Probably with Hispanic servants?"

"Probably."

The second floor was an open space, its enormous window to the south, ensuring there was light upstairs during the day. The four bedrooms were identical in size, including the master. All had been decorated with wallpaper in a muted flower pattern for two rooms, which CJ surmised was for the daughters, one room in small race cars for the son, and the master in fleur-de-lis, identical to the living room. It was more manly, but not so much so that a wife would've objected.

Karol studied the large windows and their elaborate dark oak trim. CJ noted they also needed a polishing. "Just gorgeous," she murmured. She turned to CJ and added, "So much sturdier and stronger than the windows of today."

"Definitely. Everything then was built to last."

"Plastics ruined us. They saved us in some ways, but they ruined us as well."

CJ stepped up to the window that was visible from her deck. It was quite possible that if she could see someone, they saw her looking at them through her binoculars. She noticed the window was unlocked so she locked it again. *Let them know I was here.*

"You saw someone in here?"

"Yeah, at this window."

CJ scanned the room but nothing seemed out of place. Karol bent over and examined one of the oak floorboards. "Ah, here's something."

"Just gonna have to name you Sherlock," CJ said, stepping beside her.

Karol gripped CJ's forearm and lowered herself to a knee. One of the floorboards was chipped and a speck of red filled the hole. Using her fingernail, she dislodged what looked like a candy, held it up, smelled it. "A cinnamon Tic Tac. Pretty certain this hasn't been in the floor for more than a decade, wouldn't you say?"

She handed the evidence to CJ. "It's unlikely. Someone was in here and probably dropped some of them and missed picking this one up."

Karol grabbed CJ's arm again and slowly rose with a groan. "They've been really stealthy," she said, wiping her hands on her pants.

CJ shrugged. "But what are they doing here? Squatters aren't usually so tidy—and invisible." She scratched her head and her phone chirped again with another text from Merry. *Where is my help!!!!!!*

"Let's do a quick check and be done. I don't have time for this right now. If you aren't in the cookie kitchen in the next fifteen minutes, Merry is going to blow her stack."

They quickly ducked in and out of the other bedrooms and popped into the bathroom. "I take it this was remodeled?" Karol asked, pointing to the modern faucet.

"Yes, the bathrooms and kitchen, the heating and cooling system. Everything else, though, is original. I'm hoping if we reinstall period faucets and other pieces visible to visitors, the historic preservation board will be willing to declare it historic."

"I bet they will," Karol said. She squatted and studied the old tile on the bathroom floor, thousands of tiny hexagons. "Exquisite, but definitely a bitch to clean the grout."

"No kidding," CJ laughed.

As Karol stood, using the edge of the sink to steady herself, her knees creaked. "Ah, I love getting older."

"Likewise."

Karol looked closely in the bowl. "Hey, CJ, I think I've found some more proof that someone's been here, maybe staying here."

"What is it?"

"Well, it's water." Karol touched the sink stopper with her index finger, sniffed it, and showed CJ the moisture. "If no one's here, why is there moisture in the sink?"

"That's a very good question. I'd guess someone brought a water bottle along and emptied it in the sink. Quite recently."

The bedrooms circled the staircase, which continued up to the small third floor, a single room with windows in every direction providing clear views of the mountains and the rapidly developing town of Tucson.

"This is my favorite room," CJ said as they ascended the staircase, which was as narrow as the servants' stairs.

"Oh, this is great," Karol said. "We're inside a cupola, right?"

CJ nodded. "I've heard it was an afterthought by the owner. The builder had to reimagine the stairs and the ceilings to add it on, since the master bedroom is beneath us."

CJ touched an oversize wood desk that sat in front of a small bookcase. "I'm guessing they built this desk up here," she said. "No way they could get it up those stairs in one piece."

Karol went straight to the old books that lined the shelves. "Some of these look to be very rare. Most seem to be about farming."

"Yes, they belonged to Reynaldo, the family patriarch. He was good friends with my grandfather. Let me show you something."

CJ pulled out a thick book with a red cover, *Farm Mechanics*. She opened it to the title page and pointed at the inscription.

May you find success in this new endeavor.
In friendship,
Chris

"Chris was your grandfather, right?"

"Yes, and the new endeavor was the market."

Karol looked around, frowning. "Why are these books still here? Most everything else is gone except the enormous stuff, like the organ."

CJ shrugged. "I really don't know. The house has been vacant for years. I once asked Rubio, the grandson, if I could remove the books, at least to protect them from the rain." She shook her head. "It was really weird. He said those books were exactly where they needed to be."

Karol cocked her head, her expression puzzled. "That doesn't make any sense."

"I know. I thought about just taking them anyway, not to sell them, but just to keep them safe. I didn't want to defy his wishes."

"You need a good relationship with him," Karol agreed.

"Exactly, but I'll tell you one thing. If he gets his wish and sells this land and the preservation committee doesn't save this house, the day before the wrecking ball hits it I'm coming up here to take these books out, especially this one." She pointed to *Farmer's Mechanics* and put it back in its place. "Let's get going. I know there's something going on in here, but I don't have time for it now."

Karol followed her down the steps, periodically stopping and studying the wallpaper or a decorative feature. Once they were outside she said, "I love a good mystery. And this is weird."

CJ sighed, picturing Merry doing all of her anti-anxiety techniques at the same time. They had to get to the bakery. "Well, the good news is that other than Tic Tac littering, it doesn't appear they're doing any harm to the house. I think the mystery can wait till after Ganza."

CHAPTER EIGHT

Karol had hoped to spend more time with CJ... For a lot of reasons. She wanted to know more about Ganza, she wanted Manny to see his reindeer again, and she needed to tell CJ that while Stella was waging her own war against the JOY Extravaganza, she herself was ambivalent. She just needed to tell CJ before someone else did. But now wasn't the time.

They hurried to the bakery and on the way Karol rubbernecked at the progress of the residents, many of whom were out working on their displays. Blow-up characters slowly came to life, sleighs and sleds appeared on the lawns and the roofs. When the neighbors saw CJ's vintage Ford truck, they waved and smiled. It really was a friendly place.

"Is there a theme?" she asked.

"Usually. The theme this year is kindness."

"Should be easy to get behind that."

"Yeah, the board tries to keep it simple so all the families can use their own creativity and not have to fit into a mold. We also give neighborhood awards for most thematic, most creative, best newcomer, stuff like that. Healthy competition is fun."

"What do the winners get?"

"Same thing they got in the forties from my grandfather—twenty-five dollars and their picture on the Winners Wall that's in the community center named after my grandmother."

They drove around the community center that Karol had visited the night before and passed the Aleppo pine—the location of their first kiss.

CJ glanced at her. "Bring back memories?"

Karol took a deep breath and stared straight ahead. "Of course it does."

They pulled up to the nondescript red brick building Karol had noticed the night before, unlike any bakery Karol had ever seen. When they headed for the front door, Karol distinctly heard Brenda Lee's "Rockin' Around the Christmas Tree."

"We like music while we bake."

"I do too."

They entered a small portico filled with winter wear—coats, gloves, scarves, mittens. Karol chuckled. New Yorkers wouldn't don this much outerwear until it hit freezing.

They took off their coats and hung them on pegs before entering the largest kitchen Karol had ever seen, a kitchen that looked and sounded as though it were part of a Broadway musical. There had to be forty people in the huge space. Everyone was singing along to the last refrain with Brenda Lee, shaking their hips, busting out a move as they worked.

The work was serious but the atmosphere was cheery, something Karol had never experienced, certainly not at her stately law office. Stately was what clients expected. *Or is that something I just tell myself?*

Juan, who was the closest, smiled at them as he mixed ingredients. Then he shouted to the back of the room, "Juanito! *¡Juega* 'Bohemian Rhapsody' *a continuación!*"

"You play songs that aren't Christmas carols?" Karol asked.

Juan rolled his eyes. "If it were just up to Merry, we'd be on our fiftieth version of 'Joy to the World.' A few years ago everyone made it clear that if we're working in here twenty-four seven for ten days, the music needs some variation. So we hired Juanito. He's our DJ. That kid is a walking musical encyclopedia."

Karol nodded, remembering Juanito's reference to Herman's Hermits. She stepped to the side of the room and saw Juanito atop a platform with a serious set of amplifiers, a mixer and two mounted iPads. He had a headset cradled to one ear as Queen emanated from the speakers. "He looks seriously legit, as we New Yorkers call it."

Juan smiled proudly. "Make sure you tell him that. He'll really appreciate the compliment. He got into music when he was two. He's got perfect pitch, plays piano like a fiend, holds his own on drums and guitar, and there isn't a single musical genre he doesn't love. He likes opera as much as hip-hop."

"Impressive," Karol agreed. "And he wants to be a veterinarian?"

Juan smiled. "For now. My money's on something with music. Next year he'll go to the arts school."

"Juan, baby, you're getting behind!" Merry bellowed. "The molasses people are waiting for that bowl."

"Gotta listen to the boss," Juan said as he stepped back to his position at the preparation table. He blew a kiss to Merry, who was striding toward Karol and CJ, her flowing pants ballooning with candy canes below an untucked red-striped shirt. "Just praising our boy, honey," Juan said, "and his musical gifts."

Merry blew him a kiss and planted her hands on Karol's shoulders, guiding her back out to the portico, CJ following.

She shut the door to the kitchen, muting Freddy Mercury at his most dramatic. She faced Karol, wearing an expression of utmost gravity. "Okay, I've waited decades. I'm absolutely, one hundred percent certain that if we can take our gingerbread people one level higher, like all those folks who actually reach the summit of Mount Everest, and not just that crappy outpost five thousand feet before the top, which is where we are right now metaphorically—if we can get that high, we will win the CUDL award. So, you *must* tell me Hope's secret ingredient."

Karol's jaw dropped and she looked at CJ. "There's so much in that speech I don't understand."

"Focus," Merry demanded. "The secret ingredient! Hope always made me turn away and close my eyes when she added it. She told me if I peeked she'd never make cookies with me again, so I just listened really well when she opened a cabinet or some years it was the fridge. I'd try to figure out *which* cabinet she opened; it wasn't always the same cabinet or maybe it was something that needed to be refrigerated after it was opened. But some years she didn't open the fridge, just a cabinet." Merry paused and took a deep frustrated breath, staring at Karol. "Please, I beg of you. Please tell me."

Karol had winced throughout this presentation. "I don't know, Merry. I really don't. She did the same to me the few times we ever made them together."

"She didn't leave you the recipe?" Merry asked, aghast. "I thought she said—"

"She was supposed to," Karol clarified. "At least that's what she told me. What I received was the deed to the house and her ring. I even called her attorney…What was his name?"

"Burt Ozer," Merry clarified.

Karol blinked. The attorney Stella hired. Interesting. "Well, Burt said that was all he had for me. I thought maybe she changed her mind since we'd lost touch after my mother died…"

Karol faltered, a knot growing in her throat. She thought she might be sick and she knew she was about to cry. She turned away but Merry swiveled her around and pulled her into a crushing hug. "It's okay. I'm sorry I ambushed you. I really do know how much you miss her."

"Show her the picture," CJ said to Karol.

Karol pulled the picture from her purse and gave it to Merry. "Oh," Merry proclaimed, her hand going to her mouth. "This is so precious."

"I wish I could tell you the secret ingredient, I really do. I hope the neighborhood wins that CUTLET award—"

"It's CUDL," Merry corrected. "It stands for Christmas United Display of Lights. We've come close but haven't hit it yet."

"I bet you will," Karol said. "I'll have some copies of this made so you and CJ and whoever else can have one."

"I would really appreciate it." Merry took a deep breath and clapped her hands, her face transforming with holiday cheer. "I'm so glad you're willing to help us for a few hours. Before we find you a station, I'd like you to try our latest batch and see if it tastes any different than the ones you've made over the years."

"I can do that."

Merry pointed to a door behind them and unlocked it only after looking over her shoulder. "This is a very special room. It's the decorating room."

The minute she opened the door, the smell of cinnamon and ginger flooded Karol's senses. Tables were lined up and eight of them were covered with naked gingerbread people waiting for their frosted clothes. One table was ready for sale, and Merry's gloved hand scooped up the closest person and daintily handed it to Karol, who bit off an arm. She chewed slowly, knowing Merry was scrutinizing every look and reaction.

"This is wonderful, Merry," she pronounced. "I think it's certainly as good, if not better, than mine."

Merry sighed and nodded. Karol could tell she was both pleased and disappointed. Merry looked at CJ. "I just don't get it. I've made literally hundreds of practice batches, including every spice from anise to za'atar. My poor family has been the ginger people guinea pigs for years. Believe me, there isn't any za'atar in Nana's recipe, and I'm sure it's not any of the other spices. I cannot figure it out!"

"But these are marvelous," CJ assured her, taking the other ginger person arm Karol offered.

"They are," Karol agreed, her mouth full.

Merry shook her head. "But didn't you both always feel like Hope's were a little bit better? A little tastier? A little more... gingery?" She threw up her hands. "I don't know. I'm just tossin' tinsel here. But didn't you feel it?"

Karol hated to agree with Merry as it seemed Merry was already on the edge, but she slowly nodded and then looked at CJ, who also reluctantly nodded.

They stood in silence until CJ said, "Merry, all we can do is our best." She held up a ginger person. "And these are our best—ever. Let's get back to work and make about a million more of them."

Focused again, Merry said, "Yes, back to work!" She marched out of the room, Karol and CJ following with Huey and Manny in tow—just as Blair opened the outside door and Stella charged through.

CHAPTER NINE

"We need to talk," Stella barked, charging up to Karol.

Merry interceded. "Not now. We're in the middle of serious business."

Stella glared at her. "So am I."

Merry was nonplussed. "What could be more important than the cheer, happiness, and yummy tummy feeling of a warm ginger person cookie at the holidays?"

"Yummy tummy feeling?" Stella mocked.

"Not now, Stella," Karol ordered in a tone CJ hadn't yet heard, one that conveyed superiority and pecking order.

In an instant Stella's attitude shifted from explosive to simmering at the boiling point. "Whatever you say, *boss*." She stalked away, shoving the exterior door open with far too much force.

"I'm so sorry," Karol said.

"I'll go talk to her," CJ said. "You get busy in the kitchen making those yummy tummy feelings happen."

Karol grasped CJ's arm. "There's really something we should discuss—"

"Not now!" Merry ordered, shepherding Karol away.

Karol looked back and CJ winked. They both looked away at the same time, CJ experiencing her own "yummy feeling" that had nothing to do with cookies. Before anyone could see the lust in her eyes, she hurried outside, Blair right behind her. They scanned the park but there was no sign of Stella.

"She couldn't have gotten far," CJ said. "She didn't have a car and she was in heels."

"Don't be so sure. I think she could do a half-marathon in those Manolos. Quite impressive."

CJ raised an eyebrow. "Really?"

Blair didn't try to hide their interest. It was one thing CJ really liked about her head of security. Blair played no games. They said what was on their mind and did what they said they would do. CJ treasured her relationship with Blair because it was so dependable and real.

Blair said with a grin, "You know I love a good challenge."

CJ patted their shoulder. "You manage to tame this one and I'll owe you."

Blair looked off into the distance. "She reminds me a lot of Hortense."

CJ nodded. "Oh, yes. And look what you did with her."

Hortense was a rescue reindeer that the reindeer farm had fostered at the request of Fish and Wildlife. She'd been abandoned by her owner, her story similar to house pets like rabbits, snakes and chickens who are scuttled to shelters by owners who have an idyllic and unrealistic expectation of pet ownership until reality happens.

Hortense had been wild and unfriendly, disrupting the entire copacetic vibe of the Brady Bunch reindeer. For two months Blair worked with her separately, often calling CJ with updates. CJ was thinking Blair had met their match when just a few weeks later Blair had a breakthrough and Hortense improved so much that a new family adopted her.

"I know you can handle Stella," CJ said confidently.

"Well, first I—we—need to find her."

All they had to do was circle the building. Stella was standing on a milk crate turned sideways near the delivery door, hands cupped over her eyes, trying to see through the back window into the bakery.

"What are you doing?" CJ inquired.

Stella faced them, arms crossed. "You've all brainwashed her." She pointed at the window. "I don't even know that person."

"It's the place," Blair said.

"What? What's so special about this place? It's a neighborhood getting ready for Christmas, oh, and Hanukkah too. Don't want to leave out us Jews. I know something about holiday cheer. I grew up in Upper Montclair, New Jersey. My family was respectable!"

CJ cocked her head, watching her. As Stella stood there on the crate spouting off about her pedigree, she reminded CJ of the preachers who would be invading Ganza. Taylor said she had an idea that would minimize their effect on the event, but she was still working on the details. CJ needed to...

"Aaah!" Stella cried as she lost her balance. She went left and the crate went right.

Always quick as lightning, Blair caught her before she hit the ground—but not before the heel of her expensive shoe snapped off. Suddenly she had nothing to say, mute in Blair's arms. Blair held her, and it reminded CJ of a Hollywood comedy. All she needed was some popcorn.

"Are you okay?" Blair asked.

"Uh...yeah...yeah."

Blair helped her remain upright, difficult given that one foot was now three inches shorter than the other. They swiped Stella's broken heel from the ground and handed it to her.

"Great," Stella sighed. "My best shoes."

"And not at all appropriate," Blair chided. "Don't you have a pair of sneakers?"

"Of course. They're in my locker at the club."

"The club? Like a fitness club in New York?"

Stella smirked. "Yeah."

Blair glanced at CJ and rolled their eyes as they held out a hand to Stella. "Give me your shoes."

"Why?"

"You can't walk in one heel."

Stella handed them to Blair, who checked inside the heel. "As I suspected, we wear the same size. Stay here and I'll be right back." They pointed at the crate and added, "Don't move."

Blair disappeared around the side of the building and Stella sat on the crate. She slowly raised her gaze to CJ, as if she were waiting for CJ to say something, but CJ remained silent, having learned that silence was underrated. She'd never been a huge talker, choosing instead to watch and listen. Yet the way that Stella kept shifting on the crate, looking around and glancing at CJ, it was obvious Stella *hated* silence. Since she was a person who was paid to talk, it wasn't surprising.

"In the end, none of this is going to work," Stella said.

CJ shrugged. "What do you mean?"

"She's still going to sell the house. It doesn't matter how many cookies she bakes, how much of a pull she feels to this place because of history, her rediscovered crush on you, or how many other reindeer her little dog falls in love with."

CJ crossed her arms. "Maybe."

Stella's gaze narrowed. CJ knew the expression well. She'd been told by numerous people that she was very difficult to read—especially during a poker game.

Blair reappeared carrying their Chucks. "This is all I have in my truck, so they'll have to do."

They took a knee and picked up Stella's left foot. CJ almost laughed at what looked like a very odd version of Cinderella.

Stella yanked her foot away. "I'm not wearing those!"

"It's these or my shit boots, the ones I wear into the stalls. Your other choice is to go barefoot."

"Then I'll—"

"No." Blair sat up, drawing their face close to Stella's. "I'm done with the games and the bullshit. I have things to do, a *lot* of things to do, and yet I'm still willing to take you to get some *appropriate* shoes and drop off your heels with the finest cobbler in all of Tucson because Manolos deserve the best."

Stella gasped. "Yes, they do," she said.

"However, if you want to keep on with this uber-bitch attitude, I'm going to throw you over my shoulder, carry you to the petting zoo and drop you in a pile of goat turd! Are we clear?"

CJ really wished she had some popcorn. This was the best show she'd seen in a long time.

Blair and Stella remained in a standoff, neither willing to give an inch. CJ's money was on Blair, who always claimed that humans were just animals without tails. Blair could wait out a stubborn reindeer. Stella didn't have a chance.

"Okay," Stella said.

Blair pulled away and CJ could've sworn Stella leaned toward them, like a string held them connected. Stella watched Blair slip the Chucks over her feet and tie the laces. Then Blair stood, offering their hand to Stella, who took it.

Blair looked back at CJ. "I'll be back in an hour."

Only after Stella and Blair disappeared around the side of the building did CJ burst out laughing.

CHAPTER TEN

When Karol had volunteered to help with the cookies she'd done so with dread, knowing it was the right thing to do but recognizing that she'd be surrounded by Hope's neighbors, people who adored her nana and knew Hope much better than she did. They all knew Karol as the heartless granddaughter who couldn't be bothered to attend her grandmother's funeral. Now she was selling Santa's Workshop right before Christmas! She might as well pull on a black hat and tie somebody to a nearby railroad track.

Yet as she took her place in the cookie cutter station between Jeannie Stroman and Jamaica Mansfield, two women who looked to be a generation younger, she was greeted with smiles that seemed genuinely welcoming.

Jamaica said, "I can't believe we're working with a celebrity."

"What do you mean?" Karol asked, dipping her cookie cutter into the flour and punching out a few ginger people on the large swath of dough in front of them.

"Well, you're the first person Hope shared the recipe with. The rest of us are following in your footsteps."

"Absolutely," Jeannie agreed.

"I...well, I'm just glad she had all of you as a community. Living here meant everything to her."

She bit her lip, realizing what she'd just said. *How can I sell her home? She's probably turning over in her grave.*

"She meant a lot to us," Jamaica replied.

Before Karol could put her foot further into her mouth, DJ Juanito announced, "Okay, everybody, ten-minute break. Stretch your legs. Come on up to the front and join the 'Hokey Pokey' fun!"

"Let's go," Jeannie giggled.

The two women hustled Karol into the circle, ignoring her protests. The music began and Karol hesitantly put her "right foot in" with the other three dozen folks. Usually she hated making a spectacle of herself. Never sang karaoke, rarely danced at weddings, regularly declined speaking engagements from local New York law schools. The only place she felt comfortable being on display was in a courtroom in front of a jury.

Somehow this was different. Perhaps it was the wonderful smell of the gingerbread. Maybe it was the complete and total abandon exhibited by the entire group as they "put their whole selves in," wiggling, shaking, singing, and laughing. Whatever it was, it took hold of Karol, and as they proclaimed, "That's what it's all about!" she realized that everyone was looking at her— for obvious reasons. Her left hand was on her hip and her right hand was fist-pumping the air.

"Way to go, Karol!" Juan shouted.

Everyone applauded and she buried her face in her hands. Arms wrapped around her from both sides—her new friends Jamaica and Jeannie. At least, it felt like they were friends. How could this be? In New York it took months for a friendship to form from a casual encounter.

She was still pondering that thought as they returned to the cookies. Talk among the eight cutters immediately focused on Ganza—how many people were expected, which houses would likely win the local awards, and whether or not a CUDL official would grace the JOY neighborhood with their presence.

"It's just gotta happen," Jamaica said, plucking a gingerbread form from the dough and placing it on a cookie sheet. "We all want it, but Merry wants it *bad*."

"Yes," Jeannie agreed. "Merry is very competitive, usually in a good way, but if we don't win this time…" She shuddered.

Karol froze. "You don't think she'd become violent, do you?"

"Of course not," Jamaica said. "Not with anything living."

Jeannie explained, "If the last time we lost is any indication, every fireplace in the entire JOY neighborhood will have enough firewood for the rest of winter, and Morty Riegel will have the cash for his yearly trip to Cozumel."

"Who's Morty Riegel?"

"He owns Axe to Grind," Jamaica said. "It's a competitive ax throwing facility."

Karol gazed at Merry who was over by the mixers. "You mean Merry is a professional ax thrower?"

Jamaica nodded. "And she's damn good. Got all the way to the national quarterfinals a few years ago."

Karol couldn't hide her surprise. "Um, wow. And what about the firewood? What do you mean that everyone will have enough?"

"To work through her aggression," Jeannie explained, "Merry will start chopping wood day and night until Juan hides her ax or her rotator cuff screams at her."

Jamaica picked up the full cookie sheet. "So, it would just be easier if we finally won the damn award."

Jamaica headed for the ovens and Jeannie put an arm around Karol. "You're a lawyer, so I imagine you connect dots quickly. You've probably already realized that we don't stand a chance to win the CUDL award without Santa's Workshop."

"I do understand and I'm seriously rethinking my position."

Jeannie exhaled audibly. "Good. So happy to hear you say that."

Karol stared at Jeannie's compassionate face. "I'm just surprised that everyone has been so nice."

"Well, what good would it do to be uncivil to you? It certainly wouldn't change your mind. In fact, it would probably solidify your decision. Besides…" She looked away for a moment and said thickly, "…Hope would've wanted us to welcome you home."

While Karol cranked out gingerbread people and Blair took Stella shoe shopping, CJ checked on various neighbors who were part of the HOA's Angel program, an unofficial effort by the board to help those who struggled physically, mentally, or both. Manny joined them since Dr. Charlotte insisted Mo needed some separation each day. So with Manny and Houston in tow, CJ knew Joy's Angels would greet them with smiles and squeals of glee. After checking on Mrs. Singer as she'd promised, and delivering Mr. Sherlock Holmes his prescription from the pharmacy, she stopped to see Geena Hernandez, a fourteen-year-old teen battling bone cancer. Geena went to school when she could, but the last few rounds of chemo had worn her out and she was stuck at home through the holidays.

When her mother, Vanessa, opened the door and saw Manny, who just strolled in like he owned the place, she gasped. "Oh, my gosh! He's so cute! Is it a 'he'?"

"Yup, this is Manny. He belongs to Karol, Hope's granddaughter."

"Oh, she's here?"

"Yeah, she's helping make cookies right now."

Vanessa smiled but she couldn't hide her exhaustion. Her long dark hair was pulled away from her face by a cheery red headband, but the deep bags under her brown eyes conveyed the family's current struggle.

"How's Geena doing?"

She sighed. "This time of year is hard. Her friends are great, but they're all involved in basketball tournaments and the Winter Dance…" Her eyes welled with tears. "We thought she'd be in the clear by now. Jesse was so upset after the last scans."

Jesse was Geena's father and one of CJ's favorite people. He was always one of the first to help his neighbors, so when Geena got sick, the community rallied. It was their turn to help.

"Hey, who's this with Huey?" Geena called from her room.

"I guess Manny found her," CJ said, putting her arm around Vanessa and guiding her down the hall.

Geena's room was typical for a teenage girl who loved graphic novels and basketball. Sketches of the various characters she'd created and posters of Breanna Stewart, Sabrina Ionescu and various U of A Women's Basketball teams covered her walls. Geena wanted to be an artist and she was working on her own graphic novel.

CJ immediately smiled, hoping it masked her breaking heart. Much of Geena's stuff surrounded her—sketchbook, tablet, laptop, and headphones. CJ knew what it meant. Geena was struggling to get out of the bed. *Probably the damn radiation.* Still, Geena's smile as she held Manny and petted Huey brightened the tableau and filled CJ's heart with hope. And she was dressed in sweats, her dark hair pulled back in a ponytail—not languishing in her pajamas. That was a good sign.

"Hey, Gee," CJ said. "I knew you'd want to meet Manny."

"He's adorable."

Manny had plopped into Geena's lap and Huey was spread across her bed. CJ sometimes dropped him off while she worked. According to Vanessa, Geena loved the company and CJ was glad he wasn't alone.

"How's Ganza coming along?" Geena asked.

"It's getting there. Thanks for all your help, by the way. Taylor says without you, we wouldn't have any presence on TikTok."

"No problem," Geena said, stroking Manny's chin. "That's easy."

CJ eyed some drawings on Geena's nightstand. She tried not to frown. Just steps away from Geena's bed was her art table, covered with the completed pages of her graphic novel, *Cancer Kid.* The fact that Geena's latest effort rested on the nightstand meant she felt too weak to sit at her table. The whole journey seemed like an elevator going up and down endlessly.

CJ forced a smile and gestured to the nightstand. "So, what's going on with Sadie now? Last I heard she'd uncovered Dr. Senendrin's plot to stall the cancer cure."

Geena's face immediately morphed into a smile. "Yeah," she said, reaching for the topmost drawing, "and now Sadie and her friends are forming alliances with some badass vigilante groups. They're gonna take down Dr. S and expose him."

"Very cool."

The doorbell rang and Vanessa left to answer it. CJ wasn't surprised when she heard Blair introducing Stella to Vanessa. Blair, the model of efficiency, had no doubt found Stella the perfect shoes in under forty-five minutes. CJ hoped Stella would control herself here. Geena didn't need any negative energy around her.

When they stepped into the room, Geena grinned and thrust out her hand, palm up. "Hey, Blair."

Blair high-fived her. "Hey yourself, Golden Girl. This is Stella. She's from New York, so she's naturally pushy."

"I am not," Stella barked. She nodded at Geena and then beelined for the art table. She leaned over it with her hands behind her back and studied the drawings scattered about. CJ glanced at Blair, who rolled their eyes, but Geena stared at Stella, obviously hoping Stella liked what she saw.

Geena's dresser sat next to the table and Stella's gaze drifted to the row of pill bottles that lined the top. She brazenly picked up one of the bottles and turned to Geena. "How bad's the nausea with this one?"

Geena shook her head. "Bad."

"What stage are you?"

"Two."

"They catch it early?"

"Yeah."

"Ask your doctor if you can halve the dose. It'll really help with the side effects."

Geena took a deep breath and smiled. "I will. How do you know about that?"

Stella's face softened. "My sister. She got to stage four fast. We lost her at seventeen. But you're at two," she added quickly. "You'll be fine."

"I hope so," Geena said.

Stella leaned in very close to her. "I *know* so. You need to believe that too."

Geena nodded and the two stared at each other and CJ felt something pass between them, a secret to which no one else was privy. CJ exchanged a glance with Blair, who didn't seem surprised by Stella's actions at all. There was clearly more to Stella and Blair saw it.

Stella broke the stare and picked up one of the drawings. "Who's seen your work?"

Geena shrugged. "No one, really. I started doing it as therapy."

"May I take a few pictures? I'd like to show your work to a friend if that's okay with you."

"Sure."

While Stella organized drawings and took photos, Blair asked Geena, "Are you up for visiting the reindeer?"

"Oh, yeah. Mom was going to ask you if we could come by later this afternoon, after Lily gets home from school."

Lily was Geena's ten-year-old sister, purported to be Juanito's girlfriend, although Juanito denied it.

"Absolutely. Text me when you're ready and I'll bring the cart up."

Stella whirled about and said to Geena, "It's been a pleasure and I look forward to speaking with you soon."

She whisked past CJ and Blair, said something to Vanessa who was in the living room, and left. Through Geena's front window, they watched her hurry down the sidewalk, her phone against her ear. Suddenly there seemed to be more oxygen in the room with her departure.

"Wow, she's intense," Geena said.

"No kidding," Blair agreed.

Geena looked at CJ. "Why did she want to take pictures of my drawings?"

"Well, she's from New York, so I'm guessing she knows a lot of people, possibly people who publish graphic novels?" Geena's eyes grew wide, and CJ held up a hand. "But I don't know for sure, so don't get your hopes up. That's just a guess. We've barely met the woman."

Manny jumped up and licked Geena's face. "It's okay," she replied with a laugh, stroking his head. "I've learned just to take one day at a time."

CHAPTER ELEVEN

Stepping across the threshold of Hope's house altered Karol's mood immediately. The trepidation and melancholy she'd felt trudging up the front steps evaporated once she stood in the entryway with its white wood trim and high ceiling. Inside, she turned and looked above the front door at the stained-glass image of a cloud with a rainbow. It made her smile just as it had all those years before. During her visits she'd bound down the stairs hoping to catch the sun as it passed through the stained glass, printing a beautiful patch of colors on the opposite wall.

She'd always arrived at Nana Hope's house an anxious jumble, the residue of whatever negative emotions her father had imparted about her departure—guilt or anger were the usual choices—strapped to her along with her luggage. But within twenty-four hours of her arrival, the world and her place in it made sense. Nana's comfort and care gave her clarity about her life, her mother's illness and her future. It wasn't as though Nana launched into an inquisition of school and friends, it was what she didn't say, the quiet moments they shared together that provided Karol with the time to reflect. She couldn't have named it or explained it back then but Nana's house was the one place where she was literally and figuratively at peace with herself.

"Karol?"

She'd almost forgotten CJ had accompanied her inside. "Oh, I'm sorry."

"Nothing to be sorry about." CJ looked around and said, "Honestly, every time I come in here I want to laugh and cry, all at the same time. You ready to see Santa's Workshop?" she asked playfully, throwing the switch on a portable generator. "I want you to have the full effect."

Karol wiped away a tear and smiled gratefully. A sign blinked over the living room's archway: Elf Work Center. They followed a carpet that looked like the yellow brick road. Freestanding ceiling-to-floor backdrops of green fabric created a room within the room. A long bench sat on each side of the carpet and tools and partially constructed toys rested on top with real mallets, drills, paints and brushes and sandpaper blocks. Karol imagined human elves delighting the excited children as they passed through on their way toward Santa Claus.

The yellow brick road led to a tunnel of white, which snaked through Hope's disguised dining room. Clear lights surrounded them and glimmering puffs of snow guided their way. Colorful signs announced, "You're almost there!" and "Do you know what you want for Christmas?" Karol imagined the prompting questions ensured the line kept moving.

The tunnel ended in the study, or rather Santa's House. His gold and red chair sat on a platform and was also covered in white clouds, as if the children had completed a climb to the North Pole to meet him. A photographer's gear sat tucked away in a corner to catch each child's precious moments with Santa.

Through the last arch was Hope's kitchen, which was the one room being used for its intended purpose: a prep area for the true stars of the JOY Extravaganza: the gingerbread people. As indicated on a free-standing sign, visitors passing through on their way to the exit were given a cup of cocoa and a cookie.

Karol closed her eyes as grief poured over her heart. She'd been distracted by the makeover, seeing the place through the eyes of the children, but when they arrived at the kitchen, she was nine years old again, picturing Nana Hope standing at the tall butcher block counter where she rolled out the dough. The first time she'd visited, Karol was too short to see the countertop and Nana had pulled out a red stool with Karol's name on it. She'd felt so special as she'd stepped up, standing next to Nana, who handed her one of the cookie cutters and gave her the important job of making the actual cookies.

"So, that's the whole tour," CJ said. "Once the guests receive their cookies and cocoa, they exit out the back door and follow the red rope back out front to the street. We've never had a problem with any of the displays, except for a dog stealing baby Jesus from a creche—"

"Really?"

"—But that was an isolated incident." CJ waved it off. "Just a doll. Not a person." She pointed to the back door. "Also, because guests come into the interior of a home, we have two cameras at the entry and exit points as well as extra security throughout the route. Someone's stationed at the foot of the stairs to make sure no one tries to go up and use the bathroom or engage in anything more nefarious."

"So, no nefariousness." Karol couldn't stop herself from grinning.

CJ laughed. "None." She started across the kitchen. "Why don't we go upstairs next?"

Karol exhaled and shook her head. She closed her eyes, desperately trying not to cry. "CJ, I don't think I can right now." She leaned against the butcher block, realizing she couldn't hold back.

As the tears turned to sobs, CJ drew her into an embrace. "Just let it go."

Karol cried for several minutes, and when she finally looked into CJ's beautiful eyes, her libido stirred and she was suddenly very aware of their breasts pressed together. *That's what happens when women hug!* CJ stroked her back. *To give comfort!* Their lips were practically touching. *Why not kiss her?* She leaned toward her but CJ pulled away. Hurt, she looked to the opposite wall, but she knew CJ was staring at her.

"Make no mistake," CJ said softly. "I want to kiss you."

CJ handed her a tissue and she wiped away her remaining tears. "Thank you."

When their eyes met, CJ said, "I want to kiss you, but I don't want it to be, or appear to be, transactional. I want to kiss you because I've wanted to kiss you since I was twelve, not because I want you to let us use Hope's house as Santa's Workshop."

Karol bit her lip and ran her hand across the butcher block. "I understand. Being here...It's not like I didn't cry when she passed. I bawled the whole day of her celebration of life, so guilty about not coming, so guilty because I didn't think I'd earned the right to come." Karol tearfully looked around. "But it's like she's here. And I don't just mean in this house. I feel her in the community. You'll think I'm nuts, but while I was helping in the community kitchen...I swear I thought she was right next to me."

CJ's eyes blurred with tears and she nodded.

Karol cleared her throat and took a deep breath to rein in her emotions. "Obviously, I've got some strong feelings about my time here. My gut tells me I need more information, so I should give myself more time to gather facts."

"What does that mean?"

Karol took a deep breath. "Use the house for Ganza, and we'll just see where it goes from there."

CJ's shoulders dropped, as if she'd been holding in a ball of stress that she suddenly released. "Oh, thank God. I can't even tell you how relieved I am. You have no idea how happy Merry will be."

"I think I do. Merry pretty much promised she'd rename a street after me if I let this house be Santa's Workshop for Ganza."

"I'm not sure how she'd pull that off, but I'm guessing she'd find a way." They both laughed until CJ's radio squawked.

"CJ, do you copy?" Blair called.

"I do. What's up?"

"Um, are you with Karol?"

"I am."

"Well, the two of you need to come over to the reindeer barn. We have a situation."

"A situation? What kind of situation?"

"Mo won't eat unless Manny sits beside her."

Anticipating Karol might be emotional during the tour of Hope's house, Blair had taken both Manny and Huey with her as she worked on her to-do list. CJ glanced at Karol, who'd covered her mouth to stifle a laugh.

"Think you can counsel your lovesick pooch?"

Karol shrugged. "I can try. Seems it's your reindeer that's lovesick, though."

"We're on our way."

They locked up Hope's house and boarded the golf cart. Karol leaned across the seat and kissed CJ on the cheek. "Thank you."

CJ blushed and zipped the cart down the street. "So are you hanging around or are you leaving and spending Christmas in Florida?"

"Well, I can't gather more information if I'm not here. Stella can do what she wants but I'm staying. I also want to be honest, so I'm telling you that Stella met with an attorney... Burt somebody."

"I know him. He doesn't like us very much."

"Well, if Stella's started something, I'm going to squash it."

"Thank you," CJ said, glancing at her with a smile.

Karol scanned the homes along the route. "I've never been to Ganza. Did you realize that?"

CJ nodded.

"Why do you think that is? Why didn't Nana Hope insist I come? Why didn't my father just bring me down here or fly me out solo? He could've afforded it."

"I don't know. Maybe it would've been different if Hope had been *his* mother and not just his mother-in-law."

"Perhaps."

"Hope talked about you constantly, but she never said anything about you visiting during Ganza. I'm sure she would've loved it. I imagine it was difficult for her to insist since your father wasn't *her* child."

"I think that might be true."

"I remember one time she made a little dig at your dad for some reason I don't remember, but otherwise she never mentioned him." CJ reached over and squeezed her hand, their fingers lingering together on Karol's thigh. "What matters is you're here now. And for the record, I'd like to take a raincheck on that kiss."

Karol flashed a wicked grin. "Well, I guess we'll have to find some mistletoe."

CHAPTER TWELVE

CJ and Karol found a crowd gathered around the reindeer enclosure. They were trying to be quiet, but it was hard not to laugh at the goings-on in the pen. Blair was attempting to scoop up Manny, but each time they approached the little guy, Mo stepped between them, forcing Blair to slowly retreat. They were talking sweetly to Mo, offering special reindeer treats, but Mo kept turning her head away.

One of the wranglers opened the closest gate, and CJ and Karol joined Blair near the feeding trough. The other reindeer were milling about the pen, uninterested in the little dog.

When Manny saw Karol, he trotted over to her, checking to make sure Mo was following, which she was. Karol scooped him up and Mo confronted her.

"Don't run away," Blair advised. "Just talk to her and let Manny sniff her. We never want a deer to be stressed out as it's likely the others will follow. But I can assure you that Manny hasn't been in any danger since he snuck into the pen."

Manny rubbed noses with Mo and licked her face. "Can't Manny just hang out with her?" Karol asked. "For now, would it hurt to let them be?"

Blair shook their head. "According to Stella, y'all are leaving in another day or so, after you boot us out of Hope's house. I don't want to spend all of Ganza nursing Mo's broken heart."

As if he could understand the conversation, Manny yipped twice and stared at Karol. CJ shook her head. *How did we wind up in a Disney movie?*

She said firmly, "I'm staying for the extravaganza and Hope's house will participate."

"Thank goddess," Blair said. "Does Stella know? I don't think she's going to like this turn of events. She's back downtown right now, pushing on some attorney she found."

"Burt, Rubio Orozco's attorney," CJ said.

"How interesting," Blair murmured.

Karol set Manny on the ground and he and Mo wandered back to the food trough where Mo enjoyed her meal and Manny sat steadfastly at her side, his little tail wagging in the fake snow.

"They are so adorable," Karol said.

"They are," CJ agreed.

Blair hugged Karol. "Thank you so much."

"You're welcome. Actually…I think it's what Hope would've wanted."

Blair smiled. "I think you're right."

CJ and Blair's phones pinged at the same time. CJ pulled up the TikTok feed for the JOY neighborhood and found a video Geena must have posted. She held it out so Karol could see, and on the tiny screen Manny gleefully jumped and wiggled while Mo seemed to dance, her antlers bucking up and down. Emoji hearts burst all over the screen.

"Well, I guess we're trending," Blair announced. "This should make for a great opening night. A whole lot of people are going to want to see Manny the Canine Reindeer."

"Absolutely," CJ agreed.

Blair tucked their phone in their pocket. "Back to my to-do list." They looked at Karol. "You get to tell your paralegal that

Florida is postponed." Blair indicated with their chin toward the north entrance. Stella marched toward them, carrying a large envelope.

"She looks angry," CJ said.

Karol sighed. "Yeah. I'm gonna have to play the boss card again." She frowned at CJ. "I thought retirement was supposed to free you from all the things you hated about work."

CJ snorted. "Oh, no. When I retired from the business side of our operation I just took on a different leadership position, one that didn't pay and still made me the bad guy sometimes."

"You're making me regret retiring."

CJ leaned closer and squeezed her elbow. "Don't say that. If you hadn't retired, you wouldn't be here."

"True." She smiled and whispered, "And I'm loving it."

CJ stepped away as Stella confronted Karol, hands on her hips. "I've just had one of the most embarrassing moments of my entire career."

CJ cocked her head to the side. "Now, I thought you'd retired too and your legal career was over. Am I mistaken?"

Stella glared at her. "Until my paperwork is completed by the firm and submitted to the personnel department, I'm on the job." She whirled toward Karol. "May I speak to you privately?"

Karol shook her head. "Stella, I'm not going through with the injunction. I imagine that envelope has something I need to sign and I won't."

Stella began to interrupt and Karol held up a hand. "I'm truly sorry I brought you into all of this. I appreciate how you always pick up whatever flag I'm carrying and make it your own. I wish I'd thought through my feelings and realized I couldn't handle this matter as I would with a client. Nana Hope was the most important adult in my life, but this place and these people were the most important people in *her* life." Karol rubbed her temple, as if a migraine was approaching. "I can't imagine what she'd say now."

CJ wrapped an arm around her waist. "I know what she'd say. She'd be proud that you were humble enough to admit you were wrong."

"But are *you*?" Stella asked curtly, looking at CJ with false sincerity.

CJ sighed. She was growing tired of Stella's dramatics. "What are you talking about?"

"Karol has the best instincts of anyone I know and when she saw that YouTube video, she knew in her gut something wasn't right here, something—"

"Stella, what are you talking about?" Karol interrupted.

"I gave up on the injunction, although it was quite embarrassing to tell that two-bit attorney we weren't filing. I could tell the minute I saw you with *her* that you'd bend whichever way she wanted, so I investigated another angle." She stopped speaking and her lips formed a smile worthy of the Cheshire cat.

"And?" Karol asked.

She held up the envelope. "Are you aware that the homeowners in the JOY neighborhood are *required* by the HOA to participate in the JOY Extravaganza? It's in their deed. They can be fined by the HOA and taken to court if they don't participate."

"What?" Karol glanced at CJ and withdrew a document from the envelope, which CJ recognized as a page from the CC&Rs—Covenants, Conditions, and Restrictions. Karol skimmed the document and looked up at CJ. "Is this for real?"

CJ shrugged. "Technically, yes. When my grandfather built the community, he wanted everyone to share his love of holiday cheer. People knew what they were getting into."

Stella crossed her arms and shifted her weight as if she were assuming a fighter's stance. "But what if they loved the house they saw and just didn't want endless candy canes and tinsel? What if they viewed Christmas like *normal* people? What if they were Jewish?"

"There were actually five Jewish original owners," CJ said.

"Really?" Karol asked.

"Yes," CJ said. Her cell phone rang and she stepped away to take the call while Karol and Stella huddled with the document.

"CJ, it's Rubio Orozco."

"Well, hi. What's up?" She hoped she sounded casual. She didn't want Rubio to know they were snooping around his childhood home.

"Just wanted to check in. I'm sure you're extremely busy getting ready for the Extravaganza, so I'll be brief."

"Okay."

"I've come to an agreement with the corporation that wants to buy Tierra Celestial. I know you were hoping to have the house declared historic—"

"It *is* historic, Rubio," she snapped. "We all know that. It's not my fault that the historic preservation board is so slow. I've tried to be the squeaky wheel, but they're still dealing with backlog from the pandemic. A lot of the folks they hire to look at a property aren't around anymore. They moved, died, or got out of the industry."

"I understand that but I'm going forward. I just wanted you to know."

"Are you aware that people are sneaking onto the property?"

"Squatters?"

"No, not squatters. I spotted one through my binoculars the other day, but there's no indication anyone's actually living there. Whoever these guys are, and I know there's more than one because one of our teenagers saw a different person on the property, they're taking great pains not to leave any sign they were there. It's almost like they're doing something secret, probably illegal." She stopped. He did not respond. "Do you know anything about this, Rubio?"

"No." He cleared his throat and said, "I'll make sure you're informed of the timeline for the demolition and the actual date of sale."

CJ's gut was churning. Something wasn't right. "One more thing. Remember that bookcase in the cupola? One of those books is a gift from my grandfather to your grandfather. I'd like to take that book. I'd be happy to remove all of them and possibly gift them to the Tucson Library. Just let me—"

"No, that won't be necessary," he said sharply. "Now that you mention the books, I do know one of the people you or the teenager saw on the premises was a book appraiser my assistant hired on my behalf. I just forgot and I apologize for not letting you know. I appreciate how you've kept an eye on the place, and I will make sure that when we remove the books that you receive the book you mentioned. I have to go. I'll get you that timeline."

CJ stared at her phone. In the past, when there had been a problem with Tierra Celestial like the time the wind tore off part of the sunroom's roof, Rubio's assistant let CJ know the particulars of the service person's visit so she could open the gate and close it after they left. An appraiser would surely want entry through the gate and they certainly wouldn't scrabble over the fence, landing on old wooden boxes.

Rubio was lying and CJ wanted to know why.

CHAPTER THIRTEEN

"I *knew* something wasn't kosher with this place," Stella said as she and Karol strolled around the reindeer enclosure.

Manny continued to trot along with Mo sniffing the ground and enjoying reindeer treats whenever one of the wranglers came by. Stella yammered on about her visit with the attorney, who had a long-standing grudge against the Joy family but wouldn't discuss the particulars, while Karol smiled at Manny as he basked in all the attention he was garnering.

"...and Burt didn't care for Hope all that much, even though he was her probate attorney."

Karol turned to her. "The attorney didn't like Hope?"

"Yeah, I don't know why. He didn't say."

"Considering Hope is, well, *Hope*, my opinion of him just dropped a great big notch. What exactly *did* he say?"

Stella looked away, suddenly flustered. "Um, he just mentioned her when he was talking about the big old house across the street."

"In what context?" She touched her arm. "This might be important, Stella. Think."

"Okay, after I told him the injunction was a dead end and I didn't want to waste his time, he brought up the clause in the CC&Rs. I, of course, was astounded, and he talked about a few residents who'd come to him over the years and complained about it. He urged them to file a lawsuit, but then they suddenly wouldn't do it." She pointed her finger at Karol. "That's when he mentioned Hope. She was the one who always talked them out of it. Cost him a lot of money over the years, but he said he wasn't angry with her."

Karol smirked at that. "Something's fishy."

Stella threw up her hands. "I agree. This whole place…It's too good to be true. There was something else, too. While I waited to talk to the attorney, I overheard bits and pieces of a conversation between his inept secretary and somebody familiar with this neighborhood. She specifically said JOY neighborhood and some place…Celestial…"

"Tierra Celestial?"

"Yeah, that was it. She referenced some legal code. I think it had something to do with historic preservation."

"CJ was talking about having the house across the street be declared historic. It's known as Tierra Celestial. Remember anything else, like which code it was?"

Stella shook her head. Karol folded up the document and put it in her purse. She looked out at the reindeer just as Juanito picked up Manny, who licked his face. Soon Mo was imitating Manny and licking the other side of a laughing Juanito's face. A small group of journalists stood nearby and many were taking pictures. Standing in the reindeer ring was Taylor, the communications director for the neighborhood—and a journalist. Karol had met Taylor earlier that morning in the kitchen.

Karol glanced at CJ, who was still on the phone, then said to Stella, "Come with me."

"Where?"

"To get some answers. I'm not making the mistake of being reactionary again."

"What else is there to know? It's in the document in black and white. I'll admit there are some terrific people here, but it's the principle of the matter. CJ even admitted to it."

"That's true. But what's also true is that the person I loved and respected more than anyone else in the world made this place her home. Nana Hope lived here for most of her life. I want to make sure I'm seeing the full picture before I pass judgment."

"I can help you with that," Taylor said a few minutes later after Karol showed her the CC&Rs document and explained her concern. "You'll need to meet some people, and as it turns out, some of these folks are the people I've been assigned to assist this afternoon before the final dress rehearsal."

They got into a golf cart and zipped past CJ with a wave. Karol felt the excitement in the air. Most of the homeowners were outside working on their displays, laughing with each other. Some joked and gently trash-talked across the street.

"I really don't see why this is necessary," Stella repeated.

"I should clarify something for you," Taylor said. "Yes, participating in the JOY Extravaganza was in the *original* CC&Rs of the subdivision. However, that hasn't been enforced in decades. Every homeowner here participates because they want to."

Stella leaned forward from the back seat. "I can't imagine there aren't at least a few people who don't want to participate each year, but I haven't seen a single house that isn't decorated. Could it be that some residents feel strong-armed by their neighbors?"

Taylor shrugged. "I can't speak for every single resident, but since I've lived here what I've seen occasionally is a resident who *can't* participate, usually because they've had a life-changing incident. I've never seen anyone at a homeowner's meeting stand up and say they don't *want* to participate. The Christmas spirit isn't something that just disappears. Some years it might be tough to find because something terrible happened, like the pandemic, but that's when you lean in. That's when you let your neighbors carry you. People who are depressed need the holiday spirit more than anyone else."

"Are you studying to be a life coach at U of A?" Stella deadpanned.

Taylor just smiled, but suddenly she swerved the golf cart to the curb in front of a lovely red brick ranch-style house. "Oh, my gosh. Come on!" she cried as she ran toward the driveway.

Karol immediately saw the problem—a man hanging from a gutter, the ladder he'd been using tipped over. She jumped out of the cart and followed Taylor. Suddenly a swarm of people from other homes descended on the scene and the ladder was quickly resituated. Karol expected him to come down, but once he found his footing, he hopped up on the roof and called, "Thanks, everybody!"

The group disseminated back to their own yards and Taylor and Karol returned to the golf cart, where Stella sat filing her nails. "So, what kind of insurance do you have on this little party? I'd imagine it's quite expensive."

Taylor threw the cart into drive and they breezed down the street. "Our event insurance covers the actual time frame of Ganza. If Bob, that's the guy who was hanging from the roof, had fallen, he'd have filed with his own homeowner's insurance."

"All the more reason why I imagine some people wouldn't want to participate," Stella argued.

"Of course there's always risk," Taylor agreed. "We do our best at the homeowners' meetings to encourage safety and make suggestions about how to be safe."

The golf cart turned in to a cul-de-sac, Santa Street, and pulled up next to another red brick ranch-style house. Amid its desert landscape was a long table draped in black. Seven large candles sat across the table in an electric wooden platform. Karol knew each candle represented a different Kwanzaa principle. Next to the table was a scroll, noting the upcoming festivities that would begin December 26th. Across from the table was a large chair on a platform decked in red and green velvet.

"He's Santa and celebrating Kwanzaa?" Stella asked.

"Yes, many people celebrate both Christmas and Kwanzaa."

"Didn't know that," Stella replied.

"This is Dr. St. John's house. His parents were original owners," Taylor said, hopping out of the cart and heading for the front door. Karol followed but noticed Stella lagging behind, making a show of exiting the cart and slowly walking up the driveway as if she were hurt. *Do I really want to go to Boca with you?*

Taylor pushed the doorbell and Bruce Springsteen wailed, "Santa Claus is Coming to Town."

Stella touched her temple as if her head hurt. "What is it with these doorbells?"

"Coming!" a voice called.

The longer than usual wait was explained when a tall African American man—supported by a cane—opened the door. He smiled broadly when he saw Taylor. "To what do I owe this pleasure?"

"Hi, Terrence. I'd like you to meet Karol Kleinz and her friend Stella Plotz. Karol is Hope's granddaughter. I'm giving Karol and Stella a tour of the neighborhood including some of the personal histories of the original owners."

He shook hands with them and said, "Please come in. I certainly know a lot about the history of this neighborhood."

His living room seemed comfortable, and although he appeared to live alone, the handmade quilt spread across the couch and the crocheted armrests suggested a woman's touch. *Don't be so quick to judge. Many men enjoy crocheting.* A comfortable recliner faced a large wall-mounted flat-screen TV, and they had apparently interrupted a U of A women's basketball game.

"Who's winning?" Taylor asked.

"Unfortunately ASU, for the moment," he said.

Instead of gesturing for them to sit, he led them toward the stairs and a few dozen photos that filled the wall, some black and white and some in color. All were arranged in four circular groups with a larger photo in the center. "If you want to know about the JOY, you need to see the pictures. I've put them in chronological order since I'm often called upon to discuss our history, as I also serve as the HOA's historian." He smirked at Taylor. "It seems to be an ongoing position for which there is no end date."

Taylor giggled and explained, "Terrence was the history chair at U of A for nearly two decades and is a leading expert on African American studies. If anyone knows how to accurately curate history, it's Dr. St. John."

That, Karol thought, would account for the slight formality in his speech.

His laughter was a rumble and he shook his head as he answered Taylor. "You always know how to lay it on thick."

He pointed at the first group of pictures, old black and whites of the house as it was being built and a sign that said "Welcome to the JOY Neighborhood!" The photo in the center showed a family of four standing outside the completed house—a father who looked proud, a mother whose smile mirrored Dr. St. John's, and two preteen boys.

"These are mainly self-explanatory, and that's me on the end with my family."

"Your mother looks thrilled to have a new home," Karol commented.

"She was. It was the first—and last home they ever purchased."

"They must have loved the neighborhood," Stella said.

"They did, and finding this community was an act of the divine. My father owned a textile company, and although he did rather well, and certainly had the money to make the down payment, he'd been turned away by developers—twice."

"What do you mean?" Karol asked. He stared at her but said nothing, until she nodded. "I see."

"Yes, you do, but I appreciate your question and the way you asked it. You are indeed Hope's grandchild." He shifted his weight on the support of the cane and walked up two steps to the next grouping. "Here are some of our photos with our family and the neighbors. There were several families that migrated from the east with the Joys once they heard about their plans to build a development. It's important to note that both Chris

Joy and his wife Elizabeth were licensed architects. And they both came from money." He pointed at the pictures. "You'll notice other Black families joined the neighborhood as well as Mexicans and Asian Americans, who, of course, still experienced extraordinary discrimination after World War II."

Karol scanned the pictures, noting many people of color—and four butch women. She pointed and Stella leaned in to see the photo. "Well, my, my," she chuckled. "I guess Commander Joy let just about anyone in, huh?"

Terrence pointed at each one as he said, "That's Nikki, Culp, Hoboken, and Georgy. Nikki and Culp were together, as were Hoboken and Georgy. All four of them played professional baseball. That's where they got their unique nicknames, and when they retired they settled here."

"But how did they buy a house?" Stella asked. "Women couldn't buy property solo until the seventies, and nobody was going to let a lesbian couple own a home."

"That's true. That's why Christopher Joy took their money and bought it for them. On the deed it showed him as the landowner until the law changed in the seventies." He pointed at the center photo. "Here he is shaking hands with Hoboken, who was the leader of the group, and handing them their deed."

"They must have really trusted him," Karol commented.

"Absolutely." He leaned on his cane and said, "I remember as a little boy going into Commander Joy's office. He had this bookcase with old books on it. No one was allowed to touch them, but their spines were beautiful with gold filagree, some were leatherbound…just fabulous. The story goes that when he proposed the idea of buying the property for the women, he pulled out one of the books from the top shelf and opened it. The middle of the pages had been cut out so there was a hole in the center."

"I read that people did that to hide things," Karol said, nodding.

"Exactly. So he picked up the women's money and said to them, 'I'm keeping your money right here. It will stay here until you can legally buy that house. Anytime you want to come see it and make sure I haven't spent it, you march into this office and you open the book.' Then he stuck their money inside it and put it back on the shelf. He never spent it, but as I've heard it, the women never checked either. Eventually they owned that house, free and clear." He exhaled and added, "They're all gone now except for Culp. She lives in our assisted living house."

"I think I'm gonna cry," Karol said.

Stella crossed her arms. "So what about the CC&Rs? The idea of forced participation in the decorating?"

Dr. St. John glanced at Taylor, who winked at him, then he took a few more steps up the stairs to a circle of photos all in color except for one, all taken of the St. John house during various JOY Extravaganzas. Some years they celebrated Kwanzaa and other years they staged their own version of Santa's House. The center photo showed a Black Santa Claus with a little Hispanic boy on his lap.

"Is that you as Santa?" Karol asked.

Terrence nodded but then pointed to the black and white. "And that's my father."

Karol leaned closer. Something about the photo was off. Dr. St. John's father wore a big grin with a little white boy sitting on his lap. The boy had on a heavy coat, a scarf, gloves, and boots. At the edge of the photo was a rosebush bed—and it was dormant.

"Notice something, Karol?" Terrence asked playfully.

"This photo wasn't taken in December. In Arizona the roses bloom in winter. At the very least, this bush should be covered with rosebuds."

"Let me see," Stella demanded, moving closer.

"Very observant," Taylor said.

"What gives?" Stella asked.

"I'm answering your question. Commander and Mrs. Joy arrived in Tucson in early forty-six. By mid-June they'd purchased the seventy-five acres that comprise the JOY neighborhood. The Joys built their own house first while also establishing friendships and connections with many people, including the Orozcos, who owned the farm just north, and my parents, since my father knew much about home furnishings.

"The Joys started to hear stories about discriminatory practices by some of the other developers. You have to remember this was soon after the war. All the Baby Boomers were starting their families and building the American Dream. It was a true seller's market, very competitive, and the developers could afford to turn away people of color, people who were different… anybody who pissed them off for any reason. There were no laws yet to prevent discriminatory housing practices. One day Commander Joy stopped by my parents' showroom and my father was very distressed. He told Chris they'd just been turned down for the second time."

"That's disgusting," Stella spat.

Terrence raised a hand. "Yes, it was, but it was the times and I share my mother's opinion that all things happen for a reason. They didn't get those other houses because they were meant to be here. As the Joys began subdividing their acreage, word spread among the various minority communities that a fair and honest developer had come to Tucson. The problem was most of those families didn't have the down payment readily available— my father being a noticeable exception—but a lot of white folks had the cash in hand. Of course, there were many fine white families, but there were more who were unwilling to appreciate diversity. The Joys were looking for a way to give more time to those minority families to get their funding together, but also, they wanted a way to separate the white bigots from the inclusive ones."

"And that's where the clause came from?"

"Well, actually, the general idea of community holiday displays was the brainchild of Elsa Joy, Christopher and Elizabeth's daughter, and CJ's mother. She'd created a blueprint in crayons. It's on display in the community center."

"I saw that today and wondered what it was," Karol said. She turned to Stella. "It was amazing. She had it all figured out."

"She did," Terrence agreed. "But it was *my* father's idea that Elsa's idea become a requirement, which we knew would probably knock out a few of the deplorables, to quote Hillary Clinton. We could also display photos from the first annual

JOY Extravaganza in the main office when the Joys opened for business in early forty-seven."

Stella raised a hand. "Wait. Something's not right. I just saw today at the attorney's office that the first JOY Extravaganza was held in December of that year."

"The first *official* JOY Extravaganza," Terrence corrected. "We staged an unofficial Extravaganza in the early fall of forty-six and made sure that most of the people in the pictures represented diversity. That's when this picture was taken. Fortunately, nobody noticed the dormant rosebush in the background.

"When prospective homeowners, who were mostly white, showed up in the JOY development office, they saw all these photos." Terrence laughed. "There were some rather funny— but sad—moments for some shocked white folks, especially when they saw a Black Santa Claus. Some couples couldn't run out of the office fast enough. There was lots of swearing and a lot of racial slurs…"

Terrence looked away and shook his head. Taylor stepped up and pointed to the center photo and said, "This is the first community photo of the JOY neighborhood family the day before the first real extravaganza. As Terrence said, there were a lot of people who left Christopher and Elizabeth Joy's office shocked or angry, but there were some great moments too, right?" Taylor touched his arm and he smiled.

"There were. When a Black family came in and a little child was thrilled to see a Black Santa…it was like Christmas happened for them right then. And there were white families who just saw past the racial and cultural differences, a father explaining to his kids what a menorah was, or a mother explaining to her kids why Asians have differently shaped eyes. As you might suspect, many of the accepting white families had ties to the university and were highly educated, but not all of them."

"How did the Joys know all this?" Karol asked. "Did they have a peephole in one of the walls, watching the families in the waiting area? This was long before hidden cameras."

"They didn't need a camera," Taylor said. Looking at Terrence she said, "I want to tell this part." He nodded and gestured for her to continue. "They knew what was happening in the waiting room because they had a spy, Elizabeth Joy herself. Although she was an accomplished architect and Commander Joy considered her his absolute equal, she posed as the secretary when people arrived. No one in the forties ever would've suspected a woman would be anything *but* the secretary."

"But that changed," Terrence added, "when Ming Zhao's family moved in. They'd moved to Tucson from San Francisco and owned a store there. Mrs. Zhao, Ming's mother, knew how to run an office and keep the books. The Joys hired her and she was their office manager for many years. That was partly how the Zhaos made their down payment."

"And of course the bigots couldn't stand the idea of an employed Asian person," Taylor added. "A few walked in, saw Mrs. Zhao and walked right out."

"So the clause was a mechanism for diversity," Karol said.

"Exactly," Terrence said. "Racist laws and policies were the norm if you were anything other than a white heterosexual male. Chris and Elizabeth Joy made it their mission to balance the scales, at least in the corner of the world they could control. Chris had come back from the war determined to make the world a better place." He stared grimly at Stella. "Just so you know, seventy-five percent of the homes in the JOY neighborhood are still owned by members of those original families, people who are thrilled to have this sense of community year-round and gladly participate in Ganza."

"So what about the other twenty-five percent?" Stella pressed. "The attorney I've spoken with says there have been complaints."

Taylor rolled her eyes. "Burt has a beef with CJ. He's convinced CJ turned his daughter gay. Long story. Hope used him as her attorney, but when she passed, he lost his last client from the JOY neighborhood."

"But he's still the attorney for the Orozcos," Stella argued. "The people who own the farm across the street."

Taylor sighed. "Yes, he is. And he's trying to get under CJ's skin and destroy her friendship with Rubio."

Karol noticed that Terrence had edged his way down the stairs and was glancing at the basketball game which had just entered the fourth quarter. "We need to go," she said, and they all joined Terrence at the bottom of the stairs. She extended a hand and said, "Thank you, Dr. St. John. This conversation has been most enlightening. We'll leave you to your basketball game."

"It's been my pleasure." He walked them to the door, and said to Stella, "You asked about the other twenty-five percent of people who bought in the JOY but aren't related to original homeowners. Among those people are a gay couple facing an AIDS diagnosis and a trans woman who wasn't chosen by sellers with multiple offers even when she had the highest bid." He leveled a finger at Stella. "Think about them when you raise the question of discrimination."

CHAPTER FOURTEEN

CJ loved the dress rehearsal for many reasons. It was her favorite night of the year—even more so than Christmas. Tonight would be full of wonderful surprises. While many of the neighbors subscribed to the "tried and true" policy for their yards, and each year they resurrected a winning theme, many of her neighbors loved to mix it up. Undoubtedly, at some point during the summer or fall, when she'd run into her neighbors at the grocery store or a restaurant, they'd gush about the amazing idea they were considering. She loved their energy and she couldn't wait to see what they'd created.

Tonight was also the most special night for the tight-knit community her grandparents had assembled and her parents had shepherded, the community now entrusted to her. Although the next two weeks would be about putting on a show for the greater Tucson area, tonight the neighbors would entertain each other and a very select group of guests, including two dozen donors with very deep pockets who appreciated the JOY neighborhood. There would be a catered dinner at the community center that CJ provided, and then everyone would retreat to their yards.

Lights would go on, music would play, inflatables and balloons would ascend, and the reindeer would wear their most festive harnesses.

Most of all, she loved tonight because of the very special visitors—children from various agencies who engaged with children who needed a special night, and outpatients from Children's Medical Center of Tucson. CJ understood some gingerbread cookies and a sleigh ride couldn't solve the monumental issues they faced, but for a few hours they could forget the real world and enjoy the JOY.

She stared into the mirror and adjusted her sparkly red bow tie that matched her red tuxedo with tails. She checked the buttons of her white dress shirt and pulled her green newsboy cap over her curly hair. It was an outfit she'd designed several years ago, mainly because she wanted to wear one item—her grandfather's pocket watch. She opened the special walnut box that housed the watch, a box that had been designed by a family friend—Brendan—Merry's grandfather. Inside on a blue velvet bed rested the gold watch, the initials CRJ inscribed on the case. Her grandmother had presented it to her grandfather when he returned from the war.

CJ carefully opened the watch to study the beautiful face. It still kept accurate time—and reminded her she needed to get going. She snapped it shut, attached it to her vest and gazed into the mirror. She hoped Karol was impressed. *Be honest. You want her to be more than impressed…*

She felt a nuzzle at her leg. Houston sat next to her, wearing his own red coat and his antlers. She scratched his back and told him, "You look adorable, boy."

They hopped onto the golf cart and headed for the community center. She waved at the security team stationed at the neighborhood's north entrance, knowing another team of five covered the south entrance. While the neighbors shared dinner together, they needed to know their yards were safe. Nothing had ever happened, but CJ didn't dare test fate. She knew the security staff would also have a wonderful meal—once the neighbors returned to their respective properties.

She pulled up next to Blair's golf cart and wasn't surprised to see Blair sitting behind the wheel, talking on their cell.

"Tell the reporter she's going to have to wait. I'm sorry she got the time wrong, but there's nothing I can do except send her out some cookies." They nodded. "Okay, will do." They closed their phone and looked up at CJ. "As always, you look spectacular. I'm sure Karol will be impressed."

CJ smiled and felt her cheeks flush. "Well, it's not for her…"

"Uh-huh."

CJ studied Blair, who wore their standard security vest over a black dress shirt and their special Ganza kilt, the front of which was decorated in tiny blinking light bulbs. "You look pretty spiffy as well."

"Thank you." They hopped out and offered their arm. "Shall we?"

"Yes."

The community center was already full of neighbors and the buffet had just started. The Benitez family, who lived on Christmas Card Lane, owned El Sombrero, a successful Mexican restaurant that CJ hired to cater the event each year. Pungent spices reminded her that she was very hungry, but first she wanted to greet some people—and see Karol.

The standard Christmas carols DJ Juanito had programmed through the speakers were barely audible over the boisterous laughs and chatter. The place was humming with enthusiasm and CJ smiled as she gazed around the room. Her grandparents would be ecstatic.

Some of the neighbors wore their costumes or holiday garb to the dinner, but most opted for casual underclothes—waffle-style Henley shirts, sweatshirts and sweatpants—just in case of spills. She glanced at the Claytons, the steampunk family, decked out in shiny red and green metal armbands, elaborate headdresses and chest plates. *I wonder if they'll have to feed each other.* Behind them were the Fellows, a family of nine, who each year reenacted the birth of Christ on their lawn with each family member playing a role. The fact that Warren and Stacia Fellows had adopted seven children from all over world equated to a diverse and multicultural version of the event. The world, CJ thought, as maybe it should be. It was wonderful that several neighborhood churches made a point of visiting the Fellows' house in support of their nontraditional presentation.

Many families joined the food line, but CJ noticed the board huddled in a corner with Karol and Stella. She tensed—until they all erupted in laughter at the same time. "Thank God," she murmured.

Blair chuckled. "I know. I just wondered, 'What the hell has Stella done now?'"

Karol turned, saw CJ approaching, and flashed CJ a smile that left her with—as Merry would say—a yummy tummy feeling. Karol wore black dress pants and a red silk shirt that matched her red heels while Stella wore a black cocktail dress. CJ glanced at Blair, who seemed lost in Stella's legs.

Merry blew past the group and threw open her arms to embrace them. "Hello, my friends!" She gave an air kiss to each, not wanting to smudge her hot red lipstick. She was dressed as the Snow Queen in a flowing white dress with a headpiece shaped like a snowflake. Since the release of *Frozen*, all the kids thought she was Elsa, and she was fine with that.

She whispered in CJ's ear, "Doesn't Karol look delish?"

CJ grinned and glanced at Karol, who was now engaged in a conversation with Juan and Taylor. "She does look lovely. As do you."

Merry hugged her again and pulled them into the group. Juan and Taylor were dressed like Santa's elves. Notably missing was Ming, who was no doubt handling a costume crisis somewhere.

"That can't be right," Stella was saying to Juanito.

"I'm telling you," Juanito said, "'Jingle Bells' was originally written for Thanksgiving."

Stella glared at him and whipped out her phone. "I'm looking this up."

Juan clapped his hands. "Are we excited?"

"Yes!" the group replied.

"Well, shit!" Stella exclaimed, shaking the phone in her hand. "He's right!"

"Language!" Merry chastised.

"How the…heck do you ever get mad if you can't swear?"

"Stella," Juanito said, "my parents always pick a benign word with the same first letter as the swear word they want to use. They're trying to be good role models."

"Do you know what they're really trying to say?"

"Of course. I may be homeschooled—for now—but my friends go to public school, as well as my older sister." Juanito tapped CJ's arm. "CJ?" He motioned for her to bend down so he could whisper in her ear. "You need to convince Karol to stay. Mo needs Manny."

"They're really close now, aren't they?"

"Like best friends."

"I'll work on it."

"Okay, all, let's mingle," Merry ordered. The group broke up and Stella took Blair's arm as they sauntered toward the food line.

"What was Juanito saying to you?" Karol asked innocently.

"Secret stuff." CJ gazed at her and added, "You look beautiful."

"Thank you. You look fabulous as well, except…" She faced CJ, reached to her and straightened her bow tie. "That's better."

"Thank you."

They lingered in the private moment, staring at each other, until Houston nudged CJ and she nodded. They joined the buffet line, chatting about the costumes and making easy small talk. They'd just reached for their plates when Stella and Blair rushed up to them.

"I just got a call from Shea," Blair said. "They were loading the shaved ice truck for tonight and they saw a guy in a red pickup drive onto the Orozcos' property, heading toward Tierra Celestial."

CJ sighed. "Right now?"

"Two minutes ago. It makes sense. Rubio knows tonight is the dinner. He knew we'd all spend the next couple of hours together, and since you've been asking questions…"

"You're right. I was really hoping I was wrong about Rubio's involvement and it was just vandals or squatters."

"No, CJ," Karol said. "What you and I found—the crates by the fence, the water in the sink—all were deliberate signs of deception."

"Hey, if we're going to do something about this," Stella interjected, "we need to move now. Let's go over there and confront the guy. As Karol knows, I'm on my way to a black belt in karate. I could—"

"Hold it," Blair said. "While I reserve the right to follow up on your karate exploits at a later time, because it sounds really hot, we actually can watch the guy from right here."

"We can? How?" CJ asked.

Blair winced. "Don't be mad at me, but after you told me what you and Karol discovered, I *temporarily* installed some cheap cameras."

"You what?" CJ couldn't believe it.

"Very smart," Stella said with an approving nod. "Although none of the footage could be used in a legal proceeding."

"Actually, it could," Blair countered. "We're the custodians of the property and we have that in writing. A couple of years ago we had a problem with taggers and Rubio authorized cameras, and we amended our agreement with him to include that option in the future."

Stella smiled. "Smart and cunning. I like it."

CJ rolled her eyes. The sexual tension between Blair and Stella was nearly combustible.

"I know what you're thinking, CJ," Blair said, "but Rubio is dishonest. He's not working with us anymore. All he cares about is money and getting a big, fat profit from the box store people."

CJ shrugged. "I know you're right." She pointed at one of the office doors. "Let's go in there."

They followed her into the manager's office and Blair pulled up the cameras on a computer. "They're over the exterior doors, in the corner of the master bedroom and also in the cupola."

"Why there?" CJ asked.

"Just a hunch. We know the builder had a thing for secret doors and hidden spaces, but the cupola is special. I think whatever someone's after is there."

"I'd say you're right," Stella said. "Look at camera four."

They all watched as a medium build, dark-haired man squatted in front of the bookcase. He removed all the books and then picked up the bookcase and set it to the side. He kept his back to the camera so they never saw his face, but when he turned to the side, they saw what existed behind the bookcase—a safe.

"Well, look at that," Blair said. "CJ, did you know about the safe?"

She was gaping at the screen along with everyone else. "No, but it explains why Rubio didn't want me to move the bookcase."

The safecracker kept his back to the camera for most of his work, but it was clear he wasn't having much luck; they never saw the door open.

CJ checked her watch. "Hey, we need to stay focused. This is not our priority."

"Agreed," Blair said, exiting the app. "It's all being recorded. I'll review it later tonight."

"But he'll get away," Stella argued.

"From who?" Karol asked. "If the owner of the property authorized his presence, even if the guy entered the house by climbing the fence, then by confronting him all we're doing is showing our hand. The owner will know we're onto him."

They all nodded in agreement over this sound logic.

"But why doesn't the safecracker just use a key?" Stella asked.

"He doesn't have one," Blair answered. "And he can't easily get one. Rubio is in Chicago. CJ and Merry are the only people with keys. Rubio saw no reason to keep one. If he called CJ and told her to hand out a key to all these different people, it would look suspicious, especially now that we're in a tug-of-war over the house."

"Understood," Stella said. She looked at the buffet and clapped her hands. "Well, let's eat!"

The four of them enjoyed the scrumptious Mexican fiesta, albeit quickly, and then ventured out into the night. Blair and Stella checked on the two entrances and other key locations, while CJ and Karol headed to the reindeer since Manny was all but living with them now, under the watchful eye of Dr. Charlotte.

Karol was gushing in appreciation when she shook hands with the wiry, petite butch with spiky blond hair and friendly brown eyes. She realized she'd probably be much cooler toward Dr. Charlotte if she thought the vet was romantically involved with CJ.

"Manny's fine," Dr. Charlotte assured her.

He had bounced over to Karol the minute he saw her, Mo trotting behind. She held him and he licked her face while CJ petted Mo, who waited patiently—as long as she was getting treats.

Manny wiggled out of her hug and jumped to the ground, Mo snubbing the rest of the treats and trotting beside him.

"Are you really going to be able to separate them?" Karol asked.

"Yes. Reindeer are very connected, and as much as Mo cares for Manny, when the time comes, she'll follow the rest of the herd."

"If you say so."

"Everything else going okay?" CJ asked.

"Smooth as ever. These wranglers are great."

A commotion from the entrance drew their attention and the first batch of special visitors quietly followed the queue through the stanchions to the entrance. Most of them were young children holding the hand of an adult.

CJ leaned toward Karol and whispered, "That's a group from a local homeless shelter. Watch the kids' faces. Watch the magic happen."

As each child made the last turn through the guide ropes and saw the reindeer, their eyes grew wide and their smiles wider. They knew to be quiet, but some had so much energy they had to do something so they jumped up and down in place.

Once they'd gathered around the gate, two wranglers welcomed them and explained the rules and how to feed the reindeer.

"I guess it's showtime," Dr. Charlotte said and headed into the ring to supervise alongside the other wranglers.

The wranglers modeled how to feed the reindeer and the children nodded attentively. They walked in, chose a reindeer and bravely stuck out their hands while the enormous creatures opened their large mouths and ate right from their palms.

CJ leaned in and whispered to Karol, "It always amazes me that the kids are so fearless and it's the adults who freak out."

"Really?"

"Oh, yeah, the wranglers spend more time calming adults than children." Karol laughed and CJ checked her watch. "Come on. Let's go tour the neighborhood. See how things are going."

"Um, sure." But Karol didn't move; she wiped her eyes and wouldn't look CJ in the eye. "I'm sorry I'm so emotional."

"It's okay. Really. I understand." CJ put an arm around her shoulders and led her outside. "I know of at least three therapists who suggested their young clients visit Ganza, specifically the reindeer. There's nothing like the look on a child's face when they meet, what is until that moment, a mythical creature."

"I bet the wranglers get a lot of questions about Rudolph and red noses."

CJ laughed. "Oh, you have no idea. One year they kept a running tally. Almost two thousand mentions."

Karol impulsively pulled CJ into a hug. "Thanks."

"No problem. Would you mind if we stopped at my house? I left some paperwork on my desk that Merry needs."

"Sure."

They held hands as they crossed the sprawling lawn that separated the Joy family home and the barn and warehouse. Dead grass crunched under their feet, and Karol remembered some marvelous gatherings on its greenness that the Joys had organized during the summers. She also remembered kissing CJ several times while they ate lunch at the picnic table during Karol's visits. At night sometimes they'd lie on the table and stare at the stars.

As if she could read Karol's mind, CJ pointed at the picnic table and said softly, "We spent a lot of time there."

Karol sighed. "This is a great yard for parties. One of the things you don't get when you live in the city is private outdoor space."

"Does your condo in Boca have a yard?"

"A tiny one, but there are all sorts of amenities around the development."

"That's nice," CJ replied, and Karol knew she was being polite.

CJ pulled out her keys and Karol stared at the red front door. "I remember the first time I came to your house and knocked on this door. I was terrified."

CJ looked at her, perplexed. "Why?"

"I'm not sure. I mean, your family owned the development. I thought that was a big deal. Then your mother opened the door and put me at ease immediately."

"She could do that with anyone. Hope said she was always like that."

They went inside and CJ headed for her study. Karol took in the spacious great room decorated in hues of brown and turquoise. It was tastefully done, several paintings and family photos on the walls. She studied a colorful piece by R.C. Gorman—an Indigenous woman and child standing at the edge of a cliff, the vast, royal-blue night sky before them.

She studied a wall of photos, most of them old black and whites of the family and their friends. Some looked as though they were taken at the New Jersey home. Karol saw how much CJ now looked like her mother, Elsa. There were photos of Commander Joy and Elizabeth, as well as a photo of a man with his arm around a woman—someone who looked familiar.

Her gaze swept across the space. She heard Elsa's voice shooing them outside to enjoy the fresh air. Her memory of the front door was vivid because that was usually as far as she got. CJ would appear after Karol rang the bell, basketball in hand. They'd hop on their bikes and race to the courts. Nana Hope had bought her a bike and kept it on the back porch. *Whatever happened to my bike?*

She slowly circled the room and was surprised to find a framed photo of herself and CJ. They were sitting on the picnic table, each holding a basketball, their arms draped over each other's shoulders. Karol remembered CJ's mom took the photo early in their friendship—before there was attraction and before they understood what they meant to each other. *What would've happened if I'd stayed here? If Nana Hope had raised me after Mom died? Would CJ and I have wound up together?*

"I love that photo," CJ said, returning from the study, a folder tucked under her arm.

"I'd totally forgotten about it."

"My mom gave you a copy. You don't have it?"

Karol heard the hurt in CJ's voice. She shook her head. "When I left my father's house I didn't take much. Most of my stuff was stored in the attic. I assumed someday I'd go back and claim everything but he tossed most of it."

CJ took her hand. "I'm sorry. I didn't mean to bring up a bad memory."

"No, it's fine. I just didn't want you to think I cared so little about our friendship that I'd discard a photo of you—of us. I wouldn't…"

CJ set the photo on the table and pulled Karol to her. "I can get you a copy."

When they were teenagers, they'd spent countless moments just staring at each other, mainly because they were too naive and too nervous to know what to do next. Now, at least, some experience and decades of wisdom guided them. Their foreheads touched before their lips met. It was the kiss of a stranger—but it wasn't. One led to two and then to three… And then…

CJ pulled away, but she still held Karol's hand. Karol understood. "You clearly have a lot on your mind. I can see it in your eyes."

"Yeah," CJ admitted. "Ganza consumes me. If I'm not solving problems, I'm giving interviews."

"Of course. You're the ambassador of your grandparents' legacy. It must be an incredible honor and a tremendous responsibility."

CJ squeezed her hand. "You get it. That's why I'm glad you're going to stick around."

"Oh, so you're thinking there could be some more kisses in your future?"

CJ grinned. "In *our* future."

Karol smiled as they headed for the front door where Houston sat waiting patiently. He was so quiet sometimes she forgot he was with them.

They walked back through the yard to the golf cart. With each step, the quiet of CJ's house gave way to the music and laughter of the JOY Extravaganza. It was just one street away. A shiver of excitement ran down Karol's back. She couldn't wait to see it.

CHAPTER FIFTEEN

It took every bit of resolve for CJ to focus on the bits and pieces of the dress rehearsal that still needed polishing rather than the lovely kisses she'd exchanged with Karol. They'd barely spoken a word during the ride to the north entrance, but they'd held hands the entire time. CJ occasionally stole a glance at Karol, who was craning her neck to see the various displays they passed.

"That's marvelous!" she exclaimed as she watched the Curtises' Holiday Express locomotive chug around the front yard.

"Beautiful!" she cried at the Floreses' forest of silvery trees.

Her "oohs" and "aahs" had CJ grinning. Karol was a newbie, and her reactions tonight would probably be the reactions of the thousands of other newbies who would enter the JOY neighborhood during the next two weeks. It seemed each year word of mouth spread a little further, and folks from places like Dallas, Taos, and even Little Rock, journeyed west for a little holiday vacation. They spent two or three nights walking the neighborhood and really absorbing and appreciating the themes, artistry, and effort of the homeowners.

CJ pulled into Christmas Card Court and parked at the cul-de-sac's mouth. The only activity was at the Epsteins' house where the three groups were setting up their booths to support tzedakah.

"What does *tzedakah* mean? Am I saying it correctly?"

"You are. It's the Hebrew word for righteousness and justice."

"Well, this place has a different vibe entirely."

"It's supposed to."

Karol nodded and headed to the Buddhist display in the Gilberts' front yard. She squatted to study the photos and read the sign explaining Metta, the idea of loving kindness. She glanced up at CJ. "Where's your contribution?"

CJ led her to the photos of Houston and her grandparents.

"I wish I'd known them better," Karol said. "It seemed like they weren't around very much."

"That's because as they got older they spent summers in the cool pines of Flagstaff at the reindeer farm. They wanted out of the heat."

"I get that."

"Hey, at least this is a dry heat. Florida summers are humid as heck. I remember being miserable at Disney World in July."

Karol hooked her arm through CJ's as they strolled around the cul-de-sac. "Is this your way of encouraging me to permanently stay in this nice dry heat?"

"Is it working?"

Karol shrugged. "Maybe."

"Hey, CJ! Come over here!"

Daria Epstein was waving her over. She was dressed in black jeans and a Black Lives Matter T-shirt, her green and red kinky hair flowing around her face and John Lennon glasses. Next to her was a tall, thin, dark-skinned woman also wearing a Black Lives Matter T-shirt with red sweatpants. CJ thought she recognized her as a U of A basketball player.

Daria could barely control her excitement as she said, "CJ and Karol, this is Ama Iddi, star forward for the Wildcats. She'll be *one* of the players representing at the BLM booth during Ganza."

"The JOY neighborhood has big fans," CJ said, seizing Ama's outstretched hand. "Thank you so much for being involved."

"My pleasure," Ama said. "My team came through last year, and Daria ran up to us and told us about the theme for this year. She got our commitment right away." Ama grinned at Daria and added, "She should be a sports agent."

They all laughed but then a loud voice said, "It's so unfair what's happening to my family!"

CJ and Karol turned toward the booth closest to the Epsteins' garage doors, the one staffed by a fair housing nonprofit. Every year, in memory of her grandfather, fair housing advocates were somewhere at Ganza. A woman with long straight brown hair held a toddler against her hip while she gestured with her other hand. A little boy stood next to her, staring at the driveway. His T-shirt was ripped at the bottom, but it was Christmas red.

"Nobody should look that sad while they're here," CJ murmured.

"Exactly," Karol said, taking CJ's hand and strolling up to the woman. Her eyes were red from crying, and the young worker handed her a tissue. His nametag said Howard, and when he saw CJ and Karol, his expression seemed to say, *Please help me.*

CJ introduced herself and Karol. The woman was Gayle, her two children were Savannah and David. "Hey, Howard," CJ said, "Karol and I want to talk to Gayle, so why don't you take David around the corner to see the cool train, if that's okay with Gayle?"

David's face immediately brightened and Gayle nodded. Howard mouthed a thank-you as he and David headed down the driveway out of earshot. CJ said, "Gayle, it sounds like something bad is happening with your living situation. Karol is an attorney."

"You are?" Gayle sniffled.

"Yes. What's going on?"

Gayle took a breath. "He kicked us out. Two weeks before Christmas and now we're living in our car. He tossed all our stuff onto the lawn while I was at work. David got home from school and tried to pick up as much as he could, but all the good stuff was stolen by then."

"Had you been served or threatened with eviction for late rent?" Karol asked.

"No! I pay my rent on time every month. We don't have much left after rent and utilities, but we were getting by. He had no right to kick us out."

CJ watched as Karol questioned Gayle with compassion and professionalism. Apparently Gayle's landlord realized he could command a higher rent and he didn't want to wait for Gayle's lease to legally end.

"I just don't know what to do."

Karol handed her another tissue and said firmly, "Well, I do. My paralegal and I are here for the holidays, and we're going to do everything we can to get you back in your home."

"You are?" She looked thunderstruck. "That's...so nice."

Gayle started to cry and David ran up and threw his arms around his mother's waist. "It's okay, Mommy."

"These are happy tears, Davey. These nice ladies are going to help us."

Davey smiled and held up his shaved ice. "Look what Howard got me!"

"That looks yummy."

Howard set his shaved ice on the table and said, "I made a phone call and there's a room available in a group home for families. I could only get it for a couple days—"

"That's okay, Howard," Karol said. "Assuming Gayle has all the correct documentation, I think we'll be able to get her back in her apartment quickly."

Hugs were exchanged all around and CJ and Karol left as Gayle and Howard discussed directions to the group home, Karol promising to contact Gayle in the morning. Once they were back in the golf cart, CJ leaned over and gave Karol a kiss on the cheek.

"You're amazing. Do you really think you can get them back into their apartment in just a few days?"

"Oh, yes. And if I'm being honest, I won't do much. Stella will do the heavy lifting. By the time she's through with that landlord, he'll be giving Gayle a free month's rent."

"I'd like to see that," CJ said as she turned onto Candy Cane Lane.

"It's truly a sight."

Clearly, word was spreading about Ama Iddi's appearance as more neighbors decked out in U of A attire headed to the cul-de-sac to say hello.

"Shouldn't they be at their own houses?" Karol asked.

CJ laughed. "Well, technically yes, but I'm sure someone from each family is still there."

Stella and Blair drove by with Dr. St. John in the back seat. He waved enthusiastically, wearing his U of A sweatshirt.

"I know where he's going," Karol said.

"He's a huge fan."

"I know. Taylor took us to his house today."

"She mentioned that."

Karol scooted closer to CJ and played with her curls. "You know, the longer I'm here the more I resent my father. He deprived me of something intrinsically good and more important, he deprived me of *someone* so good, better than good."

CJ pulled over near the south entrance and turned to Karol. "That's true. I really wish it had been different." She looked away as she added, "Every December I asked Hope if you were coming to visit. She always said no but she made sure she gave me a gingerbread person before she delivered the answer."

Karol sniffled and took a deep breath. "I wonder if our whole lives might've been different."

CJ stroked her cheek. "We can't know and there's no point beating ourselves up about it. You may have hated me. According to my former partner, I was a pain in the ass all through my forties."

"I was an attorney. You think I don't know about being a PITA?"

When they both stopped laughing, CJ said, "Yeah, you got me there. So, did you ever have a long-term relationship?"

"Depends on how you define *long*. For me, long-term was two years, but it sounds like you and Mary were together for decades."

"Two decades," CJ said. "Then two weeks before our twenty-first anniversary, a kid texting and driving ran a red light and plowed into her. She died at the scene and the kid walked away. Well, not really *away*, given that she was arrested."

"Oh, my God. That's horrible—all of it. What happened to the girl?"

CJ ran her hand over the steering wheel, remembering the girl sobbing into her mother's arms. "Seven months for negligent homicide. She wasn't impaired and didn't have a record. It was just a terrible choice at the wrong moment. My attorney wanted me to sue, and Mary's parents probably would've done it if Mary and I hadn't been legally married. Thankfully it was my call and not theirs. They were out for blood but Mary never would've wanted a young person's life ruined—or a family to lose their home because of a civil suit judgment. There'd already been enough loss."

"I'm so sorry, CJ."

"That's why I don't think about 'what if.' If we had been together, I never would've had that time with Mary. I don't know if there's really some force pulling the strings, and I don't think it matters." She turned in her seat and faced Karol. "I always remember what my mom said a few weeks before she died. She said, 'CJ, life is ten percent luck, twenty percent fate, and seventy percent hard work. Since you'll never know what's in play at any moment, you work hard one hundred percent of the time, and fate and luck won't throw you too many curveballs you can't handle, but there will be a few humdingers.'"

"Like her getting ALS."

"For sure. And Mary's death."

"She'd be so proud of you."

"I believe she *is*."

CJ pointed at the lights and the displays down Candy Cane Lane behind them, and the JOY sleigh passing by, being led by True and Victor, the two horses who lived in the barn.

"These past five years...since Mary died...Sometimes I do get depressed around the holidays, despite how busy I am. And when that happens, I close my eyes and just listen to everything around me, and then...I know she's here, her hand guiding me, all of us, really, probably controlling fate to some extent. Her, my mom, my grandparents...and Hope."

CJ checked Karol's expression, expecting to see some cynicism from the New York attorney, but instead she only saw tenderness, kindness, compassion. Karol stroked her cheek and said, "You are really something, CJ Joy. I didn't realize it, but I've missed you terribly."

"Kiss her! Kiss her! Kiss her!"

They both jumped, startled, and looked around. Leaning out of the Wave Shaved Ice truck were Shea and Salma. Soon the patrons joined in and everyone was chanting. Karol was laughing and CJ knew her face was red. She hated this much attention. She shrugged. "Well?"

Karol batted her eyelashes. "It is the season of giving."

She gave CJ a sweet kiss as the crowd roared.

CHAPTER SIXTEEN

Karol awoke the next morning smiling. She'd had an excellent dream, one that included CJ and a lot of kissing. *Maybe that wasn't a dream?* She'd seen more action last night than she had in years. And in public, too!

Stella had taken the rental car yesterday, but when CJ dropped Karol off at the hotel last night, there was no sign of the rental. Hmm. The last time CJ and Karol had seen Stella was when they passed Blair's golf cart with Stella in the passenger seat and Dr. St. John in the back.

Karol dialed Stella, who didn't answer. *Interesting.* She went ahead and texted all of Gayle's situation, the pertinent information and the group home location where Stella could find her. Perhaps distracting Stella would cease the conversations and nagging about Boca and Nana Hope's house. Stella loved crushing horrible landlords and she was incredibly good at it.

Manny jumped on the bed and barked, and then dashed to the door. He was ready to go out, and after he had breakfast,

Karol imagined he'd want to return to the reindeer pen and see his "girlfriend." The only problem was that Karol didn't have any transportation and she'd agreed to go with Merry to yoga. She got dressed and called CJ as she circled the doggy potty area of the hotel with Manny.

"Hey," CJ answered. "Nice to wake up to your voice."

Karol felt the yummy tummy feeling again, along with a tingle down her spine. "Well, I'm glad you don't mind because I'm in a bit of a jam."

"How so?"

"I'm due to meet Merry in an hour for yoga at the Gilberts' house, and of course, Manny would like to head back to Mo as soon as possible."

CJ laughed. "Oh, he has it bad." She paused and then asked, "Is he the only one?"

Karol grinned and bit her lip. *She is such a charmer!* "Hmm. Well, I might be coming down with a case of infatuation. What about you?"

"Yeah, that could be possible. That or my allergies."

"Oh, really?"

"Ah, you know I'm kidding."

"Yeah, I do."

Manny barked again, and Karol looked down at him sitting like a gentleman and wagging his little tail on the ground.

"So, is something wrong with the rental?"

"Only that it isn't here and neither is Stella."

"Oh, then that explains why I haven't heard Blair on the radio this morning. Usually they're up by five on Opening Day, making sure all the little problems we discovered last night are handled before the crowd surge tonight."

"Do you think Blair and Stella—"

"I *definitely* think Blair and Stella."

Karol exhaled. *I'm reunited with my first true love, but Stella's the one who hooks up first. It figures.*

"You still there?"

Karol blinked. "Yeah, sorry."

"How about I pick you up? I don't have time for yoga, but I could drop you off at the Gilberts' house and take Manny over to Mo."

"That would be fabulous."

When CJ arrived, she wore jeans and a tight T-shirt that displayed her curves. As the importance of the day was clearly distracting CJ, Karol nixed her idea of pulling her into the hotel room and skipping yoga.

She did, though, welcome the sweet, long kiss CJ offered when she climbed inside the cab of CJ's truck, displacing Houston to the window seat. They'd just turned on to Speedway when the rental car zoomed past them, Stella behind the wheel—and wearing the blouse from yesterday.

CJ glanced at Karol. "Did you see that?"

"Oh, yes. I'm going to have a lot of fun with it."

CJ laughed and raised her eyebrows. "I'll bet."

"Stella's behavior doesn't surprise me, but Blair seems so…"

"Reserved? Serious? Uptight?"

"Well, sort of."

"Blair is very reserved—and careful. As a nonbinary person completely secure with their individuality, they don't put themselves out there very often. Honestly, if they got involved with Stella—even if it was just for a fling—I'd have to reassess my first impressions of her. She's got to be more than just a pushy New Yorker with very few social graces."

Karol nodded. "Stella is much more than what's on the surface, but for a lot of reasons she's developed this very thick veneer and she doesn't get close to a lot of people either."

"Maybe they're a match?"

"Maybe."

Along with a crowd of neighbors, Merry was waiting outside the Gilberts' house with her yoga mat tucked under her arm. Karol scanned the other faces, recognizing Dr. St. John, Ming the seamstress, and Jamaica from the cookie kitchen. She exhaled in relief.

"Don't worry," CJ said, squeezing her hand. "The word's spread that Santa's Workshop has survived and you're not a terrible monster. No one's going to give you the evil eye or say nasty stuff."

"Thanks," Karol said, gathering her things and stepping out of the truck.

"Oh, and one other thing," CJ called before she shut the door.

"What?"

CJ offered a lascivious grin. "You look hot."

An hour later, a bell chimed and Karol automatically checked her watch. *How could time fly by that fast?* She'd been so focused on the yoga, the music, and the loveliness of the lavender and hyacinth around her that she'd completely forgotten the rest of the world. *Well, except for a recurring vision of CJ kissing me.*

Mallory Gilbert, the yoga instructor, a tall, tanned, woman with blond hair who probably had been a model as well as a dancer, approached and asked, "What did you think?"

"It was fantastic! Thank you for letting me come."

"You're always welcome. You're family."

Karol's eyes filled with tears. All she could do was nod.

Merry stepped beside her and squeezed her shoulder. "Did you know that Hope did yoga three times a week?"

"She did?" Karol struggled to visualize Nana on a mat, twisting her body all around. Then she chided herself for her stereotypical opinions.

"Yes," Mallory said. "She didn't do the more advanced positions, but for someone nearly a century old, she had the moves." Mallory gave her a hug and said, "I hope you'll come back before you leave."

"Speaking of Hope," Merry said, "would you like to see where she's buried? It's not a far walk, and I always like to stretch my legs after yoga."

"I'd love that."

They headed out of the neighborhood to the four-way intersection. Merry pointed at the Orozco property and said, "Can I tell you a secret?"

"Um, sure," Karol said, feeling not all that sure.

"Apparently my daughter, Noel, has been sneaking onto that property to play kissy face with her girlfriend, Heather."

Karol answered carefully, "Oh, really?"

"Yes. As president of the HOA, I have one of two sets of keys that the grandson left us, and CJ has the other set. So, Noel's taken my keys, thinking I wouldn't miss them."

"How do you know she's over there with a girl?"

"One of the neighbors saw them." She added tersely, "And he felt the need to tell me."

Karol watched Merry closely. "And how do you feel about that?"

"Which part?" Her tone was testy. "The part about stealing the keys? Trespassing on private property? Having a girlfriend and kissing her? Having a girlfriend and not telling me or Juan about it?"

"I'll go with the third part. How do you feel about Noel kissing a girl?"

Merry shrugged. "I'm fine with it. I kissed lots of people when I was her age, even a couple girls."

Karol stopped walking and faced her. "But for you that was experimentation, right?"

"Well, yes, for me..."

"How will you feel if your daughter announces she's a lesbian?"

Merry paused and narrowed her eyes. Then she nodded, as if she'd reached a decision. "I'll be fine. Juan will be fine. Honestly, we've suspected she might be lesbian or bisexual for the last few years."

Karol nodded and they continued across the street to the cemetery.

"I just wish she'd tell me, especially since other people are talking about it."

Already knowing the answer because of her conversation with CJ, Karol asked, "What about Heather's parents?"

"I'd imagine they'd have more of a problem with it."

"Maybe part of the reason Noel hasn't said anything to you yet might be because of Heather's parents."

"Ah, I hadn't thought of that. A secret is a secret. Here I was making it all about me, or me and Juan. I think you might be right, Karol. Thank you for giving me that perspective."

"And I'll just add that you should be prepared for her announcement at any time. If a community member told you about them—"

"They'll probably tell someone else."

"Exactly. If Noel learns their secret is out, she'll probably want to be the one to tell you."

"Understood. I'm prepared. I've learned life can change in an instant. Fate doesn't care about your plans. If it hadn't been for Elsa Joy making a split-second decision one Christmas morning, I wouldn't be here."

"What do you mean?"

"The story goes that on Christmas Day, nineteen forty-five, little Elsa Joy walked down to the house of my great-great-grandmother. Elsa convinced her to come down and see the Joys' Christmas lights. Marie'd lost her husband in the last days of the war and she balked at first, but Elsa was very persuasive, insistent. Once she arrived, Elizabeth Joy convinced Marie to stay for dinner, and it was on that day that she met her future second husband, Brendan North, my great-great-grandfather. It was all because a little girl didn't want a neighbor to be lonely on such a wonderful holiday."

Karol stopped and pulled Merry into a hug. "I love that story."

When they broke the embrace, Merry was crying. "Just remember, Karol, John Lennon was right. Life is what happens while you're busy making plans."

They stared at each other until they both offered a tremulous, knowing smile.

"That's why we'll accept Noel as she is," Merry continued. "We haven't planned her life and we have few expectations about her future. I just hope that she's a good person to others. I feel really bad for Heather, though. How could you not accept your own child?"

Karol took a deep breath. "Unfortunately, it's still very common for LGBTQ youth."

Merry stared at her. "I take it you know from experience?"

"I do."

Merry offered her a one-arm hug. "I'm sorry."

They walked past several rows of headstones, some dating back nearly a century. The desert landscape wasn't as lush as the green fields back east—at least in Karol's opinion—but she appreciated the attention given to each plot. Most had a flower in the permanent vase next to each headstone and there wasn't a weed anywhere. As she looked farther up the path, she saw a large headstone—shaped like a gingerbread cookie and wrapped in blinking holiday lights.

That's got to be Hope.

Merry stepped ahead of Karol and brushed away a few pinecones lodged in the string of lights. "Got to keep Hope looking good," she said with a little smile. She gestured to the two Aleppo pine trees that flanked Hope's grave. "The owners of the cemetery broke with their plan and allowed Hope to be here as opposed to the next plot that was supposed to be used."

"They knew Hope?" Karol asked.

"Not personally, but they knew the gingerbread cookies, *loved* the gingerbread cookies."

Karol dropped in front of the headstone and stared at the words chiseled on the gingerbread person's tummy:

Hope Ellen Yates

May 1, 1921 – March 15, 2020

Beloved by All

She closed her eyes and prepared for the flood of tears she expected to fall, just as they had each time she'd thought about the moment she would stand before Hope's grave. Inevitably she broke into tears and sometimes it was at a most unfortunate moment when sad tears—any tears—were completely inappropriate. So, she waited. And waited. But all she felt was a sense of calm. Then a light breeze caressed her face and she smiled. *I know you're with me right now.*

Her eyelids fluttered and her gaze landed on Merry, who wore a nervous smile and wrung her hands. She glanced at the headstone and said, "Um, I hope you don't think this is too much…or in poor taste."

Karol traced Hope's name and chuckled. Even in death Hope made her feel more comfortable, more welcomed, than anyone else ever had. When she looked at Merry's expectant face, she smiled broadly and then said, "I think it's perfect."

CHAPTER SEVENTEEN

"Unfortunately, I don't think Happy looks happy," CJ said to Doug, the head organizer of the parade floats. "He looks…"

"Like he has gas," Ming said.

"Yeah," Taylor agreed.

Doug scratched his head. "Tori ran out of plaster, so she fudged on the mouth. I'm not sure what can be done at this point, but I'll try to get one of our artists on it."

"Maybe Geena Hernandez could fix it," CJ said, "If she feels up to it. She got an A in visual arts."

Doug nodded. "I'll call her first."

He scurried off and the rest of the board finished the float tour, sans Merry. CJ knew Karol and Merry were off together, but yoga had ended nearly an hour ago, and it wasn't like Merry to miss important board meetings. Even Blair was there, albeit with effort. The bags under their eyes and the enormous thermos of coffee were a giveaway of an eventful night, at least to CJ.

"Is there anything else?" CJ asked the board gathered around her.

In Merry's absence, she served as the president of the board, an office she'd held for so many years that sometimes it was hard for the board and members of the community to remember that CJ was no longer the first person to call with an issue. Merry accepted the occasional faux pas with charm and grace.

"Have you gotten a text from Merry?" CJ asked Juan.

He pulled his phone from his back pocket. "Oh, shoot, yes. She took Karol to the cemetery to see Hope's grave and they're on their way back now."

CJ turned to Taylor. "So, do we have a plan for the preachers tonight? I know it runs contrary to our theme of kindness, but I'd love for them to become frustrated enough on the first night that they don't show up again."

"We do," Taylor said. "I can only take a little credit for the plan. Stella was the one who thought of the idea."

"Doesn't surprise me in the least," Blair replied.

"Speaking of Stella," CJ said, "where is she?"

Blair shrugged. "She said she had some business when she left this morning—"

"Wait a second," Taylor said with an enormous grin. "*Left?* As in from your place?"

Blair merely stared at Taylor.

"I hope she's not off trying to get Ganza canceled," Ming said, her eyes never leaving the seam she was fixing.

"No," Blair offered. "She's way past wanting to sabotage Ganza. Near as I can tell, something happened yesterday when she went back to Burt's office. I don't know what it was, but something clicked for her and she's going back."

"She also might be helping a woman Karol and I met last night," CJ said, "one of the attendees named Gayle. Her landlord illegally evicted her, at least that's what she said. I think Karol planned to sic Stella on the landlord."

"Oh," Juan said. "I'd like to see that."

Just then, Merry and Karol waltzed into the warehouse, giggling like sisters. CJ smiled, glad to see they were growing closer. *The more people Karol bonds with, the less likely she'll leave. Isn't that what I want?*

Merry gave Karol a quick tour of the floats and joined the group. She pointed back at the Seven Dwarves float. "Why does Happy look like he's having a bad bowel movement?"

"We're on it, babe," Juan said. "Happy will be happy by parade time."

"When is the parade?" Karol asked CJ.

"Next week. We learned it was better to schedule it in the middle of Ganza to keep up the momentum of the whole event."

Merry grabbed her tablet from the conference table and started scrolling. "Let's run through the checklist. Drivers confirmed?"

"Check," Juan said.

"Street barricades?"

"Nearly done," Blair said. "We're meeting later with the city."

"Police presence?"

"Check," Ming replied. "Lou has ten off-duty officers."

"Who's Lou?" Karol whispered.

"Ming's son," CJ replied. "He's Tucson PD."

"Who has the morning cookie tally?"

"I do," CJ said. "Up to ten thousand."

Merry shook her head. "Not enough. How many after-school volunteers have we found?"

"Roughly fifty for today," Taylor said. "Tomorrow will be better because basketball practice ends till after Christmas. Both the boys and girls teams have volunteered for the next few days."

Merry grinned with glee. "Terrific! That's the spirit!" Her grin quickly morphed into a frown. "I'm worried we won't make it."

Everyone immediately started talking at once, dispensing positive adages, special words of encouragement and general uplifting expressions. They all worked to keep Merry upbeat when her hyper-responsibility and "doom cloud" took over.

She closed her eyes and gradually their positive messages turned her frown upside down. Her eyes flew open. "Thanks, everyone! I don't know what I'd do without y'all."

"I'm going over to the baking center right now," Juan said.

"When are you meeting with the city?" Blair asked.

"Not until one."

"Okay, I want to be there, so radio me."

"What else?" Merry asked.

"Costumes are nearly ready to go," Ming said. "I've got one more alteration to make, and if Stewart splits his pants one more time…"

CJ patted Ming's shoulder. Stewart, one of the elves at Santa's Workshop, was forever ripping open the back side of his pants when he contorted his flexible torso in many directions to make the children laugh.

"Reindeer and their new plus-one, Manny, are doing great," Blair said. They looked at Karol and added, "Manny is a superstar." They grabbed the morning's paper off the table. On the front page of the local section was a photo of Mo touching noses with Manny. "I'm thinking this will get a lot more folks through the gate." Blair set the paper down and said, "Everything at the north and south entrances is ready, and we've got shuttles and drivers. Hopefully, we won't have a parking problem."

"Taylor?" Merry asked. "Anything from you?"

She grinned. "Well, the Manny and Mo show brought out the press early. This is amazing and they are adorbs."

Everyone nodded in agreement and Merry said, "Okay, everyone! Today's the day. If you can help in the kitchen, please do so, and let's be careful out there!"

The meeting broke up, scattering the board in various directions. CJ waited until Karol finished thanking Merry for a lovely morning and Merry charged off, tablet in hand. Their eyes met and Karol approached her, almost shyly.

"Hey. How was yoga?"

"Yoga was fabulous. Mallory is an exceptional teacher. Stella would love her." She looked around. "No sign of Stella?"

"No. Did she text you? Did you tell her about Gayle?"

Karol fumbled through her bag and found her phone. "Ah, yes and yes. Had my ringer off for yoga. Apparently she's texted me eight times in the last hour. They all say the same thing: *Call me.*"

Karol dialed the number and put the phone on speaker.

Stella barked, "Finally."

"You're on speaker with CJ. I was at Hope's grave."

"Oh, sorry." There was a penitent pause. "I really am sorry. Good morning, CJ."

Karol said, "Did you meet Gayle yet?"

"I met Gayle and then I had breakfast. Ask me what I had for breakfast."

CJ looked quizzically at Karol, who was shaking her head and trying not to laugh. "Okay," CJ said, "I'll play. What did you have for breakfast?"

"One jackass landlord!" Stella burst out laughing and Karol and CJ joined in. "He's taking her back, replacing everything that got stolen from when he tossed it on the lawn. Even got him to come to the shelter, pick up the rest of the family's things and return all of it to the apartment."

"No way!" Karol exclaimed.

"Oh, yes way. I can't claim all the credit. Burt helped me because he owes me."

"What? Why?" CJ asked.

"It ties together with the reason I'm really calling. You need to get that board assembled at two o'clock. No, make that three o'clock."

A voice said something in the background and Stella barked, "You just keep looking. This is a private conversation!"

"Who was that?" CJ asked.

"That's Burt. Karol, I'm telling you, this guy would never make it in the City. What kind of yahoo lawyers are out here?"

Karol and CJ exchanged a puzzled look. Karol leaned closer to the phone and said, "Stella, what is going on?"

"Isn't it obvious? I'm solving the mystery."

"What mystery?" CJ asked.

"The one you told us about. Who's in the window? Why are people breaking into the old farmhouse? Well, I know and soon I'll reveal the truth."

CJ groaned. "Stella, we don't have time for this. Ganza—"

"I know," Stella barked. "It's tonight. I got that. But trust me, if you want that pretty Victorian house to remain a pretty

Victorian house and not a pile of very old rubble, you'll get the board assembled at the house at three o'clock. Oh, and Burt says Tierra Celestial's blueprints are somewhere in your grandparents' and mother's old files. CJ, do you know where those are?"

CJ exhaled. "Well, there's an entire storeroom. I'm not sure…"

"We need those plans. Specifically the ones for the cupola."

"That doesn't make sense. The house was built at the turn of the century. My grandparents didn't design it."

"No, but they remodeled it for Reynaldo Orozco. Did you know that?"

"I didn't."

"Yes. Hold on." Stella pulled the phone away and called to Burt, "What year was that remodel?"

"Sixty-eight."

"Did you hear that?"

"Yes, but why the cupola? Does this have something to do with the safe?"

"You'll see when we meet you. Just find those plans."

"Okay."

"And bring the kid."

"Who?" Karol asked.

"You know, the amazing Juanito, the walking musical encyclopedia. I need him."

Karol shrugged and said, "Okay, we'll look for the plans and I'll do my best to convince everyone that meeting you is more important than the final preparations for the most anticipated holiday celebration in all of Tucson."

"Good. Because it is."

And with that, she hung up.

"Are you sure we should spend time on this?" Karol asked CJ as she pointed the golf cart toward a large shed at the back of her property. "Merry's not going to be happy I'm not helping with the cookies."

"She'll understand."

"I hope so. Stella's antics and her flair for the dramatic usually pay off in the end, but once in a while…"

CJ slid an arm around Karol's shoulder. "It'll be okay. Ganza is a well-oiled machine by now. That's what happens after seventy-five years of production. We have all kinds of contingencies for different problems—a float loses a wheel, a child gets lost, a reindeer gets out of the barn, although that's never happened. Everything. We've got it covered. So when Merry's about to lose it, we use our Opposite Michelle Obama strategy."

"What's that?"

"When Merry goes high, we go low, or rather, we don't get all stressed."

Karol laughed. "I get it."

They pulled up to the shed and CJ pulled out her fat ring of keys. "Now, if I can just remember which one…"

It took six attempts, but she finally found the key for the padlock. They pulled the sliding double doors open and came face-to-face with a giant stuffed gorilla with huge teeth.

Karol laughed. "King Kong?"

"Yes."

"It really looks like him."

"He belongs to Juanito. Juan's brother got it from a movie company. Rumor has it that it was used in the Jessica Lange version of *King Kong*."

"Wow. Why is it here?"

"Merry dragged it here one day and told me that if I really was her best friend I'd give Kong a home, at least until Juanito is old enough for his own apartment. I guess after a week of walking into Juanito's room and nearly having heart failure every single time, she was ready to put him in the trash. And since I *am* a great friend…"

Karol looked around. "Speaking of friends, where's Huey today?"

"At doggie day camp seeing his canine buddies. He goes every week, and on opening night of Ganza I leave him home.

Since he loves to be out and about, the only way he's okay with me leaving him at home is if he's completely tired out."

"Makes sense."

Karol peered beyond Kong where *Antiques Roadshow* collided with *Hoarders, The Christmas Edition*. Expensive items were mostly draped in tarps, like the corner of a Tiffany lamp that jutted outside the edge of its covering. The form of one tarp clearly outlined a very old car. The stuff Karol expected to see in storage—a rowing machine and a massage table—were squashed amid the massive amounts of holiday paraphernalia: a huge 3-D Santa head, a rainbow-painted cross, a table filled with menorahs of all sizes, five stacks of clear plastic boxes filled with various costumes and a mountain of holiday lights that was twice Karol's height.

"When was the last time you were in here?" she asked, stepping around a team of plastic reindeer.

"Oh, it's been a year or two. Most of this stuff belonged to my parents or my grandparents, and I just can't seem to get rid of it, along with overflow of Ganza stuff that no one else can store."

"I'd love to hear the backstory about the rainbow cross sometime."

"Sure."

"You know, everybody talks about your grandparents and your mom, but what about your dad? I remember meeting him a few times but he wasn't very talkative."

"Yeah, he took over the family business from my grandfather. He worked long hours but he found time to be with the family."

"Like the barbeques on the lawn."

CJ smiled. "Yeah. When everyone talks about Ganza, he doesn't come up much because he was in the background, growing the ice business and starting franchises for the shaved ice. Just a solid guy who was generous with his employees and loyal to his family. He taught me everything I know about management. He passed away from pancreatic cancer.

"And your mom never remarried?"

"No. Everyone in the neighborhood was her family and Hope was another mother." CJ looked away, thinking hard.

"CJ?"

After a long pause, she looked up, nodding. "I remember it now, why my family stopped speaking to the Orozcos. I didn't understand it at the time but I remember a conversation between Hope and my mom. A couple of years after Dad passed, they were talking about Rubio's father and how he'd made a pass at her and it was a lot more than just an inappropriate remark. After that I didn't go over there anymore." She looked quizzically at Karol. "Why didn't I remember that? You'd think something like that would stick."

"Not necessarily. You heard it when you were young and probably out of context."

Karol craned her neck beyond a sea of tarps. "This building didn't look this large from the outside."

"We're heading to that far corner past the stack of suns with faces. Those were from the Yule celebrations."

Fortunately the Joys' architectural work was all in the same general vicinity, but unfortunately nothing seemed to be in any distinct order. Rows and rows of deep square shelves housed all the blueprints. Karol reasoned that the wide bank of filing cabinets across from the plans kept the correspondence and ancillary materials for each project. She threw up her hands. "Where do we start?"

CJ shrugged and pulled out a roll of paper almost as big as herself. They looked around for a place to set it down.

"Over there," Karol said, pointing to a ping-pong table covered with Christmas detritus—boxes of decorations, a stack of advent calendars, and a weird-looking jack-in-the-box.

They cleared the table and unrolled the plans, which were dated 1946, for a church in Brooklyn. "Wow," CJ said. "I've never seen these, but I've heard the story behind them. My grandmother had to finish them on her own because my grandfather was fighting in Europe during World War II."

"I'll bet that was nearly scandalous at the time. Not only did your grandmother have a career, she shouldered responsibility."

"Yeah, I heard a lot of people thought they were an odd couple. Strangely enough, it was my grandfather that faced ridicule for not keeping his wife in line."

"I'll bet."

CJ rubbed her temple as a headache formed. She sighed. "We'll have to go through each cubby one at a time."

"Wait a minute," Karol said, moving to the filing cabinets. Each drawer had a label with a decade listed. "Aha!" she exclaimed. She tried to pull open the drawer for the '60s, but it was locked. "Is the key somewhere in the house?"

CJ wormed her way past an array of tarps. Karol heard things scraping across the cement floor and noticed a high stack of wooden chairs teetering in CJ's general vicinity. She grimaced, imagining a collapse that would bury CJ and remembering the mess that still lingered in her New York apartment. *And I can never bring Manny in here! He'd get lost and we'd never find him.*

CJ reappeared behind Karol, holding a small silver key. She offered a sly grin. "Would you believe holiday magic?"

Karol laughed and held out her hand. "Just give me the key. I'll open the cabinet and finally feel useful."

CJ handed her the key but held her hand. "You've been more than useful since you've arrived. You've been open-minded about changing your opinion—"

"Only after I threatened you with legal action."

"You've been incredibly generous—"

"Something I should've been doing all along."

"And I'm even more attracted to you than I was back when we were horny preteens."

Karol stepped into CJ's physical space and planted a tentative kiss on her lips.

"That is not helpful," a stern voice said.

They turned and saw Blair frowning at them. "It's opening night! And we have big problems!"

"Not the porta potties," CJ groaned.

"No, not the potties, but that would be awful too." They held out their phone. "As much as I'd like to ignore the Tierra Celestial issue, we cannot."

CJ and Karol peered at Blair's small screen. Two men stood in the cupola of the old Victorian. One was a thin Caucasian in a driving cap, the other a Hispanic man in a suit. CJ pointed. "Is the guy in the suit—?"

"Yes," Blair groaned. "That's Rubio Orozco."

CHAPTER EIGHTEEN

CJ, Karol, and Blair watched as the guy in the driving cap pulled the bookcase away and went to work on the safe. A large briefcase filled with tools and instruments lay open next to him, but everything else was difficult to discern on the small screen. Rubio hovered over the man and constantly, impatiently, checked his watch. After a few minutes he walked out of the camera's range.

"We could be using our time better," Karol suggested, "if we kept looking for those plans while we watched. I'm guessing Stella wanted us to find those plans because they might include the safe's construction."

"No need," Blair said. "Look."

They again huddled around the screen. Rubio had reappeared studying a large piece of paper he held in front of him.

"He already has the plans!" Karol exclaimed. "I'm calling Stella. I don't know what's going on, but she needs to spill the beans right now."

Karol strolled toward the door as CJ's phone rang. "It's Merry."

"Oh, she's not going to be happy," Blair moaned.

"Not in the least." CJ cleared her throat and put Merry on speaker. "Hey Mer—"

"What in the hell—I mean huckleberry—is going on! Why aren't you all in the bakery or completing your to-do lists? Is somebody fixing that poor dwarf's head? Why isn't the finishing crew *finishing*? And why do we all need to meet at Tierra just a few hours before the opening of Ganza? Who the hell does Stella think she is?"

"Language," Juan called in the background.

"No, I do mean *hell*," Merry replied. "And this time, I'm gonna say it. This time I'm spouting the grown-up word! I'm losing my cookies here—literally and figuratively."

CJ imagined Merry's normally pale face the color of an Early Girl tomato. When Merry had run her tape and CJ heard nothing but silence, she said, "Rubio Orozco is standing inside Tierra Celestial. He's attempting to open the safe in the cupola."

"What safe? Why is he here? Now?" Merry cried.

"Right now," Blair confirmed. "I'm staring at him and a safecracker. He's holding the plans of the house in his hands."

"Oh, for shit's sake!"

Blair and CJ both raised an eyebrow. This was the foulest language they had ever heard from Merry. CJ guessed Juanito wasn't nearby. CJ leaned toward the phone. "Mer, it's going to be okay. Karol is talking to Stella right now. We're going to deal with this and get back on track."

"But we don't have time for a three o'clock meeting!"

"We absolutely need to make time," Blair said. "Rubio, that bastard, knows what's happening today and that's why he thinks he'll get away with it."

"What is he getting away with?" Juan asked in the background.

CJ said, "I believe Stella knows, and I'm almost certain this involves Burt as well."

"The attorney?" Merry asked.

"Yes."

CJ heard a loud noise and looked up to see the mountain of chairs collapse—just as Karol skittered past them. "Sorry," she said.

"What was that?" Merry asked.

"Nothing," Blair replied.

Before Merry could once again turn down what she termed Disaster Boulevard, CJ asked Karol, "What did you learn?"

"Well, Stella's interrogation skills are just slightly kinder than those of a general running a gulag. She wants Burt to tell you himself, so she's sending you a Zoom link right now."

Merry groaned. "A Zoom meeting? Now?"

"It'll be fine, Merry. No need to worry," Blair said reassuringly.

As promised the Zoom link immediately popped up on Karol's phone. They all appeared in their little squares. CJ wrapped her arm around Karol's waist and snuggled closer. They gazed into each other's eyes until Merry barked, "As happy as that makes me, there's really not time for that!"

Merry's face was indeed the color of a tomato and the equally red front of her Santa shirt was dusted in flour, as were her cheeks. Juan appeared next to her and lovingly swiped his hand over each of Merry's cheeks, which seemed to calm her—until she realized that Burt and Stella still hadn't joined. "Where are they?"

"We're here," Stella said as her camera went on.

"Oh, my God!" Karol exclaimed.

While Stella's appearance was the utmost of professional, Burt looked as though he'd been through hell. His tie was bound around his head, sending what little hair he had left into a wild spiky mess, his face covered in lipstick and glitter, and the front of his powder-blue shirt had streaks of chocolate.

"What happened, Burt?" Merry asked.

A piercing scream had them all covering their ears. Then a cherubic, chocolate-covered little face leaned in front of Burt. All they could see were bright blue eyes.

"Who you?" the child asked.

"Who are you?" Merry asked in a sweet voice.

"Magellan."

"Hi, Magellan. Is that your grandpa with you?"

"Uh-huh," he said, his whole mouth opening directly in front of the camera.

"You don't usually see another person's tonsils," Blair said.

CJ's eyes narrowed. "How are you so calm?" she asked Blair quietly while the group listened to the musings of Magellan as he listed everything he wanted from Santa. "We're a few hours away from the event we've planned for a year, the list of things that still need to be done is in the double digits, and our Zoom call is being hijacked by...I would guess a four-year-old."

"I'm just enjoying the ride," Blair replied.

"Thank you, Magellan," Merry said in her mommy voice. "Now let your grandpa talk to us, please."

"K, bye," he said and disappeared.

Burt still looked comatose so Stella slid him away from the camera's computer and sat down. "You're probably wondering what happened here."

"It's crossed my mind," Karol said.

"Well, Burt wasn't being very forthcoming, and as good luck would have it, he got a call from his daughter, asking if he would watch his grandsons. You've met Magellan, who is the calmer of the two, and then there's Columbus. He's seven and—"

Another bloodcurdling scream cut her off.

When it was over, Stella finished. "He's the screamer. I said Burt would be happy to watch them. Then, I called Grubhub. Did you know you can ask them to go to a candy store and buy two hundred bucks worth of candy and they'll bring it to you?"

"News to me," CJ said.

"Well, they will, and then when I dumped it on the floor... I've never seen any living creatures move that fast, and I've watched cheetahs on safari. Those boys stuffed their faces so fast...And let me tell you, anyone who says sugar doesn't amp up kids, doesn't *have* any kids!" Stella waved her hand. "But I digress. So when Burt couldn't find what I wanted, namely the combination to the safe, I sicced his grandkids on him, armed with my cosmetics bag. And did you know candy stores sell glitter? Who knew?" She turned the camera to see the decorated Burt, and that Burt's desk blotter, calendar, and even an award shaped like a pyramid were also covered in red, green, and gold glitter.

"So, what's the meeting about, Stella?" Blair asked. "Did you get my text about Rubio?"

Stella grinned. "I did. CJ, I think your conversation with him yesterday pushed him over the edge. Here's what I've learned. Rubio's broke, at least his company is."

Merry gasped. "Broke? I can't believe it! He's got all that money."

"*Had* all that money is the right word. He's got gambling debts. It's like a bad Hollywood movie. He's in deep with loan sharks. That's why he needs to unload the house. Those guys you saw, CJ, the guy Noel and Heather saw—"

"Noel and Heather?" Juan asked. "What do they have to do—"

"Juan, honey, I'll explain it all to you later," Merry said.

"You know?" CJ asked.

"I do. I've known all along."

Stella slammed her hand on the desk. "May I please finish *my* story!"

"Now you know how I feel," Blair grouched.

Stella looked directly at Blair. "Yes, I do." She blew them a kiss and continued, "Anyway, a couple of those gentlemen poking around the house were wise guys. It's a good thing none of you met up with them."

"They were safecrackers?" Karol asked.

"Sort of," Stella said. "But better at cracking skulls than safes. The guy over there now with Rubio is supposedly the best." She waved her hands. "But that's not what I'm trying to tell you. I know what Rubio is after."

"What?" Merry and CJ asked.

"The extra ingredient to Hope's gingerbread recipe."

"No!" Merry cried. "If he gets that, he'll mass-produce the cookies!"

"Wait, Karol was supposed to get that when Hope died," CJ exclaimed.

Stella nodded. "She was. But what nobody knew is that Burt never had the recipe. Several years ago Hope asked Rubio's mother to keep the recipe safe for Karol. Of course she agreed. All Burt had was the code for the safe." Stella slowly turned to him and shouted, "Which he lost!"

"And I'm sorry!" Burt cried.

Stella shook a finger at him. "Just shut up! And instead of doing the ethical thing when Hope died, like telling Karol about his mistake so she could hire someone to unlock the safe and claim what's rightfully hers, he said and did nothing. Karol always assumed Hope hadn't given her the recipe because she was mad at her for not visiting."

Merry waved a hand dismissively. "Oh, Karol, Hope would never have done that to you. I could've told you that."

"I know that now, Merry," Karol said with a smile.

"Let me see if I can summarize," Blair said in disgust. "The most sought-after cookie recipe in America is in a safe no one can open."

"Unless Rubio can get it open with the blueprint," CJ said.

Blair glanced at their phone. "It's not helping him. Now they're both just staring at the safe door."

"It's time to get over there," CJ said.

"Folks, we have three hours until Ganza," Blair said.

"I'm on my way over," Stella said. "Let's go face Rubio and figure this out once and for all."

"Sounds like a plan," Juan said.

"Ah, and don't forget to bring Juanito," Stella reminded him.

"Why?" asked Blair.

"Because children see things we don't."

CHAPTER NINETEEN

"What if there's no way to open the safe?" Karol asked as CJ zoomed the cart toward the old Victorian.

CJ shrugged. "I guess we just keep making cookies like we always have. Selling fifty thousand gingerbread people is nothing to sneeze at."

"I know you're right, but it would just make me feel better to have what Hope wanted to give me."

"I know. I think those feelings come from a different place. I don't think they have anything to do with culinary arts."

Karol wrapped an arm around CJ and kissed her cheek. "I can't wait till we get to the part of the evening where I get to kiss you some more."

CJ felt her cheeks burn. "Me too."

They pulled up next to a black SUV, which Karol suspected was Rubio's rental, with Blair right behind them. Merry and Juan took a little longer to get there since they had to pick up Juanito, and Stella was last to arrive, dragging a disheveled and downhearted Burt out of the passenger seat. He looked worse than he had on Zoom. His expensive tailor-made suit was covered in glitter, and his grandchildren had drawn designs on his pants with two different shades of lipstick.

Merry confronted him, hands on her hips. "I almost feel sorry for you, Burt, for not following Hope's wishes..." She shook her head. "How could you?"

Burt hung his head. "I don't know, Merry."

"Do you remember anything about that combination?"

"I never saw it. It was in a sealed envelope. I know my secretary put it in Hope's file. I can't imagine what happened to it."

"I can tell you what happened to it," a voice said from the top of the stairs.

They all turned toward a Hispanic man in dressy gray pants and a dark-blue polo shirt. He was clearly used to the good life, sporting an expensive haircut and two rings with stones that glinted in the sunlight as he waved a white envelope. "I paid a lot of money, Burt, to have your secretary find this and give it to me. Unfortunately, it wasn't money well spent."

Merry harrumphed. "Rubio Orozco, I've got a good mind to come up there and tan your fanny."

Rubio suddenly smiled. "It's good to see you again, Merry." He looked at the group and added, "Merry was my former babysitter many moons ago." He scanned the crowd and frowned. "Burt, what the hell happened to you?"

"Language," Juan said.

Burt just stared at the ground.

"What was in the envelope?" CJ asked.

He pulled apart the opening and showed them. "Nothing. It was empty."

That got Burt's attention. "Seriously?" he said. "Why would Hope give me an empty envelope?"

"Maybe because she didn't trust you," Stella answered. "Maybe she knew you were just a conniving SOB." She looked over at Juanito and said, "Sorry, kid."

"It's okay. I know it stands for Son of Beeswax."

Stella rolled her eyes. "Are we just going to stand here?"

CJ said, "Rubio, can we assume your safecracker has been unsuccessful?"

Rubio nodded. As if on cue, the safecracker appeared, walking down the stairs carrying his briefcase of tools. CJ thought he looked like a wise guy, tall with a thin face, a nose like a beak, and a pointy head sporting his driver's cap. "It's like the combination doesn't exist," he announced. "I can't even get the first number. Never seen anything like it. Whoever installed that safe was the best there's ever been." He looked at Rubio and said, "I'm going across the street for a shaved ice. Pick me up there."

He headed out and Rubio looked around. "Since there's nothing left to do here, CJ, I'll be on my way. I'll send you the demolition schedule."

He started down the stairs but Stella stepped in his path. "Not so fast. Burt wasn't entirely useless today." Stella looked at Burt. "Want to tell Mr. Orozco or should I?"

Burt leaned against the car, hands in his pants pockets. He shook his head.

"Tell me what?" Rubio snapped.

Stella grinned. "We managed to reach Mrs. Simpson, the head of the Arizona Historical Society. When she heard about the potential buyer of Tierra Celestial, specifically *who* that buyer is, she called in a favor with a judge." Stella handed him a folded sheet of paper. "This is an injunction delaying demolition until the Society can fully assess the property's historic value. Considering how backlogged they are, that could take some serious time."

Rubio seized and scanned the injunction, his face paling. "Shit!"

"Language!" Juan shouted.

Rubio crushed the paper into a ball, hurled it as far as he could and blew down the steps. They all watched as he jumped into the SUV and barreled out the front gate.

"I hope he remembers to pick up the other guy," Juanito said.

Blair leaped up a few steps until they were above the entire group. "Okay. First, let's give Stella a big hand for singlehandedly minimizing the immediate threat to Tierra Celestial."

Everyone whooped and hollered and clapped while Stella took a bow.

"Now," Blair continued, "can we please return to our duties?" They checked their watch. "We have two hours until several thousand people descend on our neighborhood."

"You heard them, people!" Merry bellowed. "Back to work!"

By five p.m. darkness had descended on the community. Karol and CJ went back to Nana Hope's house and helped with the final setup of the kitchen—the joining of the industrial community kitchen that had been turning out cookies for days and the quaint, homey kitchen where the cookies would be dispersed. As they organized the pans and prepared the urns of cocoa, Karol felt—more than once—Nana Hope's presence. She could hear her laugh alongside everyone else. There was a unique energy inside Hope's home and she was drawn into it.

But what about Boca?

The rest of Santa's Workshop was humming with excitement. She met the evening's Santa Claus, Mr. Len Fong, who worked with the photographer to set up his chair and the lights. A dozen high school kids dressed as elves took up their toy-making stations, and five members of Blair's security team stationed themselves strategically through the house.

CJ squeezed Karol's hand. "I wanted you to see how this would look so you'd know how much we respected Hope's home—your home now."

Karol blinked back tears. "Thank you," she managed, but her thoughts were elsewhere. *It will always be Hope's home. Even if I decide to stay, she'll be here with me.* That thought thrilled her.

Once the workshop was prepared, CJ and Karol hopped into the golf cart and made quick stops at the north and south entrances. The north entrance was just as it should be— volunteers ready for the onslaught, but quiet for now; however, the south entrance was teeming with people. Many were dressed like carolers, and almost all of them carried a black notebook. Stella and Taylor were in the mix, chatting and…plotting?

"Hmm…what's going on?" CJ asked.

Karol groaned. "It could be anything if it involves Stella."

"Well, I'm not sure I want to know."

"Probably smart."

Taylor spotted them and waved. She was too far away so she got out her phone and called CJ. "Hey, Taylor," she answered. "You're on speakerphone with Karol."

"Hey to both of you," she said. "I heard y'all had quite the confrontation at Tierra. Sorry I missed it. Especially seeing Burt dressed up like a sad clown."

"It was something," CJ agreed. "What's with all these people?"

"Just a little scheme and surprise Stella and I—mostly Stella—cooked up."

"Do I want to know?"

"Why don't you just be at The Court about thirty minutes after we start? It'll all be clear to you then, and we'll know if it's going to work or be an epic fail."

"O-o-o-kay," CJ said slowly.

"It's all good, CJ," Taylor insisted. "See you then."

She cut out and CJ looked at Karol. "You know Stella. Should I be worried?"

Karol gazed out at the crowd, watching Stella smile and joke with a lot of the people. She looked as if she was schmoozing clients at a firm happy hour. It really was Stella at her best. "No," Karol said before she realized she was even speaking. "This is going to be okay."

"I hope you're right. If anything happens to derail our chance for the CUDL award…Well, I hope whoever is the cause can sprint like a gazelle because Merry's going to be right behind them wielding her ax."

CHAPTER TWENTY

Karol didn't think her holiday spirit could soar any higher. She'd been behind the scenes singing and dancing with the neighbors. She'd played with reindeer. She'd toured the neighborhood and been mesmerized by all the displays. Yet, as she and CJ, who again wore her holiday tux with a glittery red top hat tonight, watched hundreds of people pour through the south gate, some bringing just a can of food each, but most toting bags and bins of food, clothing, and toiletries for donation, her entire being tingled. Images of being with Hope as a child, cuddling with CJ, watching Manny play with Mo… She was so emotionally overwhelmed, her senses didn't know what to do, so they did…nothing. She stood mesmerized.

CJ touched her shoulder. "Are you okay? You look really upset."

Karol, the trained lawyer who had argued multiple times in front of the New York State Supreme Court, found herself completely speechless. She shook her head. *How can I make you understand?*

CJ took her hand and led her to the dark side of the house closest to the entrance. She pulled Karol into a close warm hug, and Karol cried. CJ whispered, "Before you can totally immerse yourself in joy, you have to forgive yourself and let go of all the negativity holding you back."

Karol closed her eyes and listened to CJ's heartbeat. Despite Karol's breakdown and the enormity of Ganza and all of the responsibilities CJ carried, CJ's heart was a simple steady beat that immediately calmed Karol. Her shoulders relaxed and her chest no longer sounded like a cacophony of church bells resonating in her. She heard Mallory Gilbert's yoga voice and focused on her breathing for a little longer. When she pulled away from CJ, expecting her to be wearing an expression of concern, she saw only CJ's lovely green eyes, the color of Christmas.

Karol gasped. "I'm so sorry. You have a million things to do."

CJ took her hand. "I'm doing exactly what I should be doing right now." She pointed to a long line of people down Sleigh Street. "How about we hit one of the food trucks. I'm starving."

"Is that line for one truck?"

"No, that's why it moves fast. Juan designed a system that has one major line and then several shorter lines for each truck. See the worker in the bright yellow vest, the guy with a Christmas tree hat?" CJ pointed to a tall man with a bushy beard, wearing an entire Christmas tree, complete with lighted star, on his head.

"Yup. He's hard to miss."

"Yeah, that's the point. That's Geena's dad, Jesse. He's watching the food lines and dispersing the long line to the right places. Someone else is circulating with menus so people are ready to order when they reach him."

"Sounds like a great plan."

"It's worked for a decade. C'mon."

They meandered toward the wonderful smells wrapped up in laughter and happy chatter. Everywhere Karol looked, people were smiling. She saw several acts of care and comfort between strangers—a family stepping aside so an elderly woman with a walker could pass, a teenager dropping to a knee to collect canned goods that rolled away when a woman's paper bag split open, a child offering their gingerbread cookie to a crying toddler whose own cookie had fallen to the ground. It was personkind at its best.

They were approaching the front of the line and deciding between street tacos and Asian fusion when an older gentleman, standing on the corner of the next block, pointed at CJ and marched toward her. He wore a red sweater and Santa hat, and Karol realized he wasn't alone—an entire group of people followed him.

"CJ, who's that?"

"What?" CJ asked, engrossed in the fusion menu.

"Him."

CJ saw the man and sighed. "Crap. Those are the preachers, and that's Brother Joe. He's the ringleader."

"Well, he doesn't look very happy."

Suddenly twenty carolers poured out from the connecting street and appeared to be following the preachers. They were just starting the third verse of "Winter Wonderland" and as they approached, Karol recognized one of the loudest singers—Stella. Karol had always admired her paralegal's beautiful voice, but on this night she guessed Stella had an ulterior motive for joining the chorus.

Brother Joe stepped up to CJ, pointed at her and then at the chorus. CJ cupped a hand beside her ear as if she couldn't hear anything he was saying. The chorus had moved right behind the preachers, and for a moment Karol worried the two groups would come to blows, the preachers using the Bibles they held in their hands as weapons.

"In the meadow we can build a snowman..." Stella chirped.

"...harassment...authorities...no right..."

"He'll say are you married and we'll say no man..."

After two more fruitless attempts, Brother Joe grabbed Jesse's bullhorn and shouted into it, "You can't smother our First Amendment rights!"

"Walkin' in a winter wonderland," the chorus chimed. "Walkin' in a winter wonderland!"

Jesse moved into Brother Joe's personal space and held out his enormous hand. He said nothing. Karol guessed he didn't need to use words to demand the return of his bullhorn. He towered over all of them. *The perfect guy to run the food line.* Brother Joe withered at the confrontation and handed over the bullhorn.

Karol noticed Blair with a uniformed Asian Tucson police officer, standing at the end of the street. Both had their arms crossed, just watching the action—for now. When Stella met her gaze, Karol nodded toward Blair but Stella just looked puzzled. Karol whipped out her phone and started texting.

Brother Joe glared at CJ. "What are you going to do about this, CJ?"

CJ shrugged and chose to answer. "Not much I can do, Brother Joe. As you've reminded me many times over the years, these are public streets, and *everyone* has the right to use them."

Stella's choir, which according to the emblem on the outside of their binders, was really the U of A Wildcat Concert Choir, rounded for home with the last chorus. CJ smiled and shouted into Brother Joe's ear, "Why would we want to stop a choir from singing such a lovely song, especially if that lovely song drowned out the horrible name-calling that sometimes borders on racism from your people?"

As the song ended, everyone applauded, and Stella took a bow. Then she shouted, "Let's all sing! *Jingle bells...*"

Soon the choir and everyone in the food line joined in. It was impossible to have a conversation, and Karol realized that had been Stella's game plan all along. Karol scanned the street and saw another small group of preachers, at least she thought they were preachers since they each carried a Bible, being followed by a different choir, one made of adults and children—with Taylor leading them. They were singing "Rudolph, the Red-Nosed Reindeer" at full voice; however, when they got within earshot of the other singers, Taylor turned and directed them to join in on "Jingle Bells." It was the loudest and most euphoric version Karol had ever heard. Everyone was smiling and cheering—except the preachers.

Brother Joe shouted, "You're all going to hell!" before he gestured to both preacher groups and they all headed down the street, presumably to the exit, but Taylor's boisterous choir continued to follow them.

When "Jingle Bells" concluded with a raucous "in a one-horse open sleigh!" with Stella going full-on operatic, everyone applauded.

Blair and the police officer, who CJ seemed to know, joined them at the food line. They gestured to Karol and said, "Officer Lou Zhao, I'd like you to meet Karol Kleinz, Hope's granddaughter."

Officer Zhao stuck out his hand. "Pleasure to meet you, ma'am. My family was very fond of your grandmother."

CJ added, "Lou is Ming's oldest son."

"Ah, then you were also a member of this community," Karol said.

"Still am. My wife and I bought a house just a block away from my mom. Once you live in JOY, it's hard to leave." He nodded at everyone and said, "I'll continue my rounds and make sure the preachers don't do anything un-Christian before they leave." He pointed at Blair. "That was a heck of a creative idea."

"Not my idea, but thanks," Blair said. Office Zhao waved and headed off. Blair turned to Karol and said, "Your paralegal is really a force."

"Oh, yes. Whenever possible, you want Stella on your side. Opposing her isn't pleasant."

Blair stared down the street and finally muttered, "I would imagine that's true." They leaned toward CJ and quickly whispered something in her ear before heading back to their golf cart. CJ looked quite surprised and she shook her head as if ridding herself of whatever Blair whispered.

"Do I want to know?" Karol asked.

"Fusion or tacos?" CJ asked.

Karol studied her, and when it was clear CJ wouldn't break confidence, she said, "Fusion."

Despite the interruption by the preachers, the rest of the evening was joyous. They took a ride in the horse-drawn sleigh, caught a performance by the Claytons' steampunk band, and stopped in to see the reindeer, or rather the "Mo and Manny Show," where there were as many people huddled around the ring staring and pointing at the reindeer and her canine boyfriend as there were waiting in line to pet and feed one of the reindeer. There were also four security guards—two observing the crowd and two checking bags and backpacks before they were allowed inside.

As they climbed back into the golf cart, Karol said, "I want to go back to The Court. I want to make sure those nonprofits know to reach out to me if they have more situations like the one with the evicted renter last night."

"I hate to say it, but I imagine they encounter those situations nearly every day."

Karol nodded. "I have some leverage that I think could reach across the country, one nonprofit helping another. Maybe Howard's group could start lobbying the legislature to change the housing laws, which are much stronger in other states, New York included."

CJ smiled and cocked her head. "You really know how to use your superpowers for good, don't you?"

"What are you really saying?"

CJ leaned across the seat and kissed her softly on the cheek. Although the kiss was delicate and sweet, the wave of heat it sent to Karol's core was not. She knew she was blushing all the way to her ears. CJ whispered, "I think you're a completely different person than the woman who fired off that terse and threatening email about ceasing and desisting."

She leaned into CJ's shoulder and replied, "I'm still that person but not with you. Not with this place. Not with Hope's legacy."

CJ sat up and faced her, the sexual tension broken. For a second Karol worried she'd said something wrong. *Please don't let her be angry.* CJ sighed and tears pooled in her eyes. "I'm so glad you see it. That you see what Hope meant to all of us."

"I do."

CJ grinned and started the golf cart. She checked her watch. "Off to The Court and then we end the evening with cocoa and cookies."

The stop at The Court took longer than expected. When CJ saw Janice Johnstone staffing the Legal Aid booth, she knew Karol and Janice would form an instant bond. Janice was a recently retired judge with a reputation for fairness and a lack of tolerance for bullshit. Soon several workers from the other booths were crowded around Karol as she explained some of the recent federal-level changes to housing law practice.

CJ just hung back and listened to some of the two-way radio chatter. At the moment, Taylor was recounting the exodus of the preachers and the ten different singing groups from U of A and the greater Tucson area who had agreed to come to Ganza.

"You should've seen it, Merry. Brother Joe was so angry I thought he might punch someone."

"Isn't he the one who served two nights for drunk and disorderly before he saw *the light*?"

"Exactly," Taylor said. "Talk about a hypocrite."

"You did good, kid," Juan chimed in.

"Thanks, but really, this was all Stella's idea."

"Not true," Stella said in the background. "I just mentioned the idea of a choir. You were the one who went out and recruited ten groups *and* got them to commit to five nights."

"They're coming again?" Merry asked. "Well, bless my holy holly. That's great!"

"Yeah," Taylor said, "we know the preachers will be back. They won't think that a bunch of college kids would show up more than once. I figure they'll be back at least twice more and maybe then they'll fade out."

"Terrific!" Merry said. "Hey, did y'all stop by and see how Geena fixed our gassy dwarf? You know, the one who looked like he had diarrhea?"

"So, it's all good?" Ming asked, using her favorite phrase.

"It's better than good," Merry said.

Long ago, Blair had accepted that it was impossible for Merry to restrain herself from chatting on the radio. The compromise had been that the phrase "Important! Listen Now!" would precede any necessary or emergency communication. As Ganza was so well executed, the phrase was rarely uttered.

The chatter went silent. CJ smiled at the crowd surrounding Karol. Some people took notes or wrote down Karol's cell number, and by the time they wrapped up, Karol and Janice had a lunch date for early next week. Janice waved at CJ before returning to the booth.

"Look at you. In town for just a couple days and you're making friends right and left. Think you'll make friends this fast in Boca Raton?"

Karol threw back her head and laughed.

"What?" CJ cried.

"You're not exactly subtle."

"I know. Your timeline doesn't give me that luxury."

CJ had meant to sound lighthearted, but judging from the look on Karol's face, she hadn't succeeded. She took a deep breath and they rode to Santa's Workshop in silence. She opened her mouth to apologize a few times, but what did she have to apologize for? *It's the truth!* In a discussion about organization, Karol had shown CJ all of her Google documents with her various lists that detailed everything for her and Stella's successful migration to the Sunshine State. She'd obviously been planning the move for years. How could CJ compete with that? Especially with Stella. CJ was sure Stella could convince Karol of anything. Then she looked at Blair. *That might change, though.* After Blair saw Stella with the preachers, they had whispered, "I think I'm in love." It would be bitterly ironic if Stella stayed and Karol left.

"Hmm," Karol said, breaking the awkward silence. "I can smell the cookies from here."

That made CJ smile. "Yeah."

She pulled up behind the JOY trolley that operated during Ganza, chauffeuring folks with ambulatory issues or small children to the major sights—the reindeer, The Court, the food trucks, and of course, Santa and Santa's Workshop. They watched excited families board and exit. The children headed inside pointed at the cookies in the hands of the departing kids, their parents reassuring them there would be a cookie for them too. The ones leaving babbled on and on about their favorite part of the Workshop.

CJ felt Karol watching her. "I love watching the kids—their energy, their innocence, their…hope." When Karol didn't reply, CJ glanced at her. She was staring at the house, a single tear rolling down her cheek. CJ reached over and caressed her face, wiping away the tear and bringing Karol back from wherever she was.

Karol kissed her palm and swung out of the golf cart. Just as they started up the walk, the radio crackled. Juanito's amped up voice said, "Help! Emergency!"

CJ and Karol stopped and CJ grabbed the radio from her pocket.

"Don't say 'Help,' dork," a calm voice chastised. "We're not in danger," the voice added loudly and slowly.

"Don't call me a dork!"

"Who's that?" Karol asked.

"I'm pretty sure the one asking for help is Juanito, and the calmer voice is Noel, Juanito's older sister."

"Hey, you two," Juan snapped. "No fighting on the radio. This is for serious conversation only."

"You've got to be kidding," Blair interjected.

"Well, adult business," Juan amended.

"What are you two fighting about?" Merry asked. "I don't have time for games. These cookies aren't going to hand out themselves."

"Juanito, where are you?" Blair asked. "And why are the two of you calling us?"

"Actually," Noel said, "Heather is with us, too."

"Oh, hi, Heather," Merry said sweetly.

"Hi, Merry."

CJ could hear the strain in Heather's voice from speaking publicly, even if it was just two words over the radio.

"Okay, so why did the three of you call us and where are you?" Blair pressed.

"Give me that," Noel directed. "We're over at the barn and we're using Dr. Charlotte's radio."

"And…" Blair said. "Is there an emergency? Is someone hurt?"

"We've figured out how to open the safe at Tierra Celestial. So, is that an emergency?"

CHAPTER TWENTY-ONE

There were gasps and exclamations immediately following Noel's announcement. "What's in it?" Taylor asked. "How did you get it open?"

"It just came open," Juanito said. "And it's not the safe everybody's been trying to open. That one's a fake!"

"That's not the safe?" Merry exclaimed. "How...where?"

"Look," Noel interjected, "you've got to see this to believe it. Juanito found it. He gets the credit."

"Juanito, what's inside the safe?" Blair asked.

"Two sealed envelopes."

"Okay," Blair said in their most authoritative voice, "while opening the safe is interesting, important, and fabulous, it is *not* an emergency. We have one hour left in our opening night and probably an hour after that to secure the area. I suggest we meet over at Tierra Celestial at eleven sharp. Until that time, Juanito, Noel, and Heather, can you just hang out until we get there?"

"Sure," the three replied in unison.

Juanito laughed. "I've got my phone to play games on and I'm sure Noel and Heather can take another *tour*."

"Shut up, Shorty!" Noel snapped.

"Noel! Don't be disrespectful to your brother and Juanito, don't tease your sister," Merry said in a tone Karol had not yet heard. "And when we get there, those envelopes had better still be sealed or I might deck someone's halls."

"Ooh, violence," Stella warned.

"No, quite the opposite," Merry replied. "If I deck someone's halls, it means I literally turn them into a human Christmas tree for thirty minutes. Wrap tinsel around their arms and legs, hang ornaments on their clothes, and stick a bright red nose on their face."

"It's awful," Noel said. "A warped version of corporal punishment close to child abuse."

"Sounds like it," Stella grumbled.

"We won't open the envelopes, Mama. It's a federal offense to tamper with someone else's mail," Juanito said.

"Who are the envelopes addressed to?" Blair asked.

"One is addressed to Karol," Noel said.

Karol went wide-eyed and whispered, "It's got to be the secret ingredient."

CJ grinned. "Probably."

"The other is addressed to Rubio," Juanito said.

"Interesting," CJ murmured. "That one's got to be from his mother." She said into the radio, "All right, let's follow Blair's instructions and wrap up our party and meet over there."

They all signed off and Karol and CJ, hand in hand, resumed their stroll up Hope's front walk. The yard, covered in imported snow, had been divided into two parts: on one side, families waited in an impromptu line to sit in the massive sleigh and have their picture taken, while on the other, kids had snowball fights and built snow people with the hats, twigs, carrots, and buttons provided in large, marked boxes. Volunteers dismantled snow people as fast as they were being built so everyone had a chance to participate.

Just inside the front door was the end of the line that snaked through the workshop area and snow tunnel, finally arriving at Santa's chair. CJ led Karol into the workshop and over to the far side where they could watch the elf volunteers put together real toys, engage the children in conversation and answer constant questions about the workshop, Santa Claus, and the North Pole. A symphonic version of "Joy to the World" followed them into the tunnel, but the further they went, the giggles, laughter and chatter of the excited children drowned out the music. CJ pulled Karol behind the photographer capturing each child who sat on Santa's lap or stood next to Santa, which Karol realized was the preferred choice.

She pointed at the young man currently facing Santa and whispered to CJ, "That's a good idea, giving them a choice. I always thought sitting on his lap was creepy."

CJ nodded. "Me too. A lot of kids have personal space issues and we want to honor that."

Karol looked around, and she knew she was about to cry—again. She couldn't believe the craftsmanship necessary to make everything happen. It was…perfect. She closed her eyes and felt Nana Hope wrap her in a strong hug, the kind she'd gotten every time she arrived and every time she had to leave the JOY neighborhood.

CJ squeezed her hand and said, "There she is."

Karol blinked and followed CJ's stare to a woman in a black blazer and a green shirt tucked into designer jeans. Her dark hair was shaved on the sides and the long bangs hung nearly in her eyes. She wasn't as old as CJ and Karol, but she wasn't a youngster either. Although she stood near the father and daughter just ahead of her, Karol realized they weren't together—but the woman wanted it to appear that they were. Karol glanced at CJ with a puzzled expression and CJ muttered, "CUDL judge. Don't look at her and let's keep going."

They headed into the kitchen where several women and men dressed in red pinstriped aprons handed out gingerbread people and directed guests to the patio for their hot cocoa. Their voices all ran together save one: Merry's distinct and especially sugary "Merry Christmas and Happy Holidays!" stood out as she gave the children their respective gingerbread person in a gesture rivaling the presentation of the crown jewels. When she looked up and saw CJ and Karol, she smiled. CJ turned toward the wall and said into her radio, "Santa is at the workshop."

Karol watched Merry, who was obviously wearing an earpiece, because Merry's jaw dropped, and so did the cookie she was presenting to a five-year-old. Fortunately, the little boy's father had quick hands and caught it before it hit the floor. Merry remained still as a statue.

"Merry," CJ whispered.

Nothing.

"*Merry!*"

The CUDL official was just entering the kitchen, pausing to take a panoramic photo with her phone. Merry remained gobsmacked, and CJ started toward the judge, but Karol grabbed her arm and whispered, "Let me handle the judge, you go end Merry's catatonic trance."

CJ nodded and moved along the wall behind the table. Karol gravitated to Hope's small butcher block island in the center of the room, a framed photo on the top. She held the photo and rubbed her hand along the edge of the wood.

"You look like you know this place," a voice said.

Karol looked up at the judge, no longer taking photos, her hands stuffed in her pockets. "I do. This was my grandmother's home for decades." She pointed at the picture and added, "I spent a lot of time right here."

The judge gazed at the photo and leaned forward to read the narrative text that accompanied a great shot of Hope smiling over her rolled out gingerbread, a cookie cutter in her hand.

The judge pointed to the photo. "Is that you next to her?"

"What?"

"Right there."

Karol leaned forward and saw her eyes peeking over the block. She couldn't have been more than five... *My mother. She must've brought me here. Why don't I remember?*

The next thing she knew was the judge saying softly, "May I offer you a tissue?"

Karol blinked and realized she was crying. The judge held up a travel pack of tissues. "Thank you," Karol said, plucking one from the pack. "I didn't even realize I was in that photo."

"I see the resemblance," the judge said. She looked around. "Are the cookies any good?"

Karol gestured to the lines of folks waiting. "Well, not to brag, but I've made them for friends and family for decades, and I've never had a complaint. You'll have to be judge."

The woman's expression changed for a split second. "Indeed."

"Thank you for your kindness," Karol said, dabbing at her eyes.

"No problem. From what I can see, kindness seems to have a life of its own here."

"I only arrived two days ago, but you're exactly right. This place makes you feel, well, joyous."

"You don't live here?"

"No, I'm from New York. Just here for the holidays."

"Me too," the judge said. She offered a little wave and got in line. Karol heard Merry's unmistakable voice and saw she was back to her usual self. The judge chose Merry's line and Karol looked over at CJ, who'd returned to her spot against the wall. CJ surreptitiously crossed her fingers, and Karol did so as well. When it was the judge's turn, Merry flashed a megawatt smile, presented a gingerbread person, and told her where the cocoa was located.

"Thank you," the judge said simply.

They all watched as the judge bit off a foot and stopped, her gaze on the floor. Karol held her breath. *Oh, God, what if she's found a hair or a bug?* When the judge looked up, her eyes were closed and she was savoring the bite. Karol quickly—but casually—returned her gaze to the photo.

She sensed the judge's return and looked up, smiling. She pointed at the missing foot. "What do you think?"

The judge waved the cookie. "It may sound cliché, but this is the best cookie I've ever tasted."

Karol all but jumped up and down. Using the same restraint as in court after a particularly persuasive closing argument, she just smiled pleasantly. "I think so too."

The judge looked around, then leaned in and said, "You can tell your friends it's in the bag. I'm not supposed to say anything, but I know the jerks who've judged this neighborhood before. And 'jerks' is a nice term. JOY has had this award stolen from them for the last time. They lost a few years ago because a reindeer shed his antlers right on a judge's foot. Can you believe it? Believe such a stupid excuse for not giving them the award? Like they could control that?" She winked and took another bite. "So amazing," she mumbled as she headed out to the patio.

Karol watched through the back window as the judge got her cocoa and left. She looked over at CJ's panicked face and gave her a solid two thumbs-up. CJ thrust an arm in the air and Merry let out a bloodcurdling scream.

"What was that?" Blair demanded over the radio.

"We got it!" Merry shouted. "The CUDL!"

"What? How do we know that?" Ming asked sharply. "This is supposed to be a blind competition."

"Who cares!" Merry said. "The judge told Karol."

CJ handed Karol her radio. "The judge thought the JOY had been robbed before so she didn't want us to wait."

"Did you say *us*?" Taylor asked.

"As in you're part of the group?" Blair added.

"As in you're *not* going to Boca?" Stella shouted.

"Yes," Juan said. "Inquiring minds want to know."

Karol took a deep breath and pressed the talk button. "I'm considering my options carefully. I said 'us' because all of you have made me—and Stella, if she'll admit it—feel at home here. Regardless of where we live, we know we can be here."

"What about Hope's house?" Merry asked.

Since Merry was only ten feet away, Karol looked over at her, a sweet smile on her face. "I'm not selling the house. I haven't figured out my life, but for as long as I'm breathing, this will remain Hope's house. And I'll be selling my apartment in New York instead, Stella."

Merry started clapping and doing her happy dance—until she suddenly slipped and Karol and CJ watched her feet fly into the air.

"Crap!" CJ shouted. She ran behind the cookie table shouting into the radio, "Dr. Charlotte, we need you at the workshop, and Juan, Merry just took a big spill."

"I'm coming right now!"

"CJ, keep us informed, please," Ming asked calmly.

Merry was flat on her back and muttering, "Son of a biscuit. How in the heck did this happen? Flunk, flunk, flunk. Gorp, dang it!"

Karol studied the kitchen hardwood and found a red bead near the baseboard. She looked at Merry's sweater, much of it covered by her apron. She held up the bead. "Merry, does this look familiar?"

Merry groaned. "Jiminy Christmas. I've sewed that bead back on three times!"

Dr. Charlotte's golf cart arrived quickly, but not before Merry had uttered a fulsome litany of G-rated swear words, cried about how hard it would be to finish cookie baking, wrapping presents, and making Christmas dinner, all a tradition for her extensive family that lived outside the JOY neighborhood. She'd just lamented the likely loss of their New Year's Eve party and was turning toward Valentine's Day when Dr. Charlotte rushed up.

It turned out that Merry only had a sprain, so Dr. Charlotte wrapped her ankle and showed her the crutches she'd thought to bring. And she insisted Merry go to the ER since she'd hit her head. Merry said no, but then Juan arrived and backed up Dr. Charlotte.

"Fine, I'll go, but I'm not going until after we go see the safe at Tierra Celestial."

"And then we'll go right to the ER," Juan said.

"Yes," Merry agreed. "Maybe my big handsome firefighter could carry me through the big swishy doors."

"You know it," Juan said, and they shared a long lingering kiss, unaware of Dr. Charlotte rolling her eyes as she packed up her kit, while CJ and Karol tried not to laugh.

CHAPTER TWENTY-TWO

Merry spent the last half hour greeting children as they entered Santa's Workshop, her ankle propped up on a snowman's outstretched arm. "Hurry on in now," she shouted. "We're closing in ten minutes!"

It took nearly thirty more minutes to politely shoo all the visitors out of the neighborhood. The residents knew to shut down their displays, turn off their house lights and go inside to further encourage departure while Blair's security detail swept the ten streets for stragglers, potential prank pullers and others out for no good. Karol and CJ were part of this team.

"Ever had a real problem after hours?" Karol asked as CJ whipped the golf cart into Christmas Card Court.

"Only twice and both times it had to do with people visiting, nothing about the neighborhood. One was a domestic dispute between an estranged couple. An abusive husband following the ex and their son here and kept it going. Fortunately, security pulled up just as he was trying to kidnap the kid."

"Oh, my gosh!"

"Yeah, it was a little scary. The other time somebody got locked in a porta potty. Poor lady had been in there for two hours. She'd gone off on her own, leaving her teenagers to walk around by themselves, agreeing to meet at the south gate at closing. So she doesn't show up, and we all start looking for her."

"Didn't somebody hear her? If I got locked in a porta potty, I'd be pounding and screaming bloody murder."

CJ trained her high-powered flashlight on the areas between the houses as the cart slowly circled the cul-de-sac. "That's the funny part. Each street takes a turn hosting the porta potties. We're trying to get a central location for next year but that year it was on Brenda Lee Boulevard where the Steampunk show is located. It was so loud no one heard her, not even people in the potties next to her. She gave up after an hour, closed the potty lid and sat down. She fell asleep for a while, and when she woke up it was quiet. She started pounding and Harlan Byron Luther Tremaine found her."

"That's quite a name."

"Yeah, that's his show name, but he's really Mickey Clayton, the Steampunk dad. But other than those two issues we've never had a problem with visitors. Now, our prank-playing teenagers are another story."

"I don't think I could take a nap in a porta potty."

"Well, she was a trauma nurse so she'd seen, touched, and smelled things you and I will never know. Plus, she'd worked a double shift and was trying to be nice to her kids. Once she sat down, she just dozed."

CJ handed the flashlight to Karol and turned onto Winter Wonderland Way just as her radio squawked. "Blair and CJ," Taylor called. "We've got some pranksters over here outside the barn."

"I'm just around the corner," Blair growled.

CJ sighed and made a U-turn. "We need to get over there. If Blair gets there first, it won't be pretty."

"Actually, I'm worried about them now."

"Why?"

"Remember, Stella is riding with Taylor."

The golf cart zipped down the streets and Karol waved at many of the neighbors who were still outside, closing up their displays. *It's like they're tucking their children in for bed.*

"What are you thinking about?" CJ asked.

"Not really anything in particular. I'm just...being. That's what Mallory Gilbert talked about at yoga. We spend too much time in our heads. Just enjoy. Don't overanalyze."

"That must be hard for an attorney."

"It is."

"Seems like this place has grown on you."

CJ kept her gaze on the road as they turned toward her house, but she felt Karol's stare and when Karol brushed her fingers on the back of CJ's neck, a shiver went down her back. She knew she was in love—again—with Karol. But she'd learned that sometimes that wasn't enough, especially now that she was much older. Options, opportunities, and goals were elusive. The here and the now was real.

They pulled up to the barn next to Blair's golf cart. Blair leaned against it, enjoying a shaved ice.

"What the hell?" CJ murmured as she got out of the golf cart.

Blair dropped a spoonful of blue raspberry in their mouth and motioned to two other cups on the passenger's seat with their empty spoon. "The girls just left and I got those for y'all. Mango for you, CJ, and Karol, I wasn't sure what you'd like, so I got cherry."

"Good guess. That's one of my favorites."

CJ accepted the offered treat and pointed toward the barn. "What's going on?"

"Hey, red sweater guy, you missed a pile!" The shout pierced the quiet of the night.

"That's Stella," Karol said.

"I'm out here," Blair said, "because I had to see the looks on your faces when you go inside. And before you ask, the reindeer have all been herded into their stalls for a short winter's nap, away from the bullhorn."

They entered the barn just as Stella, who was standing in the center of the bleachers, shouted through her bullhorn, "Let's liven this up for your parents! How about something from childhood? I'm sure you all remember 'Up on the Housetop.' Let's sing! And nonsingers get to come back next year and enjoy this lovely activity."

Stella sang out the first line and then the seven teenagers inside the reindeer greeting area picked up the second line, although their voices sounded melancholy—not cheery. Probably because they each held a shovel and were scooping up the large piles of reindeer poop that the wranglers had deposited on the perimeter of the greeting area to be picked up at the end of the night. The wranglers, though, sat in the bleachers below Stella, enjoying the antics in the ring and the shaved ices in their respective hands. Also present were a group of adults—the kids' parents. Their expressions varied from amused to furious, but they were enjoying their own shaved ices. Scampering about the ring was Taylor taking numerous photos of the teens, who all complied when she said, "Say cheese!"

CJ pointed and said, "I guess this will be all over TikTok tomorrow?"

"Oh, yes," Blair said. "When I arrived, the kids were already working. Apparently, they were planning on running garlands through the reindeer antlers. Taylor and Stella caught them carrying the garlands in from the barn's back door."

Blair explained, "The garlands would probably be harmless, but if a reindeer started eating one or became anxious, we could have a real problem. We don't allow any shenanigans when it comes to the reindeer. The humans must understand that although we allow guests to pet and feed them, these aren't domesticated creatures. So, the black-and-white line is very clear." They raised a hand. "Sorry, I'm on my soapbox."

"I completely agree," Karol said.

"Stevie basically told me about the garland idea the other night," CJ said. "And Steve, his father, and I both said he'd better not."

"Well, I don't think he'll ever do anything like it again. Stella had Taylor contact all the parents who got down here pretty quickly. Stella formally cited some forgotten law about mishandling of wildlife. The kids were scared shitless they were all going to prison."

CJ turned to Karol. "Is that really a law?"

Karol shrugged. "No idea."

"So Stella bought them all shaved ices and they agreed the kids have poop duty for the rest of Ganza. *Then* she and Taylor finally saw fit to call me."

"I've got an idea!" Stella bellowed through the bullhorn. "Let's take a two-minute break..." The teens looked cheered until Stella said, "Yes, set down your shovels, and let's all do 'Up on the Housetop' once more with the gestures that I'm sure you all know because you grew up in this community."

Stella started them off, and CJ thought it was the poorest, but funniest, rendition of the song she'd ever heard. Blair pulled out their phone and tapped the screen. "Okay, we have a problem."

"What?" CJ asked, still laughing at Stevie's version of Santa's "ho, ho, ho" gestures.

"Take a look."

CJ and Karol leaned in. It was the camera Blair had installed in the cupola of Tierra Celestial. Juanito, Noel, and Heather were arguing—with Rubio Orozco. "I thought he left," CJ exclaimed.

"Apparently he came back," Blair said. "If I had to guess, I'm thinking he put in a few cameras of his own. He might've seen Juanito figure out the safe and came back from the airport."

"No one else seems to be there," CJ said. "Are our officers still around?"

"No. They went back before shift change."

"Let's go. Stella clearly has this under control."

CJ flashed Stella an okay sign and she saluted in reply. Then she barked at the teens, "Okay, shovels up. It's my turn to serenade all of you with one of my favorite holiday tunes from that great film, *White Christmas*. The song is 'Counting my Blessings' and parents, feel free to sing along."

"She really has a great voice," CJ said.

"You should see her after a few martinis. She gives new meaning to the term table dancing." She paused and then asked, "Are you worried about Rubio? Do you think he'll hurt Juanito?"

"No, I don't think so. He's not really a bad guy."

Blair was calling the board members over the radio as they pulled out on the street and headed for the gate.

The black SUV had returned and CJ and Blair parked behind it. Pulling up behind them was Ming and her police officer son, still in uniform.

"Where's Merry and Juan?" CJ asked.

"I called them," Blair replied, "but I'll bet it takes a minute for Juan to get the car and load Merry."

"Well, we shouldn't wait," Officer Zhao said. "If Rubio is in debt and owes money to bad people, he might be capable of anything. Let's go, but everybody stay behind me. He doesn't seem to have a weapon, but I'm not taking any chances." He unlocked the holster for his gun, placed a hand on it, and led the way through the house.

CHAPTER TWENTY-THREE

By the time they started the climb upstairs, they could hear Rubio shouting,

"Kid, for the last time…"

"Hands where I can see them!" Officer Zhao shouted, drawing his weapon as he reached the top of the cupola's stairs.

"Whoa! Whoa!" Rubio shouted. "Officer, nobody's armed here. Wait…Lou, is that you?"

Officer Zhao sighed deeply and holstered his gun. Then he motioned for everyone behind him to come upstairs. "Yeah, it's me, Rubio."

"Long time, no see!"

"Yeah, I think the last time was at the Zeta Pi barbeque when you locked me in the trunk of Teddy Greenbaum's Volvo."

Rubio hung his head. "Well, you know…kids. Sorry." He smiled and added, "You look good."

"Thanks. You too."

They all barely fit inside the small room, but once CJ saw Heather and Noel looking bored and sitting together in the window seat, she knew no one was in any danger.

As if she could read CJ's mind, Noel said, "Where's my mom? Can we go now?"

"No," Blair replied. "Not till we figure out what's going on." They turned to Rubio. "What are you doing here?"

"I was in the airport lounge. I got an alert that someone was in the house. I looked at my security footage and saw the kids were here. Not a big deal. These two," he said, pointing at the girls, "have been here several times and they weren't studying Victorian architecture, if you know what I mean."

"Shut up!" Noel hissed, jumping off the window seat. Heather coiled into a ball and tucked her head into her hoodie. "Don't you see you're upsetting Heather? Not everybody is cool with lesbians, especially certain parents."

"You better not be referring to us, young lady." They heard Merry's voice before her head popped into view. She was using one crutch while Juan supported her on the other side. Merry lifted her crutch and poked Rubio's chest with it. "And you, you better not have done anything to my children or my daughter's girlfriend—"

"Not helping, Mom," Noel said, pointing to Heather, who seemed to have shrunk even smaller.

Merry limped over to the window seat, motioned for Noel to move and sat down beside Heather. She patted Heather's knee and began whispering to her.

"Rubio, finish your story," Blair said. "I take it you have security cameras throughout the house?"

"Of course."

"You think you might've mentioned it?" CJ asked.

"Why? It's my property."

"He has a point," Officer Zhao said. "Go on."

"The next time I picked up my phone and looked at the cameras, I couldn't see the kids. I thought maybe they'd left until I realized the bookcase in front of the safe looked weird. Then the boy appeared in the screen, holding an envelope."

"*This* envelope," Juanito announced, pulling the envelope from the back pocket of his jeans.

"Were you trying to take that from my son?" Juan growled at Rubio, followed by a string of Spanish words CJ didn't understand but which evoked Spanish replies from Rubio.

"No, no, Papa," Juanito said.

"Why did we hear you all arguing when we got here?" Ming asked.

Rubio crossed his arms, looking uncomfortable.

"Are you going to tell them or am I?" Juanito asked.

"Oh, for shit's sake," Noel whined.

"Language!" Merry, Juan, and Karol said in unison.

"Shorty, quit being dramatic," Noel said.

"Fine," Juanito said. "Mr. Orozco and I, as Hispanic men—"

Noel burst out laughing. "Men?"

"Zip it," Merry said, her arm wrapped around Heather.

"As I was saying, as we're both Hispanic men, we share the trait of stubbornness. I'm almost ashamed to say it, but Mr. Orozco still holds the fictitious belief that Yoko broke up the Beatles. It's just not true!"

The entire room groaned.

"It's true!" Rubio said. "I don't care what Peter Jackson revealed in *Get Back*. He has his own biases."

Karol raised her hand. "As much as I enjoy a good musical debate, Juanito, can you explain how you opened the safe and if that envelope is addressed to me, may I please have it?"

"Of course," he said, presenting it to her.

Karol stared at Hope's unmistakable handwriting. She wiped away a tear and said, "Okay, before I open it, how'd you find it?"

"It was all about the bookcase. And really, Heather gets some credit." No longer in the fetal position, Heather sat up straight and smiled when Juanito mentioned her. "She has an interest in agriculture, so when she saw the books on the shelf, she naturally started looking through them and found something weird." He picked up a dark leatherbound book and handed it to her. "Heather, why don't you explain?"

She sat up even straighter and Merry patted her shoulder. "Well, this book is titled *Growing Roses in the Summer*, and of course we don't grow roses in the summer here in Tucson. Why would you need a book about something you can't grow? Then I remembered Dr. St. John's story about the trick they played when they started the JOY Extravaganza and took the photos in June. So then I opened the book and found a pocket inside it, and inside the pocket I found this." She opened the book and pulled a small notebook from the pocket inside the front cover. "The writing looked really old and strange. I couldn't figure it out so I gave it to Noel."

"And since I know a lot about handwriting—"

"Because you're a natural forger," Juanito joked.

"No, dork, because as a student assistant in the front office, the assistant principal asks me to check out the notes kids bring in to see if they're forgeries. *Not* because I've ever done it." She looked at Juan and then Merry, who both nodded. "So, this book was written by the original owner and is filled with secret information, all about the secret passages here—"

"There's more than one?" Rubio asked and everyone looked puzzled by the remark since they all knew Tierra Celestial had its share of secrets.

"Did you know there's a tunnel under the house?" Noel asked.

Everyone talked at once until Blair whistled. "Let's hit the highlights and move on. I've got to get back and make sure a bunch of teenagers aren't covered in reindeer poop."

"Yeah, I heard your girlfriend really had them going," Juan said.

"She's not my girlfriend!" Blair cried.

"Sure," Merry said.

"Our point," Juanito interjected, "is that there's a lot more to this house." He took the notebook from Heather and presented it to Rubio. "Why would you want to tear down such a cool place? Perhaps you've heard of the Winchester Mystery House in San Francisco? It seems Tierra Celestial is a lot like that place, and I know I'd pay money to know all its secrets even though I don't get much for an allowance."

"Young man," Merry said, "you know we're in negotiations right now. If you want to earn more, you need to do more, like clean your bathroom. That includes your toilet."

Juanito shook his head. "Not going to happen."

Rubio thumbed through the notebook and glanced up at all the eyes watching him. "I'll take this under advisement."

"So," Juanito continued, "one of the entries in the book is about the safe." He pushed the bookcase away, pulled back the picture of a cat playing the piano, and revealed the door of the safe. "This looks like a safe, right?"

Everyone agreed on the obvious answer.

"It's not."

"What?" Rubio cried. "I paid thousands of dollars for people to crack a safe that never opens?"

"Apparently," Blair said, laughing. "So, if that's not the safe, where is it?"

Juanito gestured to Noel. "Why don't you tell this part since you figured it out."

Before Noel could begin, Merry started to cry.

"Honey, what's wrong?" Juan asked nervously. "Is it your ankle? Do we need to get to the ER right now?"

"We could at least prop it up," Karol offered.

Merry waved them off. "Don't mind me. I'm just thrilled to see my kids maturing right before my eyes."

Noel rolled her eyes. "When I looked through the book, I found a sketch of that painting."

Juanito pushed the painting back in place and they all stared at it. CJ realized she'd never really noticed it, given that there were so many cool things to see in the cupola and the painting was bad and odd. An orange tabby, wearing a cowboy hat, sat at a black upright piano like the ones they had in saloons... *Like the one downstairs.* He's smiling at the audience with a grin like the Mona Lisa, and his completely out-of-proportion front toes are perched on the keys.

"I always thought it was my mother's bad attempt at art," Rubio said.

"No, it's much older than your mother," Ming said. "I saw this painting as a child back in the sixties."

"Well, how old it is isn't the point," Noel said. "I'm betting it's as old as the safe because the cat's revealing the combination."

"I don't see it," Officer Zhao said, squinting as he examined the painting.

Everyone else grumbled their agreement. Juanito moved the bookcase back into place, taking great care to center it. He retrieved the book from Heather and the small notebook from Rubio, which he tucked inside the book and returned it to its exact place on the shelf before he said, "The key is the bookshelf. I'm guessing no one ever really bothered with it, right?"

CJ nodded as she said, "I pulled out that book on the middle shelf, the green leather one, because my grandfather gave that to Rubio's great grandfather, and I wanted to show Karol. Other than that, no." She pointed at Rubio and said, "In fact, you told us to leave that bookcase alone."

Rubio sighed. "I did. I knew the safe was behind it and I didn't want to share that fact with anyone outside the family."

"But you found out about my grandmother leaving her recipe with your mother. And you wanted it for yourself," Karol said.

"I'll admit that. But I thought it was in that safe, which apparently isn't a safe."

CJ crossed her arms. "Has it ever occurred to you, Rubio, that your mother didn't share things with you because you can really be an ass!"

Juanito looked at Merry. "Aren't you going to call 'language,' Mom?"

"No, Rubio's an ass, son. It fits."

Juanito pointed at the painting. "Look at the cat's paws. It's all about where the toes are. Starting with the one to the far left, what note on the piano is he playing?"

"That's a C," Karol said.

Juanito scanned the first row of the bookcase and removed a book. "This book is titled *Canning and Preserving*. What's next?"

"An E," Ming replied.

Juanito continued down the row and pulled out a black leather book. "*Evermore*. And it goes like that. Do you get it?"

Everyone shook their heads. "Why don't you just do what you did that makes the safe open?" Blair said. "Wherever it is. We need to move this along."

"Sure."

Juanito removed five books and put his hand on the sixth. "Watch the floor by the bookcase." He pulled out the sixth book and the bookcase rose a foot—to reveal a shelf.

"Holy shins!" Merry cried.

"Wow," Rubio said.

The shelf held one item: another envelope. Juanito picked it up and handed it to Rubio. CJ glanced at the handwriting, recognizing Rubio's mother's bubblelike letters. Rubio tore open the envelope, unlike Karol who still held hers unopened as if it were fragile. The envelope held two papers, and CJ could tell one of them was embossed with a notary stamp. They all watched Rubio, who remained expressionless—until he didn't.

"Shit!"

"Language," Juan warned, pointing at him.

Rubio thrust the papers in Juan's face. "Your wife got to call me an ass. You read that and tell me if *shit* isn't warranted."

Everyone watched Juan who read along as Rubio did—until he laughed. "Well, I see why you said shit."

"How about clueing the rest of us in?" Blair asked.

"I don't need to listen to this." He glared at Officer Zhao. "Am I arrested or in trouble?"

Officer Zhao gestured at the stairs. "You're free to go."

Rubio vanished down the stairs, shouting a litany of swear words until he slammed the front door.

Juan held out the papers to CJ. "I believe these belong to you."

"What?" CJ said as she started to read the handwritten letter.

"What does it say?" Blair asked again.

"Well, it's from Valentina, Rubio's mother. It's dated about six months before she died."

"That would've been right after she started chemo," Merry said.

"Exactly," Ming agreed.

CJ started to read:

Dear son,

If you're reading this, it means you've found the secret safe as well as the notebook that contains all of Tierra Celestial's secrets. As I write this, I know two things: I'm dying and you're not here. I don't know if and when you'll be back. Your father and I had great hopes you would restore this property to its glory. I still remain cautiously optimistic, but I'm realistic. If this place no longer interests you, I'll give it to people who do care—and they're right across the street. Attached is a codicil to my will. If you present this document to my attorney in Phoenix on or before two years of my passing, the house and land are yours, and I know you'll do right by our family. If you don't find it before the stated timeframe, and it's found by accident or by a construction worker during the leveling of Tierra Celestial, which I imagine is what you'll do with our beloved home, my entire estate transfers to Carol Christmas Joy (CJ). My attorney has the necessary paperwork and details for her.

I love you always, Rubio.

Mom

"Wow," CJ said. She looked at Karol. "Can she do that?"

"Of course," Karol said. "It's her property. I imagine Rubio will turn this into a custody battle, but he'll lose."

"I have a question," Noel asked. "Why was Karol's letter with Mr. Orozco's letter on the hidden shelf?"

"Probably because Hope trusted Valentina to keep it safe," CJ concluded. "It could've been in there for years."

Blair cleared their throat. "I know there's much more to discuss about this turn of events, but I need to get back to the barn where Stella's staging her own version of reindeer games. Before I go, I'd really like to know, Karol, what's in your envelope, if you're okay opening it in front of all of us. I know I speak for everyone when I say Nana Hope was the heart of the JOY."

"I know, Blair, and thank you for saying that. You've all been so good to Stella and me…Of course I'll share this with you."

Her hands shook as she slowly opened the envelope. She unfolded a sheet of Hope's linen stationery. Whatever Hope had written was incredibly brief because she immediately handed the note to CJ and closed her eyes. CJ read it and passed it to Blair. It went around the circle until it returned to Karol. Everyone was silent, even the teenagers, even Juanito. They stood in silence, like a prayer circle, lost in their memories of Nana Hope. Ever busy and responsible Blair was the first to speak.

"I've got to get back," they said, hugging Karol before they tore down the steps.

Lou Zhao hugged Ming and said, "I've got to sign out at the precinct."

"Well," Merry said, "mystery solved." She stood and Juan helped her with the crutch. She looked at Karol with an enormous smile, tears in her eyes. "I believe I have that missing ingredient in my cupboard."

"I think I do too," Karol said, her voice barely above a whisper.

Before they headed back down, Merry motioned for Karol to give her a hug and then they started down the steps. CJ heard Juanito say, "This is just like 'One Tin Soldier,' that song from the sixties."

"You're right, *hijo*," Juan agreed. "As usual, you're right."

CHAPTER TWENTY-FOUR

Karol and CJ were the last to leave Tierra Celestial. While CJ checked all the doors and windows, Karol called Stella. "So will you be taking the car again tonight?" she asked.

"If you don't mind. Blair leaves so early in the morning."

"And you don't do early."

"Not *that* early."

"You both looked extremely tired this morning," Karol teased. "Perhaps you should sleep a little—maybe between… activities."

"We stayed up all night talking."

Karol laughed. "Right."

"No, really." Her voice was earnest. "We just talked. I know that's hard to believe. Yeah, there was some touching and kissing, but I had a lot of questions. They're so different from anyone I've been with, and I wanted to learn and understand."

"Wow, I'm…"

"Surprised? Floored? Speechless?"

"Yes, all of those. You've been with every type of person, male or female, and you've never needed a conference before you jumped into the sack."

"Ah, but you said *man* and *woman*. Blair doesn't subscribe to either label. They're unique."

"So tonight is part two of the conference?"

"Hell no. I plan to rip off that little kilt the second they shut the front door." They laughed and then Stella said, "What about you? How will you be spending your evening?"

CJ locked the front door and hustled down the steps. She looked so dapper in her tux and tails...

"Uh, earth to Karol."

"Gotta go."

She dropped her phone in her purse just as CJ wrapped her arms around Karol's waist and spun her in a circle.

"Whoa. Be careful. We're not as young as we used to be."

After one turn, CJ lowered her back on the ground. "Don't I know it. But you're light."

They gazed up at the grand old house, cheek to cheek. They couldn't see any stars because of light pollution, but Karol was far too distracted by CJ's wandering hands. She knew if she looked into CJ's beautiful green eyes, her restraint would fizzle.

"Let's go back to my place," CJ whispered, and in one motion she unhooked Karol's bra.

"Oh, wow. I'm impressed."

"I've come a long way since the night we fumbled around on Hope's couch."

"I'll say."

CJ kissed her and her tongue flicked inside Karol's mouth. It was salacious, and she was so focused on their mouths and lips, she didn't realize CJ had snuck a hand under her blouse and loose bra until the tips of CJ's fingers caressed a nipple. She moaned in pleasure and pressed against CJ. She wanted her. She wanted it all.

CJ's phone rang with Blair's ringtone, Gaga's "Born This Way." CJ groaned. "I've got to answer this." She fumbled for her phone. "What's up, Blair? You're on speaker."

"I thought I'd remind you that Rubio also installed cameras around the house, and while I'm enjoying your little uh, show, I may not be the only viewer. And don't forget to pick up Manny. While the two of you may spend the night together, Dr. Charlotte won't approve a sleepover." Then the line went dead.

CJ and Karol gasped simultaneously and started to laugh. Karol pulled her into a bear hug and pressed her lips to CJ's ear. "I want you."

They arrived back at CJ's and Karol zipped up the stairs to pee while Manny explored CJ's house, sniffing every rug and doorway until he found a snoring Houston asleep on his dog bed in the study. CJ tucked Manny against him, locked up the house, grabbed a bottle of champagne and two glasses, and headed upstairs. Karol had carried her tux jacket and top hat upstairs already, and CJ couldn't wait to shed the bow tie and dress shirt as well.

I want it all off and I want her to undress me.

Her bedroom door was slightly open and she heard Nancy Wilson's sultry jazz voice sing "Teach Me Tonight." Karol had found the remote control for the soundbar. Both Hope and CJ's mother shared a love of jazz, and they'd passed that love to CJ. *And apparently to Karol as well.*

She slid inside—and nearly dropped the champagne. Karol had opened the French doors leading onto the balcony, hopped onto the second barber chair and swiveled it around so when CJ entered, the first thing she saw was Karol wearing only the top hat and CJ's tux coat with tails. The December moon washed over her, illuminating her glorious chest and casting shadows below her waist. It was clear, though, that Karol had draped her right leg over the arm of the barber chair, and much more of her would be revealed when CJ moved closer. Once she stopped swooning, she opened the champagne and poured them each a glass, her gaze constantly flicking to Karol.

"Hurry," Karol said, blowing her a kiss.

She's wearing lipstick. Oh, God.

CJ wiped her sweaty palms on her pants and stripped off her bow tie and shoes before approaching her. Suddenly she felt completely out of her league. She stopped midstep and closed her eyes.

"CJ, look at me. It's okay."

When CJ opened her eyes, Karol's sultry and sexy pose was gone, and she sat ramrod-straight with her hands folded on her naked thighs. "I didn't mean to be so forward. I just wasn't sure if you'd find me sexy. I sometimes—"

"How? How could I *not* find you sexy?" CJ gestured to herself. "Look at me? I look like a Christmas penguin in this getup. But you, oh, my God. I'm so turned on right now...I just worry you'll be disappointed."

Karol shook her head. "No way." She slid off the chair and let the tux jacket, which was two sizes too big for her, drop to the floor, leaving her naked in a glittery red top hat. CJ held out a glass of champagne and they toasted. Then Karol emptied hers in seconds and set the glass on CJ's dresser.

When she started to remove the top hat, CJ said, "Oh, no. Leave that on," drained her own glass, and pulled Karol to her.

CHAPTER TWENTY-FIVE

CJ leaned back in her barber chair and watched the sunrise. She glanced at the empty chair beside her. The last few mornings Karol had occupied the seat, enjoying the break of dawn while CJ enjoyed the sunlight bathing Karol's beautiful face. She'd love to share her coffee, her balcony—her life—with Karol if that's what Karol wanted. But she didn't press. The rest of the JOY neighbors were doing enough of that. Merry was talking as if the decision was already made and had booked a meditation retreat for her and Karol. Taylor said "Please?" in a begging voice every time she saw Karol, and Juanito just kept talking about Manny and Mo. Since everyone else was doing the hard press, CJ didn't feel the need. *But does she know how much I want her to stay?*

CJ had told Karol she loved her. She'd said she should stay. *I said it, didn't I?* She scratched her head. She thought she had... *Am I sure I did?* The last week had been a blur. The two weeks of Ganza were individual flurries, and each night presented its own set of issues, although they were no longer under pressure to perform well for the CUDL judge, and thanks to Taylor and Stella, the preachers had given up.

The last major hurdle remained: the parade. Doug had assured the board they were ready. Happy the dwarf no longer looked unhappy. The dragon was ready to celebrate Chinese New Year, the tribute to the Hohokam was amazing, and Reginald Collins had finally finished his annual submission: The Procrastinator.

Reggie owned a successful chain of "boutique" convenience stores specializing in unique snacks. He'd written a sizeable check to the JOY HOA for the right to have a float in the parade. It was the same every year: Reggie sitting on his lawn chair in the center of an undecorated flatbed pulled by his son's truck. Piled next to Reggie was a mountain of snacks from his store that he fired out into the crowd with his homemade cannon, like the one used by the U of A to launch T-shirts into the crowd during basketball games. He named his submission The Procrastinator since he never showed up until the day before the parade and it was the most minimal submission ever entered.

CJ had an idea. It would take some work, and while Doug was always up for last-minute changes, some members of the board hated surprises—namely Blair. CJ doubted, though, that this change would bother them that much. She called Reggie, who loved her idea, and then she called Juan, who was about to finish his shift at the firehouse.

After she told him what she was planning, he said, "Yeah, I got a few guys who could help make that happen."

When it was time to line everyone up on the street, Doug positioned Reggie's float right before Santa, who always ended the parade. CJ stared at her handiwork. It was somewhat subtle...

"I hope it works," Doug said to her as he made his last-minute inspection.

"What's going on?" Blair asked. "Why is Reggie this far back?" They rifled through their iPad, looking for the parade schedule, and CJ touched their arm.

"Take a look at it."

Blair finally looked at the float and immediately smiled. "Well, okay."

"Places everyone!" Doug called.

CJ had never been in the parade. In fact there were some years she didn't even get to see the parade because some critical issue popped up. She took one last look at her float and hopped up on her barbershop chair. She wiggled in the seat until she was certain Juan and his buddies had securely fastened it to the flatbed. She leaned over and tried to wiggle the other barbershop chair—the one she hoped Karol would occupy—once she saw it from the sidewalk. Geena Hernandez had made a sparkly sign that said, "Reserved for Karol."

Reggie had only asked one small favor—that they each pick up a cannon—apparently Reggie had two—and fire out snacks on his behalf. He'd told CJ in his Texas drawl, "Y'all make a cute couple. I hope she says yes."

"Oh, I'm not asking her to marry me, at least not yet."

Reggie grinned and puffed on his cigar. "Sure."

That stuck with CJ and she'd replayed the conversation several times. As Reggie's son started the truck, he gave her a thumbs-up and pulled behind the giant dragon. From her perch, CJ could see lots of people lined up on Angel Avenue, applauding and whooping it up as the first floats passed. She wrung her hands. *What if this is a dumb idea?*

They edged closer to the "Welcome to the JOY Neighborhood" sign. CJ looked around for Karol, finally spotting her just past the intersection with Santa Street. Merry had told Karol and Stella that CJ was handling a neighbor issue and she'd join them as soon as she could.

That time had come as Karol, who'd been completely invested in taking phone photos of each float, didn't notice CJ until Reggie's float was right in front of her. Suddenly she looked up from her phone. CJ flashed what she hoped was a convincing smile. She pointed at the other chair and Geena's cool sign. She could see the gears turning in Karol's mind—but Karol didn't move. Stella, whose jaw had dropped at the sight of the float, quickly recovered. CJ couldn't tell what Stella was saying, but her pointing was enough. She was lecturing Karol, encouraging her to go. Karol seemed to break out of her trance and laughed.

CJ finally took a breath as Karol ran to the float and Jesse Hernandez, whose family was standing next to Stella, helped her onto the flatbed. Karol went to CJ and leaned close enough to be heard. "Are you sure?"

CJ caressed her cheek. "Oh, honey, I've never been surer of anything."

Their kiss ignited a roar from the crowd. Then when the truck rumbled forward, Karol set the sign between them and hopped onto her chair. CJ handed her a cannon and Karol reached into the giant bucket of snacks Reggie had provided. She showed CJ a package of Key Lime Coconut Patties, a Florida favorite, then she loaded them in the cannon and dropped and fired them at Stella, who easily caught them. She stared at the package, looked up with a sad smile, and nodded.

CHAPTER TWENTY-SIX

Karol laid the spring flower bouquet against Hope's headstone and sat on her yoga mat in front of her. Twice a month, after yoga, Karol came by the cemetery and talked with Hope. Sometimes Merry came with her and sometimes not. She kept Hope updated on the neighborhood events—like the day the reindeer left, and Manny and Mo had to part. Dr. Charlotte and Blair had taken great care to mix Mo in with the herd, gradually separating them. As Mo was led up the ramp, Manny barked.

Blair had gasped, worried Mo would leap off the ramp and out of the pen since reindeer could vertically jump twenty-five feet. Instead, Mo looked at Manny and as if accepting her fate, followed Barry into the truck. Karol learned from Blair that reindeer had good memories, and when Mo came back, it was highly likely and a consolation that she would remember Manny.

She also told Hope about her "Second Act" as the Operational Manager for Full of Joy, the neighborhood's nonprofit. Karol loved organizing and she couldn't imagine a more important role than helping people escape food insecurity.

Sometimes she talked through important issues and decisions—her and CJ's wedding plans, her burgeoning work with Tucson housing nonprofits, and Stella's probable relocation to Arizona since she'd never actually made it to Florida. Sometimes Karol just wanted Hope to know how much she missed her.

She sighed and touched the top of the headstone, as if doing so connected her further with the best human she, and many others, had known. "Hope, you would've laughed so hard at what happened during the CUDL ceremony. The judge who gave us the award went on and on about your cookies and the amazing community we are.

"Well, you probably remember the group of high school pranksters we have here in the JOY. Stevie and his friends? You would've thought Stella's punishment of poop scooping would've knocked them in line, but oh, no.

"So, the ceremony was held in the community space, where they have those catwalks over the stage and the audience. Apparently, Stevie and his friends, one of whom is the manager of the shaved ice place, spent the early morning turning ice cubes into snow. Right before the ceremony, they drive the ice truck up to the back of the building and get into the catwalks. As the presentation begins and the judge speaks, it starts to snow! People are dusting off their shoulders and looking up. Soon it's coming down really hard and the kids are pelting snowballs at everyone below. Merry grabs the microphone, trying to restore order—until the *judge* hits her with a snowball. Then it's on! The whole thing is mayhem…and that's okay. It's totally joyous.

"When there isn't any more snow, the teenagers immediately start wiping off seats and cleaning up. Soon order is restored and the judge tells a story I didn't know. How Elsa Joy convinced her father to make the JOY neighborhood a reality. You've probably heard it before, but the very day he returned home from the war, Elsa shared her plan for the JOY neighborhood. But just as important, she'd created five rules to live by in her community."

Karol wiped her eyes. "I don't know why I'm crying. For such a young kid, she sure was observant." She sighed. "I won't say the rules out loud. You know them. You lived them."

She told Nana Hope her plan for the day, which included completing her unpacking list, then she kissed her hand and laid the kiss on the top of the headstone.

On her way back to meet Merry in the community kitchen, she waved at the neighbors mowing, clipping, and sipping lemonades—and stronger beverages—out on their lawns.

Rule Number One: Say hello to everyone you see every day.

She heard a voice call, "Karol! Karol!"

She turned to see Geena Hernandez coming toward her as quickly as she could, given the cane she still used to steady her. "You're not going to believe what's happened!"

Karol realized Geena was waving a paper in her hand.

"I just got this in the mail. I'm going to be published!"

She held out the letter to Karol, who pretended to be surprised. "Congratulations! This is so wonderful and exciting."

Rule Number Two: Share in the happiness of others.

"I know. I'm still shaking."

Stella had told Karol a month ago that she'd lobbied on Geena's behalf to one of the top publishing houses with a fledgling graphic novel department. Not only would Geena be published, but she'd also be the *first* for the company, a fact Karol wouldn't share with Geena, as she didn't need any more pressure now that her cancer was in remission.

"Stella really came through for me."

Rule Number Three: Do good deeds as often as possible.

"Have you spoken with her?"

"Yeah, I called her earlier right after the mail came. We chat and visit constantly."

Karol smiled. "I'm glad you two are connecting."

Geena nodded. "She's cool. Intense, but cool."

"I agree."

Geena's phone rang, and she rolled her eyes. "My mom. I've got to get home, but I just wanted to share this with you." She threw her arms around Karol, who'd grown accustomed to the bear hugs exchanged between JOY residents. She answered the call and nodded a goodbye. Karol watched her go, confident that she'd rid herself of the cane soon.

Rule Number Four: Give hugs frequently.

As she crossed the park, her phone rang. *CJ.* "Hey, honey."

"Hi, babe. When you see Merry, will you please remind her of the tax stuff I need for the board?"

"I will, but do you think she'll know what stuff you're talking about? Merry's not all that together about taxes."

CJ laughed. "In this case she will be because I put it in a big envelope and wrote 'tax stuff' on it."

"Okay. Will I see you for lunch?"

"Yeah, why don't we go eat over by the rock at Tierra Celestial? I want to see how the remodel is coming."

"Okay, I love you."

"Love you too."

Rule Number Five: Say I love you as often as possible.

She headed into the community center kitchen and noticed the frame that hung near the door was crooked, most likely because everyone touched it as they entered, a new pre-baking ritual to honor Nana Hope. Karol stopped and took a moment to straighten the frame that held two items: the photo of Nana Hope making cookies with CJ, Karol, and Merry alongside Hope's note that she'd left for Karol, revealing the secret ingredient:

One large cup of kindness.

Bella Books, Inc.
Women. Books. Even Better Together.
P.O. Box 10543
Tallahassee, FL 32302
Phone: (800) 729-4992
www.BellaBooks.com

More Titles from Bella Books

Mabel and Everything After – Hannah Safren
978-1-64247-390-2 | 274 pgs | paperback: $17.95 | eBook: $9.99
A law student and a wannabe brewery owner find that the path to a
fairy tale happily-ever-after is often the long and scenic route.

To Be With You – TJ O'Shea
978-1-64247-419-0 | 348 pgs | paperback: $19.95 | eBook: $9.99
Sometimes the choice is between loving safely or loving bravely.

I Dare You to Love Me – Lori G. Matthews
978-1-64247-389-6 | 292 pgs | paperback: $18.95 | eBook: $9.99
An enemy-to-lovers romance about daring to follow your heart, even
when it's the hardest thing to do.

The Lady Adventurers Club - Karen Frost
978-1-64247-414-5 | 300 pgs | paperback: $18.95 | eBook: $9.99
Four women. One undiscovered Egyptian tomb. One (maybe) angry
Egyptian goddess. What could possibly go wrong?

Golden Hour - Kat Jackson
978-1-64247-397-1 | 250 pgs | paperback: $17.95 | eBook: $9.99
Life would be so much easier if Lina were afraid of something
basic—like spiders—instead of something significant. Something like
real, true, healthy love.

Schuss – E. J. Noyes
978-1-64247-430-5 | 276 pgs | paperback: $17.95 | eBook: $9.99
They're best friends who both want something more, but what if
admitting it ruins the best friendship either of them have had?

Printed in the USA
CPSIA information can be obtained
at www.ICGtesting.com
JSHW080850261023
50926JS00001B/3